FALL OF HOUSTON

T.L. PAYNE

NO OTHER CHOICE
Fall of Houston Series, Book Two

Copyright © 2020 by T. L. Payne
All rights reserved.

Cover design by Deranged Doctor Design
Edited by Melanie Underwood

No part of this book may be reproduced in any form or by any electronic or mechanical means, including information storage and retrieval systems, without written permission from the author, except for the use of brief quotations in a book review.

Don't forget to sign up for my spam-free newsletter at www.tlpayne.com to be among the first to know of new releases, giveaways, and special offers.

❊ Created with Vellum

*For Octavia Avielle
My ray of sunshine in a very dark year.*

Contents

Preface	vii
1. Will	1
2. Betley	9
3. Will	14
4. Savanah	25
5. Will	34
6. Will	46
7. Isabella	56
8. Savanah	63
9. Will	69
10. Savanah	76
11. Will	84
12. Will	93
13. Will	104
14. Will	114
15. Cayden	122
16. Isabella	129
17. Will	134
18. Will	139
19. Will	146
20. Will	154
21. Will	160
22. Will	169
23. Will	175
24. Will	183
25. Will	190
26. Will	199
27. Will	205
28. Will	211
29. Will	219
30. Savanah	224
31. Will	231

Sample Chapters	237
Also by T. L. Payne	255
About the Author	259

Preface

Real real towns, cities, and institutions are used in this novel. However, the author has taken occasional liberties for the story's sake, and versions within these pages are purely fictional.

Thank you in advance for understanding an author's creative license.

"Texas is a blend of valor and swagger." — Carl Sandburg

ONE

Will

DAY FIVE

Explosions throughout the night had rocked Will Fontenot from the most restful sleep he'd had in the five days since the electromagnetic pulse attack. He had at first thought the explosions were the refinery fires reigniting. He'd hoped that's all it was, but the sound of automatic rifle fire poked holes in that theory. He'd chosen to believe that they were safely away from whatever it was. But how long would that last?

Will stared through the mosquito netting at the ceiling in Isabella D'Angelo's Houston, Texas apartment. At least the noise from the explosions and gunfire had distracted him from the constant buzzing of dozens of tiny vampires swarming the bed. When the rain from Hurricane Epsilon finally stopped, hordes of mosquitos had been unleashed like hounds straight from hell.

With communications down, Will had no way of knowing how much rain had been dumped on the area, but it was enough to cause significant flooding as predicted. Along with the flooding came the unbearable heat and humidity. With the electric grid destroyed and no way to run the air conditioner, all the apartment windows had been left open. The screens were no match for the bloodsucking creatures. They weren't the only creatures unleashed on them. Every time the door to the apartment opened, swarms of flies launched their invasion. The flies were horrendous. The thought of where they'd been was nauseating.

In a city of two and a half million, and with hundreds of thousands of people stranded on grid-locked evacuation routes attempting to flee Houston, the death toll from the storm was likely immeasurable. Some would have found shelter from the two hundred miles per hour winds, only to be inundated by flooding. Downtown high rises that hadn't burned would likely now be filled with those stranded evacuees.

Will had yet to venture out, not wanting to risk exposure to the toxic floodwaters. Still, a few bodies were visible from the third-floor balcony of Isabella's apartment. Will had wanted to shield his thirteen-year-old son, Cayden, from the gruesome sight, but with no one coming to collect the bodies, that wasn't about to happen.

For the most part, Will had kept busy planning his and Cayden's escape from the city. He had yet to get a chance to speak with Isabella about coming with them. He had planned to approach her the morning after they'd arrived at her apartment. He was looking for a good time to broach the subject, but with her boyfriend around and his bandmates sprawled out on her living room floor, along with the people coming and going from the apartment all day and night, there hadn't been an opportunity. He needed to do it soon though. He was anxious to heed Kim's and Betley's warnings and flee Houston as quickly as possible.

Will shifted in the bed and winced. His entire body still hurt. His knee was swollen, he had a dinner-plate-sized bruise on the left side of his abdomen from the bullet he'd taken to his body armor, and a matching one on the right side from the boot of the guy back at the law office. Will held up his hand and examined his busted knuckles. He wasn't in great shape, but he didn't want to waste time sitting around when he could be out finding the supplies he and Cayden would need to make the one-hundred-and-fifty-mile ride to his sister's farm north of Lake Charles, Louisiana. With the waters receding, soon it would be safe to travel. And even though he hadn't had enough time to rest and recover from his battle with the Chinese Communist Party's enforcers, he was planning to head out at their first opportunity.

Without a watch and with a cloud-filled sky, he had no idea what time of day it was. He'd been up most of the night pacing the floor, trying to figure out how they'd go about getting out of the city. He'd just settled back down to nap, but his mind had refused to shut off.

"Will. We're heading out," Isabella called from the hallway.

"Okay. I'll be out in a minute," Will said. The night before, they'd discussed the need to find food. With so many mouths to feed, that would be a monumental task.

Will rolled over on the bed to face Cayden. "How long was I out?"

Cayden was seated with his back against the oak headboard. His knees were drawn up to his chest and in his hands was a paperback book.

"Not long. Maybe thirty minutes."

"Where'd you get the book?"

Cayden pointed to the nightstand as he flipped the page.

"Is it any good?"

Cayden shook his head.

"But you're still reading it?"

"I'm bored out of my mind," Cayden said.

Will hadn't had time to be bored, but for a thirteen-year-old who was used to constant external stimulation in the forms of music, video games, and the internet, he imagined the lack of technology would be torture.

Will climbed out from under the mosquito netting, threw his legs over the side of the bed, and pulled on his boots.

"I'm going out with Isabella. We're going to—"

Cayden cut him off. "I know. I heard."

"You'll be okay here?"

"If I say no, will you take me with you?"

Will thought for a moment, considered bringing Cayden along, and then dismissed the idea. It was too risky—too much could go wrong.

"No. I guess not," Will said. "Anything, in particular, you'd like me to find for you?"

"The internet," Cayden said sarcastically.

"I wish I could, buddy. I could keep an eye out for a better book."

"Sure."

Will wanted to say something—to ask Cayden how he was doing—emotionally. The words stuck in his throat. He struggled to approach the subject, just as he had all the other times he'd wanted to open a discussion about how his son was coping with things. Cayden would say he was fine, like always. Will had no clue how to get him to open up and discuss what he was feeling. He tried to think of what Melanie would have said. But he was not his wife. What Cayden needed was his mother, and she wasn't here.

Will's face scrunched as he lifted his hands above his head to slip on his tactical vest. He was grateful that Betley had outfitted him with the gear. He had no idea what or who they would encounter after leaving the apartment, but the equipment would hopefully give him an advantage. Will checked the ammunition in his rifle and pistol and ensured the tactical knife was secured on his belt before grabbing the doorknob. Before turning it, he turned back to Cayden. "I won't be long. We're going to check out a few apartments nearby. If you need me, just yell. I'll be able to hear you."

Cayden let out a heavy sigh.

"I know you're not a little kid. I'm just saying, you know, the world has changed. We have to look after each other."

Without looking up from his page, Cayden shrugged one shoulder and nodded.

It was the response Will expected. It was the one he would

have given at his age. He kept reminding himself of how awful he was to his parents during his teen years. Will wasn't sure that he could bear it. How was he supposed to know what was Cayden being a typical teen and what was him punishing him for killing his mother?

His eyes fell to the water bottle sitting on the oak nightstand next to Cayden. He pointed to it. "Use a coaster. You'll leave a water ring on the wood. You know better than that. We're guests here. We have to respect other people's things."

Cayden sighed loudly and snatched the bottle from the nightstand as Will stepped into the hall and closed the door.

Will stepped over the sleeping bodies littering the floor of Isabella's stylishly decorated living room and made his way to the kitchen where Isabella and her live-in boyfriend, Kevin, were seated at the kitchen island. Kevin's tattooed hands were wrapped around a coffee mug. Sleeve tattoos ran down both muscular arms. Kevin's appearance reminded Will of the drummer from the rock band, Nickelback. He had similar colored, light brown hair and chiseled good looks.

Will threw him a slight nod as he approached. The smell of rotting meat from the fridge was gone. In its place were several competing aromas emitting from three differently scented candles burning around the room. It was almost as bad as the odor from the fridge had been.

Isabella swatted a fly on the wall and turned toward Will. "Did you finally get some sleep?"

"Some," Will said. He glanced back at Isabella's other house guests snoozing soundly nearby and wished he could sleep like that.

Isabella yawned and held out a mug. "It's not good, but it's caffeinated."

Will took it, smelled the coffee-like substance, and tipped the cup. It was awful. But he needed the pick-me-up, and it would do the trick. He'd had cold coffee before, but it had been brewed first. Soaking coffee grounds in room temperature water didn't have the same effect.

Isabella's cat, Otis, jumped into the air attempting to catch one of the giant flies swarming the trash can. To Will's surprise, he caught it in mid-air. As fat as he was, Will wondered how the black and white feline could move so fast. As Otis moved to his perch on top of the microwave to stare out the window, Will put his empty mug in the sink and joined him. The parking lot below was still covered in knee-deep water but the sun was out. It was only a matter of time before the water receded and they could be on their way. But first, they needed supplies for a trip across southeast Texas.

Will's clothes were still damp from his trek through the floodwaters to Isabella's apartment. His socks were hanging over the back of a chair in her guest room. With the humidity as high as it was, there was little hope of getting his clothes to dry any time soon. He knew that wet feet could lead to all sorts of foot problems, and with the long trip ahead of him, Will had reluctantly borrowed a pair of socks from Kevin. Will stared down at his boots. He didn't want to get the socks wet going back out into the water. His real concern was all the toxic chemicals it would contain.

"Can I borrow a couple of trash bags?" Will asked.

"Sure. They're under the sink," Isabella said.

Will grabbed several, along with a roll of duct tape he found under the sink, climbed onto one of the bar stools, and pulled off his boots. Kevin tilted his head to the side and stared at Will as he slid the black trash bags over his feet and wrapped duct tape around the top, and then pulled his boots back on. He thought about applying the duct tape directly to his skin, but pulling it off would hurt like hell. Maybe if he taped the trash bags up tight enough he might avoid getting his skin soaked with bacteria, viruses, parasites, and toxic chemicals. It was worth the try. He hoped the water wasn't any deeper than his knees, or it wouldn't work.

"That's a great idea," Isabella said. She crossed the room and pulled two trash bags from the box. "Can I have some duct tape?"

Will cut Isabella two lengths of tape and stuck them to the counter. As he was fashioning a bag to carry the finds from the scavenging, Isabella attempted to tape the bags around her thighs. The tape stuck to her fingers, and as she tried to pull it free, one of her acrylic nails popped off. "Dammit," she cursed.

"Here, let me," Will said, cutting another strip of tape. He knelt in front of her, wrapping it around her thigh, securing the trash bag to her jeans. When he glanced up, their eyes met. She looked so relaxed and at ease, considering all she'd been through. A smile broke through her lips. The corners of Will's mouth curled up, and he smiled back. He felt the intensity of her gaze, and heat rose behind his cheeks. Kevin cleared his throat, and Will's gaze flicked to him. Kevin puffed out his chest and glared back. The dark blue veins were visible in the man's thick neck. Will stood and backed away from Isabella.

"Look, Kevin. Isn't this a great idea?" Isabella said, turning to face him.

Kevin shrugged.

She seemed to be oblivious of her boyfriend's jealousy or maybe chose to ignore it. Will couldn't. He wasn't about to get into something with the man. He wasn't afraid of a fight, but he wasn't in any shape after the battle he'd been in with the Chinese mafia. He couldn't take the chance of becoming so injured he couldn't make the trip to Louisiana. Kevin furrowed his brow, pushed himself away from the island, and left the room without answering. Isabella was quiet a moment before turning back to Will.

"It might help provide some protection against all the nasties in the water, though," Isabella said. "Thanks, Will." She picked up a canvas tote from the counter and headed toward the door. "Are you coming, Kevin?"

Kevin sighed and joined her at the door. As the two went outside, Will put the empty milk jug and juice containers they'd been gathering into a trash bag and headed for the stairs. Will, Isabella, Kevin, and a couple from a second-floor apartment gathered on the landing outside Isabella's apartment. The plan was to start on the adjacent building's second-floor apartments and work their way farther and farther out until they found enough to supply them for a few days, or at least all they could carry. After Isabella's initial response to his supply gathering on their way to find shelter from the storm, Will was surprised at her willingness to go into other people's homes to scavenge what they needed to survive now.

Will descended the stairs behind Isabella and Kevin. He closed his eyes as the water rose first past his boots and then above his knee, stopping just below the top of the trash bags. So far, so good. His feet were dry.

At the bottom of the stairs stood a stocky Hispanic man in his mid-thirties and a young, slender Hispanic woman. She was short and attractive, dressed in shorts and a tank top.

"Will, this is Gus Ortega and Jacinta Alvarez. Gus is the manager here. He has the keys, so we won't have to break down any doors," Isabella said.

Gus gave Will a nod and then pointed to Will's legs. "Smart."

TWO

Betley

DAY FIVE

After arriving at Ellington Field Joint Reserve Base, FBI Agent James Betley had been escorted into the medical clinic to have his wounds taken care of. His leg hurt even worse after being cleaned and stitched. The doctor had given him a local, but that wore off after an hour and the doc was unwilling to provide Betley with anything stronger than ibuprofen for the pain. Betley assumed that was because he hadn't been interviewed yet. They'd want him clear-headed for the questioning. Betley just wanted some relief and a little sleep. Was that too much to expect? At least he'd been given a clean change of clothes to wear.

After his visit at the clinic, Betley had been taken to an office deep in the heart of a Coast Guard's multistory building. Hours passed as he waited to brief the Central Intelligence Agency officials about what had occurred with his informant, Kim Yang. He'd fallen asleep with his head resting on the desk. He jumped when the door finally opened.

A tall and slender woman Betley guessed to be in her early thirties rounded the desk and took a seat in the faux leather office chair.. "Agent James Betley, I'm Analyst Rachel Stephens," she said,

Betley straightened, ran a hand through his dark brown hair, and wiped the drool from his mouth with his sleeve.

As Stephens gathered pen and paper, Betley looked her over. Her brown hair was kept in a tight bun. She was a strikingly attractive woman, even without makeup. Betley shot her his lady-killer smile, but from her body language, she was all business.

"I've been reviewing the material on the flash drive you claim to have received from your informant, Kim Yang," Stephens continued.

Betley had conducted enough interrogations to recognize her technique. She was playing the skeptic, putting distance between their roles, and attempting to throw him off balance.

Betley tried his best to look relaxed but his neck and shoulders were stiff. He placed his palms on his thigh and inhaled and exhaled slowly. "And what did you find?" he asked. He expected her to tell him it was classified and refuse to give specifics. After all, he lacked the clearance for the level of information Kim claimed would be on the flash drive.

"Well, Ms. Yang did a very good job of documenting the theft of petroleum refining trade secrets," Stephens said.

Betley raised an eyebrow. Why would Kim's reports on corporate espionage be on the drive? That was unexpected. Perhaps she'd made a copy of the thumb drive she took from Hui Shi and Shan Huang. He stared at the backs of his bruised hands. The image of the member of the Chinese mafia who'd stabbed him in the leg flashed before him. The man had wanted that drive pretty badly to have followed them through a raging hurricane even after Kim had been killed.

"Why don't you tell me why it is that you believe that Kim Yang had information pertaining to the attack we've experienced and a possible insurgency. That is what you told Lieutenant Sharp, is it not?"

"That is what Kim Yang told me," Betley said. After he'd

described what Kim had told him as far as he could recall, Stephens stood and walked to the door.

"Wait here. I'll be back," she said.

Betley waited and then waited some more. He had never been on this side of an interrogation and he didn't like it. Not one bit. Maybe Stephens needed to be reminded that they were both on the same side.

Betley was weak from blood loss and weary from battling the Chinese mafia that had come after Kim. He needed food—real food—and a shower. After those things and some sleep, he'd be much more helpful to Stephens. The fact that she'd chosen to treat him like an adversary instead of a colleague had him concerned. Had Kim played him? Had she lied about what she'd found? But what about the blueprints and schematics of the power plant and pipelines leading to the Houston Ship Channel? Those were not part of Kim's work at the refinery. And why would they send mafia goons if they didn't believe she had something significant?

There was a knock on the door and then a soldier appeared. "Please come with me, Agent Betley."

"Why? Where am I going?"

"I was instructed to escort you to the SCIF," the soldier said.

Being allowed into the Sensitive Compartmented Information Facility was a step forward. Perhaps they would now read him in on what else they'd found on Kim's flash drive.

A man in a white button-down shirt, black slacks, and red tie greeted him at the door. "Agent Betley?"

Betley nodded.

"I'm Analyst Warren. If you'll come in here, we just have a few more questions, and then we'll let you go get some rest."

The analyst led Betley down a short hall. At the end was a soldier standing guard in front of a single steel door. Analyst

Warren showed the soldier his badge, and the soldier opened the door, closing it immediately after Betley and the analyst stepped into the vestibule. Steel mesh lined the walls from floor to ceiling. The analyst then opened a second interior door. The interior walls and ceiling were lined with acoustical panels. The padding provided soundproofing between the SCIF and the outside. The space was a lot smaller than Betley had imagined it would be. Stephens was hovering over a man seated in front of a computer screen. She glanced up, nodded toward a chair in the corner, and returned her attention to the screen.

"You're sure?" Stephens asked the man.

"That is all that's here," he replied.

Stephens turned her attention to Betley as Warren spread a stack of papers out on a table in the middle of the room. "Tell me again how Kim came into possession of the blueprints for the power plant and the Houston Ship Channel pipelines?" she asked.

"She said she stole them from Huang's safe. When she entered the room, Huang shoved a duffle under his desk and out of view. Before being suddenly called away, he placed the bag into his safe and hurried from the room."

"And Kim knew the combination to Huang's safe?" Warren asked.

"She'd watched him unlock it several times to retrieve cash he was paying her for stolen trade secrets," Betley said.

"And Kim somehow managed to get the duffle out of his house, and that's when she contacted you?" Stephens asked.

"She contacted me from her car moments before the EMP. She said she was being followed, so they knew she'd taken it," Betley said.

"Here's our problem, Betley. There's nothing on that drive related to an insurgency or targets they plan to hit. Having the schematic in your possession lends validity to your claim, but we need the other memory device. We have sent our people back out to the storage facility to try to locate it. But they came back empty-handed. I need you to walk me through it again. Don't leave anything out. I need to know Kim's every move from the moment she called you until she was killed. Can you do that for me?"

Betley's head ached by the time he'd recounted every moment he could account for. "Once the Chinese mafia showed up, things got crazy pretty fast. I can't say where she went from the time she left my unit until she was shot."

"And the three civilians that were with you on the bridge; they were present when Kim Yang was shot?"

"Yes," Betley said.

"Sharp said the girl gave you her address."

"She did," Betley said.

"Why would she do that?" Warren asked.

Betley glance from Stephens to Warren, then back to Stephens. "Because I'm a handsome son-of-a-bitch."

THREE

Will

DAY FIVE

Gus led the group across the courtyard and up the stairs to the apartments which he was sure weren't occupied. As Will stepped into the deeper water, his pants legs became soaked. He lifted his leg above water and cursed under his breath. Pieces of debris had poked holes in the bags. What he would give for a good pair of waders.

Will waited at the bottom of the stairs as Gus and his girlfriend went up to confirm that no one was home. Isabella pulled her thin jacket tight against her as a light rain began to fall. Her boyfriend just looked bored or stoned. Maybe both.

"Jaz, hold that flashlight while I open the curtains," Gus said, disappearing inside an apartment. A moment later, Gus reappeared in the doorway. "All clear," he called.

Before Will even stepped inside, he knew no one was home. There'd be no way anyone could have stood the smell that emanated from the place. With the electricity out, the items in the refrigerator had spoiled, and the odor was unbearable. Almost as bad as the smell of Isabella's bathroom.

Will headed for the laundry closet in the hall where the hot water heater was located. He pulled his T-shirt up over his nose, and after filling the two milk jugs for him and Cayden, he filled the two-liter soda bottles and then the sixteen-ounce water bottles.

"If there are any containers that we can carry water in, I need those," Will called into the kitchen.

Kevin appeared with a couple of empty orange juice jugs.

"Are they finding much food?" Will asked.

"Yeah, but I doubt we'll ever see any of it," Kevin said.

"That's not nice," Isabella whispered as she walked up behind him.

"Whatever. You'll see," Kevin said.

Kevin disappeared into the bathroom across the hall. Will heard cabinets opening and closing.

"There's nothing wrong with Gus and Jaz. They'll share whatever they find. Kevin just doesn't like them for some reason," Isabella said.

"Maybe we should split up, just in case," Will said. He had no way of knowing if Kevin was right or not, but he hadn't come outside and taken the risk just to go away empty-handed.

"I don't know. If you want to, that's fine, I guess," Isabella said.

Will handed her two jugs of water and headed for the door. "I'm going to check out the one across the hall."

"That's Mr. Hernandez. I don't know if he's home or not. I didn't get an answer when I knocked before the storm, but he's hard of hearing," Gus said.

"He doesn't have a car or any way to evacuate. How would he leave?" Jaz pointed out. "I thought I saw a light in his window last night."

"We should check on him, then, right?" Isabella suggested. She banged on the door. If the man were in there and alive, he'd have to be totally deaf not to have heard her. She stood back and waited. He didn't answer. "I think we should go in and make sure that if he's in there, he's all right."

Gus jingled keys, finally located the one he was looking for, and inserted it into the lock. Before Gus could even turn the knob, the door opened. A face appeared in the crack. *Not* Mr. Hernandez.

"Who are you?" Gus asked. His tone was not friendly. Will stepped to the side and placed his hand on his holstered pistol.

"Who the hell are you?" the pretty young woman asked.

"I'm the apartment manager. Where's Mr. Hernandez?" Gus asked.

She looked back over her shoulder into the room. "He's sleeping."

"Wake him up," Gus demanded.

Will didn't like where this was headed. Gus's reaction seemed a bit extreme. But he knew the old man. Will didn't.

A man's head appeared above the woman's. "I don't know who the hell you think you are, but you need to leave," he said, slamming the door in Gus's face.

"I think we should go, Gus," Jaz said, tugging on her boyfriend's arm.

"Something ain't right in there, Jaz. You know it, and I know it. Hernandez doesn't have family nearby. Those folks are up to something," Gus said.

"She's right," Kevin said. "Let's mind our own business and get back to finding food."

Gus wheeled around and got in Kevin's face. "Listen here. You do what you like, but I'm getting inside that apartment and finding out what the hell is going on in there."

Will was torn. His gut told him something wasn't right with the couple but on the other hand, they weren't cops, and there wouldn't be any backup coming if they got into something with them. As much as he would like to help, Will just couldn't risk not making it back to his son.

Will stepped around Gus, Jaz, and Isabella and walked next door. "What about this one? Are they home?"

Jaz shook her head. "Give them the keys, Gus."

Gus ignored her and shoved the key back into Mr. Hernandez's door and pushed it open. "Holy hell. What the—"

Jaz stepped through the door and screamed.

Isabella pulled her pistol from its holster and moved to the side of the door. "What is it?" she called.

Will rushed over and flanked the opposite side of the door frame. He didn't like it. The couple could shoot through the thin walls, no problem.

"What did you do to him?" Gus asked.

"He's old. He died in his sleep," the man said.

The girl was crying hysterically.

Will stepped through the door. An elderly man was lying on a sofa in his pajamas. Except for the odor, Will would have thought he was sleeping. He covered his mouth and nose with his arm and backed out the door. He waited for the others on the steps where the air was somewhat better.

"They're going to come back with us. They can't stay here with that body," Isabella said.

"What?" Will asked. It was her apartment. It wasn't up to him, but he had no clue where she thought she would put two more people. They could barely move in there as it was. Ten people in a tiny two-bedroom apartment would be bad *with electricity*. Without it, it'd be unbearable.

"They're going to stay in the apartment across from Gus and Jaz. I think he wants to be able to keep an eye on them," Isabella said.

"Okay. What about the food? Are we still searching the rest of the vacant apartments or what?"

"Will," Gus said, tossing him a set of keys. "They're for that building there." Gus pointed to the building to their right. "No one should be home in those units."

"What are you guys doing?" Will asked.

"We're taking these two back to our unit, and then we'll catch up with you," Jaz said.

The young woman glanced back over her shoulder and smiled as Gus and Jaz led them across the courtyard. Will didn't return the gesture. She was young and attractive. There was nothing about her that should set off alarms, but she had. He couldn't pinpoint it. He didn't trust her or her boyfriend. He wondered if he should say something to Gus and Jaz. But what? The only thing he had to go on was that his intuition told him that something was off with them. Will had the sudden urge to give up on searching the rest of the buildings and get back to Cayden.

"Are you ready?" Kevin asked, pointing to the apartment unit across the way.

"Yeah," Will said, telling himself that he was being paranoid. He needed the supplies so he and Cayden could leave. The sooner they got on the road, the better he'd feel.

"Right behind you," he added.

Upon returning from getting the young couple set up in an unoccupied apartment, Gus and Jaz rejoined the search for food and supplies. Isabella and Kevin took one apartment while Jaz and Gus took another. Will went on his own to the apartment at the end of the walkway. After scavenging through three apartments, Will had enough cans of green beans to last him through the apocalypse. It was apparent they were the residents' least favorite food. He couldn't fathom why people bought that many if they didn't like them.

He'd save the peanut butter and one-pound bag of rice for his trip. Everything else was too heavy. He'd located a few non-food items that would be useful, like a roll of duct tape, yards of nylon cord, and a nice little stainless-steel pot with a lid to boil water and cook the rice. He was checking off the list of items he'd need for himself and Cayden to survive outdoors for the several-day trip. Soon, they'd be ready to go if the damn water would just dry up.

Gus and Jaz emerged from the apartment next door. "Did you find much?" Jaz asked.

Will held out his canvas tote filled with green beans. "Just these."

Jaz scrunched up her face. "They're something at least."

"What about you guys?" Will asked.

"We found some dried soup mixes. We could put the green beans in it and stretch it to feed quite a few of us."

She'd said us. There went Kevin's assertion that they'd hog it all to themselves.

"Yeah. I guess that's true," Will said.

He felt bad for not telling her about the rice and peanut butter but they might not understand that he and Cayden needed food to get away from the city. He also felt bad that he was taking food that they'd need to survive, which would force them to have to venture farther from the apartment complex in search of more.

"What's next?" Isabella asked, rising from where she'd taken a seat on the steps.

"I'm beat. I'm ready to head home myself," Kevin said.

"I'm going to step back in here for a moment." Will pointed a thumb over his shoulder.

"Need some help?" Isabella asked. She didn't wait for a reply before joining Will in the living room.

Will was pulling books off a bookcase near the window.

"Nope," Will said, throwing a book onto the nearby chair.

Isabella picked it up. "This is a good one. What? Are you not into romance?"

"I'm into romance. Just not romance novels and not for my son," Will said.

"Oh, you're looking for something for Cayden." Isabella pulled a Harry Potter novel down and handed it to Will.

"He read that with his mom when he was like ten years old. I think he'd like something a little more mature."

Will grabbed *Ready Player One*. "How about this one?"

"I think he'll love it."

Will took it, dropped it into his bag, and turned to go.

"Here's one you might like," Isabella said, a grin spreading across her face.

Will took it and turned it over to reveal the cover of *Fifty Shades of Grey*. Whoever said not to judge a book by its cover was wrong. A flush began to grow behind his cheeks and he shoved it back into her hand.

Isabella threw her head back and laughed.

"Who reads that stuff?" Will asked.

"What? Too steamy?"

"Too pornographic to have around my kid," Will said.

Isabella dropped the book onto the chair and followed Will to the door. Before stepping through, she punched him on the arm. "Hey, I was just kidding."

"I know," Will said.

"Kidding about what?" Kevin said as they stepped outside.

"Oh, nothing. Will was looking for books for Cayden," Isabella said.

The scowl on Kevin's face told Will he thought it was more than that.

"Are we ready to go back now?" Kevin whined.

Gus turned and scanned the courtyard between the apartment buildings. "We've pretty much cleaned all these units out. At least the ones without a foot of water in them."

Isabella looked into her backpack. "This isn't going to last very long." She reached out and grabbed the strap of the bag hanging over Kevin's shoulder. He swung away. Will could hear something rattling inside the bag. Whatever it was, he didn't want anyone seeing.

"We really need to hit a grocery store or something," Gus said.

"Won't they be underwater too?" Isabella asked.

"Yeah, but the cans will still be good. It's a shame about all the other food just going to waste while folks are starving."

"So are we calling it a day then?" Will asked. He was anxious to get back. He didn't like leaving Cayden that long.

"I think so. I mean, we should draw a map and make a plan to hit all the stores around here," Gus said.

"That might be dangerous," Jaz pointed out.

"I know."

"We could wait until the water recedes," Isabella said.

"We won't be the only ones searching those apartments across the street," Jaz pointed out. "There are a couple of groups in there alone. I saw them from my window yesterday. They were doing the same thing we are. They have a head start on gathering supplies. It won't be long before they strike out to hit the stores."

Will considered that bit of information. How many hungry and desperate people were they competing with for supplies? Thousands? Hundreds of thousands? The sooner he got away from the city the better in his view. Waiting for the water to recede may not be his best plan of action, considering the danger posed by hordes of wretched and hungry people. Some of them may be desperate enough to want to fight over those green beans that he'd found.

There was no way he could carry enough food for himself and Cayden to make it to Louisiana. He'd need to find more on the way but with so many others doing the same, he could see it might get pretty dicey out there on the road.

Isabella turned and descended two steps. She stopped and turned back, eyes wide. "Did you see that?"

"No. What?" Jaz said, stepping down next to her.

Isabella pointed to a spot near where the trash dumpsters had been shoved up against a truck in the parking lot. "There. See it?"

"No. What?" Jaz leaned forward and stared where Isabella had pointed. She jumped back two steps. "What the hell is it?" Jaz said, her pitch high.

"Oh, my God," Isabella said, turning and running back up the stairs. She grabbed hold of Will's arm, spun him around, and buried her head in his back.

"I don't see anything," Kevin said, as he passed Jaz and moved toward the bottom of the stairs.

"You better not—" Isabella started to say.

Kevin spotted the alligator just as it lunged for his leg. He placed both hands on the railing and hopped into the air. When he landed, the alligator snapped again, barely missing his foot and biting into the metal spindles of the banister.

Isabella was screaming in Will's ear. "Shoot it! Shoot it!"

Jaz screamed and ran back up the stairs as Gus descended them. Gus yanked Kevin up and away from the deadly jaws before it could strike again.

Will stepped to the edge of the landing and attempted to aim his pistol at the alligator, but Gus and Kevin blocked his shot. There was no way for him to shoot the gator without hitting the men. The giant beast attempted to climb the concrete steps as Kevin and Gus retreated. Will stepped around the men and took aim, just as the reptile gave up and disappeared from view.

"I am not going back into that water. No freaking way," Isabella said.

"Me neither," Jaz replied.

"We can't stay here all night," Gus said.

"The hell we can't. You can go out there and get eaten by a gator if you want," Jaz said.

"We'll give him time to move on and then hurry back to our place," Gus said.

Will walked to the bottom step and scanned the water. There was no sign of the gator. It was at least two or three o'clock in the afternoon by now and Will was exhausted from the heat and humidity. He was wet, smelly, and hungry. "You guys can wait around here, but I need to get back to my son."

Will clenched the trash bag filled with supplies under his left arm and gripped his pistol in his right hand before stepping into the murky water.

"No, Will. It's still out there," Isabella said, stepping down to the middle of the staircase.

"I can't let every obstacle prevent me from doing what I need to do," Will said. "You have a pistol and a knife. If it comes for me, shoot it." Will took in the parking lot. With all the debris floating on the surface of the water, it was impossible to spot a gator snout. His heart raced as he stepped into the water, half expecting to feel the giant jaws clamp onto his leg. He took off as fast as he could move toward Isabella's building.

"Wait for me," Isabella yelled.

She descended the steps, pistol gripped in both hands. "Do you see him anywhere?"

"No. Let's hurry though," Will said.

"Wait up," Jaz said. "Let's go, Gus. I don't want to be eaten by no gator."

Kevin beat them back to the apartment. He was inside peeling off his wet socks by the time Will and Isabella had dropped off the canned food items to the neighbors across the hall and made it back inside Isabella's apartment.

"Thanks for the help, Kev," Isabella said sarcastically.

"I figured you two didn't need me," Kevin sneered.

Will left them to straighten out their differences and headed back to the guest room to find Cayden and peel out of his wet clothes. Too bad the trash bags hadn't worked as well as he'd hoped.

The band members were still sound asleep on the living room floor. They'd slept through all the screaming outside. Will wondered if Cayden had heard them?

"A close call?" Cayden asked as Will entered the room.

"You saw?"

"Yep. I heard Isabella scream."

"The water is likely full of creatures from the bayou," Will said. "You just need to be watchful." He didn't want Cayden to be too frightened to go if he decided to get on the road before the floodwater receded.

"I'm glad you didn't shoot it. Its home was disrupted too. It was likely more scared of you guys than you were of him."

Will smiled. "I wasn't scared." He retrieved the book from his bag and flopped it down on the bed next to Cayden. "Isabella thought you'd like it. If you don't, blame her."

Cayden's eyes lit up. Will wasn't sure if it was because of the book or that Isabella had chosen it. He wondered if Cayden might have a little crush on her. She was attractive and Will had daydreamed about his science teacher when he was thirteen. It would be quite normal to find Isabella alluring even though she was his mother's age. That's when it dawned on him. Will's insides twisted. Was Cayden clinging on to her as a mother figure? It was too heartbreaking to think about. His brain was exhausted from trying to find a way to survive. He didn't have the energy to think about how leaving Isabella behind in a day or two might affect his kid. He'd talk to him about it—later. Right now, he wanted to grab a nap while the band was sleeping. They could be in for another very long night.

FOUR

Savanah

DAY SIX

There'd been no sign of the police. Neither Wade nor anyone from Mayor Thibodeau's office had come by to check on them. That was because they were busy fending off attacks by Jason's family. Word had come by way of a cousin, warning Jason to stay away from town until the Blanchards were securely in charge of city hall.

There'd also been no sign of the rich kids on all-terrain vehicles. Savanah waited on pins and needles for the parents of the boy they'd buried out back to come knocking on her door. They hadn't. Well, not that they could get to the door. She and Jason had spent the last three days securing the property from intruders. Spurred on by the idea of the spike strip they'd placed along the driveway, Jason had expanded the concept to the fence line along the road. There was nothing to stop someone from hopping the fence from the neighbors' side. But so far, none of them had seen anyone lurking around.

Apart from Jason living in her barn, nothing much had changed for Savanah and her children. They carried out their chores, milking the goats twice a day, feeding the chickens and pigs as usual. Savanah had even made soap. This would be for washing clothes. Which now, with Jason, there were more of.

"Mom," Keegan yelled, "Kylie ran into me and broke the eggs."

Savanah poked her head through the door of her outdoor kitchen to see Keegan squatting over the egg basket on the ground. Kylie was chasing after one of the barn cats.

"Kylie, you have to be careful. Those eggs are extremely valuable now."

"No, they're not. You can't even sell them at the store now," Kylie said, catching up with the kitten.

"Kylie, put the cat down and go to your room," Savanah said. Her daughter tossed the kitten aside and slowly walked to the house. "I will be there to talk to you after I help your brother pick up the eggs you broke."

"I didn't mean to get her in trouble," Keegan said.

"It's all right. You did nothing wrong," Savanah reassured him.

After they picked up all the eggshells, Savanah tossed them into the pigpen and turned toward the house. She'd made it halfway up the back walk when she heard yelling in the direction of her neighbors, the Bertrands. Savanah stopped and listened. Someone screamed. Savanah took two steps in that direction and turned.

"Keegan, run and get Jason. Tell him there's trouble at the Bertrands. Hurry!"

Jason met Savanah at the fence that divided her property from her sixty-five-year-old neighbors. Charles Bertrand had lived on the property all his life. His second wife had five children that Charles had never got along with. Selfishly, Savanah hoped that any trouble they were having at the moment had to do with family and not the residents of the gated community down the road.

Jason parted the barbed-wire fence and held it open for Savanah to climb through. They ran toward the barn at the back of the forty-acre property. Jason stopped near the front of the barn, and they listened.

"You ain't taking shit from me," Charles said. "I'll burn it all to the ground before I let you step foot inside my house."

"Put that down, old man," a young male voice said. "Ain't nobody got to die here today. We just want a little something for my hungry kid brother, is all."

"It's them," Savanah whispered.

"Sounds like it," Jason said. He flicked the safety off his pistol and stepped around the side of the barn. "Stay here. Let me handle this."

"But—"

"Stay here. I'll handle it," Jason interrupted.

Savanah watched as Jason disappeared around to the front of the two-story white-clad house.

"I'd put that down if I were you," Jason said.

"Really? Seems like we have you outnumbered, Jason," he said, in a thick south Louisiana drawl.

"You think you know me?" Jason asked.

The kid snorted.

"I know who you are. I know who your family is. I not scared of you."

"You should be," Jason said.

"Yeah. Why is that?" the kid asked.

"Because I'm going to do to you what I did to your friend, and then I'm going to dump your body in Mr. B's pond."

"You think so?" the kid asked. "You think you can shoot us all?"

"I don't have to. Only you."

One of the teens came into view, and then another. They were backing away. They didn't want any part of what was about to happen—the little cowards.

"We'll be back," the kid said. He held a hunting rifle in his hands as he backed toward the road. "We're coming back. This road is ours. After we have everything we want from it, we're going to move into town and take what your family has too."

"Big talk from a punk walking away," Jason said.

"You'll see."

"You and what army? Your six-year-old brother?" Jason taunted.

"You'll see," the kid repeated.

Savanah didn't like it. The kid was too cocky. He could have just been beating his chest because he was embarrassed, but somehow, Savanah got the impression that the kid might be telling the truth, and something big could be about to happen.

"You guys all right, Mrs. B?" Jason asked.

Mrs. Bertrand had her arms wrapped around herself and was trembling. She did not look okay.

"Thank you for coming over when you did. I don't know what would have happened if you hadn't," Mr. Bertrand said.

"I know what would've happened," Mrs. Bertrand said. "The same thing that's happened to others along this road. I don't know what the hell the sheriff has been doing, but no one from the deputy's office has been out to check on us. It's like the wild west. We're on our own."

"We're here for you, Mrs. B," Savanah said, wrapping her arm around the woman's shoulders.

Savanah knew that it was pure luck that they'd been there at the fence separating their two properties and heard the yelling. If they'd been a few minutes later, the Bertrands would have ended up dead like the Johnsons. Something needed to be done to those murderous kids. She just wasn't in the position to do it herself. Not when there was a chance she'd leave her children orphaned and alone to fend for themselves, or worse, having to rely on their father.

"We need to find a way to secure our homes from those punks. We need to work together and watch out for one another," Savanah said.

Jason turned to face the road. The Bertrands' house sat less than fifty feet from the street and they didn't have a fence along the front of the property. Anyone could just walk straight up to their front door any time they liked. He stepped into the driveway and made a circle, examining the layout of their land. It was all open, with only a few trees here and there. Someone could shoot into their house from any angle. There was no way to secure the place.

"What are you thinking?" Savanah asked.

"It's not defendable," Jason whispered.

"So, what can we do for them?"

"Other than moving them the hell off this property?" Jason asked.

Savanah glanced back at the elderly couple. "Is that a possibility?"

"It's the best option, but would they do it?"

Mrs. Bertrand looked frightened enough to go, but there was no way she'd go without her husband.

"Only one way to find out," Savanah said.

"No way. I can't leave my animals for them to just waltz in here and take," Mr. Bertrand said.

"Bring them with you," Savanah said, glancing at Jason.

Jason shrugged. "I don't see why not. It would be some work to move their chicken coop, but I think if we take out a section of the fence, we can just drive the cattle over onto Savanah's pasture."

Mr. Bertrand looked like he was considering it.

"I know it sucks, but how much sleep do you think either of

you will be able to get knowing they could come back at any time?" Savanah asked.

"I haven't slept since the lights went out. Every noise has me up checking for intruders," Mrs. Bertrand said. "Please, Frank. I'm exhausted. There's safety in numbers. You said that."

"What about our house, our belongings, and my shop?" Mr. Bertrand asked.

"We can move as much of it over as you'd like. We can board up the house—make it harder for them to break in."

"I don't know. A man works his whole life on a place, and some snot-nosed kids just walk in and run him off his land. It ain't right," Mr. Bertrand said.

"It's not permanent." Savanah sure hoped it wouldn't be. It was going to be crowded with two extra people, and—more particularly—all their stuff. "It'll just be until the sheriff gets out here and arrests those kids."

"Someone needs to go down there to his office and tell him to get his ass out here then," Mrs. Bertrand said. Her pale blue eyes were filled with anger and Savanah didn't blame her. They'd had their sense of security ripped from them. Savanah hadn't had that since she'd discovered Derek dealing drugs, but she understood how it felt.

"We should go and talk to the rest of the neighbors. Maybe between all of us, we could come up with some way to protect everyone while we wait."

"Maybe I should go into town and—"

Savanah held her hand up and interrupted him. "No! No, Jason. We'd be trading one problem for another. We'll likely have to deal with them at some point, but that's not the answer."

"Okay."

Jason sounded like he was still entertaining the idea. He was blind when it came to his family. He had the misguided belief that since he was kin, they'd come to save them but not want to claim the area as their territory. Savanah didn't buy that for a second but she admired Jason for wanting to help. He had willingly put himself in this situation. He didn't have to be here. But she was glad he was.

"Will your tractor start, Mr. B?" Jason asked.

"Of course. I keep all my equipment in top shape."

"Let's see what we need to do to move that chicken coop then," Jason said.

They spent the entire day moving the Bertrands' canning pantry items over to Savanah's. Savanah was impressed. The couple still maintained a garden as if they were feeding their two boys. Kendra counted and inventoried as they stacked the quart-sized jars on the shelves and then the floor. They'd moved one hundred and twenty-five jars of tomatoes, tomato sauce, okra, peaches, and a variety of other fruits and vegetables. By the time they'd finished, the pantry was so full they could barely even open the door, and they hadn't even started on moving the dry goods over.

Karson and Jason helped Mr. B herd the cows over to the corral by the barn for the night and it was dark by the time they'd move the last of their things over. They ate soup from the can for dinner and moved Kendra's things to the room in the attic. She didn't seem to mind giving up her room to the couple.

Once the Bertrands and the children were settled in for the night, Savanah joined Jason out by the barn. She found him seated in a lawn chair just outside the corral, watching Mr. B's cows.

Savanah overturned a bucket, slung her rifle over her back, and took a seat beside him. "Do you think they'll be back tonight?"

"Nah, not tonight. Did you see that kid almost pissed his pants when he saw us? He's a coward, praying on the elderly and weak. He knows we are neither," Jason said.

"Where in the world are those kids' parents? Where do they think all that food is coming from, the grocery?" Savanah asked.

"They don't care. As long as they eat, they don't care where it's coming from," Jason said.

"I refuse to believe that. Maybe we should go and talk to them—tell them what they've been up to out here."

"That's a very bad idea," Jason said.

"Why? It might work"

"Have you forgotten that we have one of their sons buried in your back pasture?"

That was like a gut punch. She hadn't forgotten. She was just desperate for this nightmare to end.

They sat quietly for a long time, listening to the frogs croak, until Jason announced he wanted to patrol the fence line. Savanah stayed and tried to think of some other way to reach the gated community's residents. They needed to know if the parents were complicit in their kids' crimes before they talked to the neighbors about what to do about them.

Twenty minutes later, Jason returned. He'd been smart and announced himself well in advance of approaching her in the dark. "See anything out there?" Savanah asked as he settled back into his lawn chair.

"No. All seems quiet. Except for those big-ass bullfrogs down at the gully."

Savanah laughed. "They may be noisy, but they're good eating."

She pictured her two sons shining their little flashlights on the bank and Keegan diving to catch one. Her kids loved playing in the water—when she allowed them to. They had to be so careful of alligators, even in small gullies like the one that ran behind her farm.

An idea formed. "Jason, I have an idea."

Jason didn't answer. That's when she noticed his head lolling to one side. She reached out and touched his arm. None of them had gotten much sleep recently. Exhaustion was kicking their butts.

"What?" Jason said, sitting up straight in his chair.

"It's nothing. I just had an idea about how we could spy on that gated community and maybe find out what they're planning."

FIVE

Will

DAY SIX

By day six, it finally stopped raining. It had been another sleepless night. This time, he'd been awake listening to Isabella and Kevin's heated fight. That hadn't been the only explosion, either. Somewhere in the distance, something had blown up. He'd checked from the bedroom window but couldn't see anything. He'd thought about going and looking out the windows in the living room that faced south but decided it would be too awkward, considering the love birds were in there having a quarrel.

Sometime in the early morning hours, the band decided to move downstairs to one of the other unoccupied apartments. Will wasn't sure what would happen if the tenants that lived there returned but it wasn't his problem.

Thankfully, Cayden had slept through it all. As the sun was peeking through the slit in the curtains, Will tiptoed down the short hall and poked his head into the living room. It was vacant. Isabella and Kevin must have worked out their differences and gone to bed. As he made his way across the living room, Will wondered how he could ditch them and go out scavenging on his own. He pulled back the curtain and shielded his eyes from the sun. After his eyes adjusted, he lowered his hand and stared out at the thick black smoke coming from the direction of the Gulf Freeway and Beltway Eight interchange.

"What's on fire now?" Cayden asked from behind him.

"I'm not sure. It's too close to be one of the refineries reigniting."

"Something burning?" Isabella asked, rubbing her eyes as she entered the room.

"Could be vehicles on the freeway," Will said.

"What would cause that? Aren't they soaked from sitting in water for days?"

"I'm not sure, really. I heard an explosion last night. It looks like it's still burning, whatever it is."

"Maybe we should go check it out," Cayden suggested.

"No, it's too risky." Will turned away from the window.

Isabella yawned and stretched her arms above her head and Will couldn't help but notice how fit she was. He glanced over at Cayden and their eyes met. Will couldn't read the look on his face. Was he upset that he thought Will was checking Isabella out? He wasn't, he told himself. She had a boyfriend. Isabella turned her back to them and Cayden nodded toward her. "Ask her," he mouthed.

Will checked over his shoulder. It was the first time since they'd arrived that they'd been alone. He didn't want a confrontation with her boyfriend, though after her fight with him last night, Isabella may be more open to following them to Louisiana. He wished he'd talked to Cayden about it—prepared him for the possibility that she'd say no and explained all the reasons so he'd know it wasn't because she didn't care.

Will hesitated a little too long, trying to think of just the right thing to say, knowing it might be a tough sell to convince her to follow two relative strangers one hundred and fifty miles under the circumstances.

"Isabella, my dad and I want you to come to Louisiana with us," Cayden said.

Isabella turned to face him. Her mouth was open, but no words came out. She looked at Will and then back to Cayden. "I… um… I," she stammered.

"It's not safe here, Isabella. You can see that. Help isn't coming. Things are only going to get worse in the city. You can come with us. We can have each other's backs," Will said.

"I… I don't know. I mean…"

"My aunt Savanah is really nice. You'll like her. Her farm is great. They have chickens, ducks, goats, and lots of other animals. She makes her own soaps and lotions. They've lived without electricity for a few years. We can make it there. It's far enough from the city to be safe," Cayden said.

"And she'd have room for another mouth to feed? I don't know. What if I got there and she objected?"

"She won't. I assure you," Will said.

Isabella stared off down the hall. Despite the fight the night before, she had a boyfriend and they hadn't extended the invitation to Kevin. It hadn't even crossed Will's mind that she'd expect him to be included. He wouldn't. He couldn't. He didn't trust the man. There was no way he would put his son at risk out on the road with the irresponsible man. He'd get them all killed.

"Just think about it," Will said. "We're planning on leaving when the water goes down."

She returned her gaze to him and Cayden, but the deer in the headlights look told Will that she was torn and scared. He didn't blame her. They both knew what they'd face out there. It would be dangerous. But it was going to get deadly in the city very soon.

"I'm going to go get dressed," Will said, breaking the tension. "I want to check out the grocery store today before that other group that Gus mentioned has a chance to clear it out."

Isabella shook her head.

"What?" Will asked. Did she now have a problem with looting again?

"I can't believe it has come to this. It's just—"

"I know," Will said, softening his tone.

He understood the moral dilemma—the blurred lines between right and wrong. He wasn't sure he knew the difference anymore. Where did one draw the line when fighting for the survival of those you cared about?

She lowered herself to the chair and buried her face in her hands. Her shoulders shuddered. Cayden moved to her side and placed his hand on her back.

"I just want things to go back to normal. I hate this. All of this," Isabella said through tears.

Will thought about saying what was easy. He could lie to make her feel better, if only for a little while, but what good would that do in the long run? Would burying their heads in the sand make the inevitable somehow go away?

"I have a feeling that things will never go back to normal. I think that somehow, we have to find a way to live in this new world," Will said.

He couldn't bear her pained expression and looked away. She wasn't built for this. He could see that. Who was? She needed hope. So did Cayden who was seated on the sofa, hunched over with his elbows on his knees and his head in his hands. Will wanted to know what was running through his son's mind. He'd let him down—again. Instead of safely riding this out at the lake house, he'd got his son into this nightmare and now they were in a fight for survival.

"I do think things will get better. We'll find a way to make it better. Right now, though, we have to survive. We need food to do that, and this is the only way to eat right now."

Isabella stared at Cayden for a moment. She ran her fingers through her long brown hair. Tears glistened in her eyes and Will was afraid she was about to fall apart again. He couldn't handle that.

"I know," Isabella said, standing. "I'm going to go get dressed. I'll push the shopping cart."

Cayden stood and turned to Will. "Can I come? I kinda don't want to stay here by myself."

Will chewed on his bottom lip. He didn't want to take Cayden. It was too dangerous, but Isabella's spat with Kevin had driven the bandmates downstairs and Will didn't know them well enough to knock on the door and ask them to watch his kid. Besides, they were all likely passed out cold after last night.

"I guess I don't have a choice," Will said.

Cayden pumped his fist up and down and ran down the hall to the bedroom.

"He's never been that excited to go to the grocery with me before," Will laughed.

"The EMP changed a lot of things. Looks like your relationship with Cayden is one of them," Isabella said.

That wasn't true. What did she know? She was virtually a stranger to them. Isabella had no idea what their relationship had been before all this. Will wanted to ask about her relationship with Kevin, but he refrained. That was a little too personal. He'd learned more about them during their fight than he'd ever cared to know. They'd said horrible things to one another. Kevin had called her poor white trash and said she'd never be anything more. She'd called him lazy and self-absorbed. Will thought the comment about how bad he was in bed had been a low blow. The man seemed to have a very fragile ego.

Will was grateful that he and Melanie had never fought like that. Melanie was direct and never spiteful when they argued. She'd say what was on her mind, let Will know where he'd screwed up, and how to fix it. He'd apologize for being an insensitive idiot and vow to do better. The makeup sex had made the whole thing worth it—God, how he missed her.

It must have shown on his face because Isabella was staring at him. "He's really proud of you, you know. He told me so."

"Proud? Of what? Looting? Killing?" Will asked. He'd done nothing that he was proud of.

"How brave you've been and how determined to make sure he survives this," Isabella said.

Was it brave for a father to protect their kid? He'd done what any parent would have done. That didn't make him a hero.

"I don't know if I ever thanked you—for pulling me from my car and saving my life several times."

"You did," Will said. He glanced at her and then turned away. "We looked out for each other. You had my back out there too."

Isabella walked over to the sink and stared out the window. "I can't stop thinking about it."

"About what?" Will asked.

"All of it. The accident and almost being burned alive, the carjacking, that poor girl with the mental issues that attacked me—all the killing." Isabella turned to face him. Tears streamed down her cheeks. "Every time I close my eyes, I see them staring back at me. I can still feel the blood on my hands. I've scrubbed and scrubbed, but it's still there in my mind."

Will took two steps toward her. He understood. He knew about the flashbacks. He had them too. When he was awake, he busied his mind thinking of ways to survive, but when he tried to sleep, the faces he saw were of those innocent college kids that had been so senselessly murdered. They were just in the wrong place at the wrong time. He should have done more to protect them. He'd known that dangerous men were after them. They'd put them in the middle of their war, and now the kids were dead.

"I hear that young girl in the bar crying after her brother…"

"I know, Isabella. It's really hard, but we need to stay focused on today and what we need to do to survive. Dwelling on it won't make it any easier."

Will took a seat on a stool at the small island. He wasn't the one to give her advice about how to deal with trauma. He obviously sucked at it himself. He knew he was screwed in the head. There was nothing he could do about it.

"I think about Fahima the most," Isabella said in almost a whisper.

That surprised Will. They'd left her alive and well back in the mechanical room.

"I hate not knowing," she said.

"Not knowing?"

"What happened to her? If she made it? How she's doing now if she did?"

Will hadn't realized they'd bonded so much in the short time they'd been with the woman. But obviously, she'd made quite an impact on Isabella.

"She'll be fine," Will said.

"How do you know? You can't know that."

"We left the door to the upper floors open. If the water rose too much, she would be able to get high enough to avoid it."

"How will she eat and find clean water?"

"Fahima is a survivor. She's survived situations that would break us. Fahima knows how to take care of herself out there on the streets."

"But she likely relied on one of the shelters for food," Isabella said.

"There's food in the apartments. She's likely doing the same thing we are," Will said.

Isabella was quiet for a long moment.

Will stood and pushed in the stool. He didn't want to think about Fahima. He knew her chance of surviving this was not good. Isabella was right. Without food supplies from charitable organizations, Fahima would be fighting the hordes of evacuees for what meager supplies weren't ruined in the flooding downtown.

"Fahima is probably tougher than we are. She's been through a lot. We've been through a lot," Will said.

"I'm ready," Cayden said as he appeared in the living room.

"I need to get dressed and grab my flashlight. I'll meet you downstairs," Isabella said.

No Other Choice

Will and Cayden waited at the bottom of the steps for Isabella and Kevin to join them. The trash bags Will had taped around Cayden's legs came up to his groin. They'd double bagged to make sure nothing seeped through. Will shined the flashlight into the murky water, looking for any sign of the alligator that had nearly taken Kevin's leg off the day before. He removed his knife and handed it to Cayden.

"Here, put this on," Will said, strapping the Velcro of the sheath through Cayden's belt loop. "Can you reach the snap?"

Cayden unsnapped the sheath and retrieved the fixed blade knife. He smiled. "I'm good."

Will didn't like taking him. He didn't like it one bit. "Keep your eyes open for gators and snakes."

Cayden nodded and placed the knife back into its sheath.

The door above opened, and Isabella descended the stairs. Her hair was wet and pulled back into a ponytail. Gone were the dark circles under her eyes from crying. It was the pink lipstick that threw him. He watched her descend the stairs. The trash bags on her legs made a swishing noise as she walked. Will smiled, and she smiled back. She wore a pink backpack and carried two canvas tote bags. When she reached the bottom step, she handed one of the tote bags to Cayden.

"Have you seen Gus and Jaz yet?" she asked.

"Not yet," Will said.

He'd barely said it when the door to their apartment opened, and out they stepped. Jaz was dressed in pajamas and fuzzy slippers. It was clear she wasn't going. Gus was dressed in fishing waders and long sleeves. This time, he was prepared for wading through the murky water. As Jaz helped Gus with the straps to his pack, the couple from the dead man's apartment came to the door.

"You guys heading out again?" the guy said.

"They are. I'm staying," Jaz said.

"We're going to check out the grocery store," Gus said. "You want to come?"

The couple looked at one another. The guy shrugged. "Not really. It sounds dangerous."

"Suit yourselves," Gus said, turning his back on them.

In one way, Will was relieved. On the other, he didn't like that they weren't expected to pull their weight, but in the end, it wasn't his call. He wasn't the one that would be sharing resources with a couple of deadbeats.

"All righty. Let's get going," Isabella said, stepping into the water. Her tone conveyed she found it irritating too.

"Wait, where's Kevin," Cayden asked.

Everyone stared at Isabella. "He's sleeping."

"Well, let's go wake his little ass up," Jaz said, turning to head up the flight of stairs leading to the third-floor apartments.

"He's not up there," Isabella said.

"Where is he?" Jaz asked.

Isabella shrugged one shoulder. "I don't know. We had a fight. He walked out. I assumed he'd joined the band in the vacant apartment."

"Nope. We would have heard them," Jaz said.

"All these are locked up tight. I have the keys," Gus said.

Isabella threw her head back and looked down her nose. "Then, I have no idea. And after the ass he made of himself yesterday, I don't care."

Will couldn't say he was exactly sorry to see Kevin and the band leave though it was selfish, he knew.

"Can we go now?" Isabella said, walking past Will.

She didn't look all that upset. Maybe she was glad they were gone as well.

"You sure we should leave with those two across the hall?" Will whispered. He didn't know why, but he'd somehow felt better about them staying there when he'd thought the band was there to watch them. That made no sense now that he thought about it. But not much did these days. He was tired and stressed. He couldn't rely on his spidey sense in these unprecedented times. No one was acting normal. Whatever the hell normal was, anyway.

"I asked Hector to come to sit with Jaz and keep an eye on our place," Gus said.

"You're concerned about that couple we found at Mr. Hernandez's apartment yesterday?" Isabella asked, rubbing her temples. "Did they do something?"

"No. We just don't know them," Gus said.

Isabella nodded. "I get that." She started to turn and wobbled. Will caught her arm to steady her.

"Are you feeling all right?" Will asked.

She looked flushed. She'd been through quite a lot, physically and emotionally, and had never received medical attention for the injuries she'd suffered in the car wreck. They weren't eating and drinking properly, and the stress was hard on the body.

Will touched her forehead with the back of his hand. "You're burning up."

"What?" Jaz said, backing away from her. "I don't want it, whatever it is. I got a bun baking in here." She rubbed her stomach. "I can't get sick."

She didn't look pregnant to Will, but Melanie hadn't looked like she'd been expecting almost until she'd given birth to Cayden.

"Let me see your arm," Will said. "Your burns could be infected."

"They're fine. I put antibiotic cream on them this morning and I've been keeping them covered," she protested but gave Will her hand anyway. He peeled back the bandage. It looked nasty, but the smell was what told him it was infected.

"What about cuts or scrapes to your legs or feet? If you have open wounds, this nasty water could make you really sick," Will said.

"No. I inspected myself when I cleaned up last night. My clothes were still dry under the trash bags."

"Do you feel nauseated?" Will asked.

"Maybe a little."

"I think you should stay here. Let the others go check out the grocery store," Jaz said through the T-shirt covering her mouth and nose.

"She's right. Stay here. Get some rest. I'm going to see if I can find some antibiotics." Will leaned close and whispered, "Ask Cayden to stay with you, please."

Isabella smiled.

"Cayden, your dad would like for you to stay and babysit me. Would you mind?"

Will sighed heavily and looked at Cayden.

Cayden smiled and bobbed his head.

"Lock the door, Cayden. Don't let anyone in—not even Kevin—not until I get back," Will said. He placed his hand on Isabella's shoulder. "You okay with that. After last night, I kinda don't want my son caught in the middle of round two."

"He's not coming back. Even if he does, I am not opening the door," Isabella said.

"I imagine he has a key. Better slide the door chain over," Will said.

"I will, Dad," Isabella said, smiling as they turned to head up the stairs.

Cayden rushed to her side and ran his hand around her waist. Will watched them climb to the third-floor landing, where they disappeared from view. He listened for the door to open and close. A second later, Cayden came to the window and called down. "It's all locked up tight."

"We'll be back soon," Will said.

He didn't like this situation one bit. If they didn't need supplies for the road trip and antibiotics for Isabella, there'd be no way he'd leave Cayden behind. But somehow, he believed that Isabella would watch out for his son. He kept telling himself that it was just a quick run to the grocery store. He'd get in, get what they needed, and get back. After that, they'd get on the road out of town.

"Do you have a weapon of some type?" Will asked.

Gus held up a baseball bat.

"What the hell are you going to do with that, old man," said a male voice behind Will.

Will spun around. Two twenty-something men approached them.

"I asked Javier and Rudy to come. They live in that building there." Gus pointed to one of the apartment buildings across the small courtyard. "They know how to handle themselves."

Will wasn't sure, but if Gus was willing to trust them, what choice did he have? This was important. After this, he could very well have everything he and Cayden would need to make it to his sister's. He wanted to be ready to go the minute the water receded enough to travel.

"All right. Let's do this then," Will said.

SIX

Will

DAY SIX

The doors to the large chain grocery store were broken, as were all the windows. The awning above the door had been shredded by the hurricane-force winds, and a tree branch protruded through one of them. Packaged foods were floating on the surface of a foot and a half of water.

Gus went in first, followed by Rudy and then Will, while Javier stood outside, watching for anyone approaching. As soon as Gus flicked on the flashlight, Will knew anything that wasn't inside a can or a jar would be ruined. Rudy rushed past the checkout and disappeared.

Gus pushed aside a cardboard display and turned to his left toward the canned foods aisle.

"I think we should stick together, just in case we run into trouble," Will said.

"I got your back, bro," Gus said.

Will pushed aside the floating debris in front of him and grabbed a shopping cart. "Good to know."

They filled Will's cart full of soups and stews and then stocked Gus's cart full of peanut butter, jelly, tuna, and canned fruit. There was no bottled water or sports drinks, but there was plenty of juice.

Will pulled several cases of juice box drinks from the top shelf. Those would be good for travel. He needed beef jerky, nuts, energy bars, anything with a lot of calories that was lightweight and would sustain them for several days.

Will and Gus were searching for batteries when they heard voices. From the sound of it, there were at least three males. Gus immediately headed toward them.

"What is it?" Will asked.

"Rudy. He's arguing with some dudes."

Will pulled his pistol and stepped out behind Gus. He glanced back at their shopping baskets. There was nothing in that store worth dying for, but he'd agreed they'd have each other's backs. He'd expect Gus to come to his aid if he needed him. He just hoped he wouldn't be dealing with a whole neighborhood of people and that they could talk their way out of the situation without exchanging bullets.

As soon as Will rounded the aisle, he saw Rudy standing toe-to-toe with three young Hispanic males.

"We were here first. You need to get your punk-ass outta here," the shorter of the three said. The kid, no more than five feet three inches tall and less than one hundred forty pounds, with thick, curly black hair, stood at the end of the aisle with his chest puffed out.

Rudy had his hand on his waistband. Will knew this wasn't going to end well. He scanned the store for others that might be with the kids. He needed to know how many of them he would have to fight to get out of there.

"Ain't no five-o coming here to save your bitch ass," the kid said.

Gus stepped forward. "Bro, there's more than enough here for everyone. There's no need for any of that." He walked toward them.

The kid took a step back and relaxed his shoulders slightly. The two with him turned and ran.

"Miquel? What the hell are you doing?" Gus asked the kid.

"Same as you, old man," the kid said.

"Old? I got your old man right here," Gus said, grabbing his crotch.

Rudy pointed to the kid. "You know this dude?"

"Yeah. He's my homeboy's nephew," Gus said.

"Is Daniel here with you?" he asked the kid.

"Nah. Daniel got shot yesterday. Didn't you hear?"

"How the hell was I supposed to hear? The phones are out," Gus said.

"Nobody came to tell you?"

"No. What happened?"

"Some bitch-ass Asian dudes jumped him over near the Gulf Freeway last night. We were at home and Daniel came running in saying someone was planning to blow up the interchange."

"Wait? What?" Will asked

"Do you need hearing aids, pops? I said someone was attempting to blow up the freeway." The kid turned his back to Will and continued. "Anyway, Daniel and a bunch of us went to check it out. Those dudes shot first. They had AKs and shit. Daniel wasn't the only one hit. Those Asian dudes took out five of our guys."

"What the hell are they doing over here?" Rudy asked.

"Don't know, man," the kid said.

"Did they succeed? Did they blow up the freeway?" Will asked.

The kid looked over his shoulder. "Did you not hear those explosions last night?"

Will had. He'd hoped it was another one of the refineries or something. It had to be the people from the list Kim stole.

Without a word, Will turned and walked back to where he'd left the shopping cart. He could no longer wait for the floodwater to recede. He needed to get Cayden and get out of town today before the insurgents could trap them in the city.

As he pushed the cart through the debris-filled water heading for the door, a shot rang out in the parking lot. Javier, the kid that had remained outside to keep watch, was crouched behind an overturned sedan. To his left were two soldiers. They were returning fire at someone out of Will's view. A round hit the building just to the right of the door, sending Will scrambling for cover behind a display of rental carpet cleaning machines. Will bumped his head hard on the metal shelving, the pain of the impact causing him to see stars. He shook it off as he ran in a crouch toward the back of the store in search of an exit. Will heard Gus and Rudy yelling Miguel's name. A second later, Rudy ran by.

"What happened? Is Gus all right?" Will asked.

"The kid. He's been shot," Rudy said before disappearing through the front doors.

"Wait, Rudy," was all Will got out. He didn't wait around to see if Rudy got mowed down by whoever was fighting outside. He ran back to where he'd left Gus.

"Gus!" Will yelled.

Gus appeared in the aisle. "Help me, Will," he called out.

"What the hell happened?" Will asked.

"Two of the Asian dudes ran up on us. They shot Miquel. I need to get him home."

"Where are they now? Are they still in the store?" Will asked.

"I don't know. They ran off."

Will began unstrapping his body armor.

"What are you doing? Grab his arm and help me," Gus said.

"We need to apply pressure to his wound or he's going to bleed out," Will said, pulling his T-shirt over his head and stuffing it into the wound in the boy's abdomen. He held it tight as he slid an arm around the kid's waist. "Some dudes are shooting out in the parking lot. They're probably with the ones that shot the kid. It's not safe to leave out that way."

"I have to get him home to his family. I need you to help me," Gus said. He sounded desperate. Will glanced down at his hands pressed against the boy's abdomen. By the looks of things, there was no way this kid was going to make it. Going out there would be a suicide mission.

Gus shoved his arms under the kid's shoulders and legs and picked him up.

"Gus, wait," Will said.

"I'm taking the kid home. You do what you want."

The front of the store exploded with gunfire. The battle was now inside the store. Any moment, it could be him bleeding out on the floor.

"All right, let's hurry out the back. I sure hope no one is waiting to ambush us," Will said, and he picked up his body armor and slung it over his shoulder.

As they stepped through the loading bay door, three guys ran up. Will pulled his arm back and went for his pistol, but Gus shook his head. "It's okay, I know them."

"What the hell? Did you shoot Miquel?" one of the men asked as they approached.

"No. Shut up and help me carry him home," Gus said as he and Will headed toward the road.

"Over here. Put him in my ride," the tall skinny kid said, pointing to an older model four-door Chevy.

Someone opened the car door, and Gus slid into the back seat first. Will did his best to keep the pressure applied to the wound as two of the kid's friends lifted him into the back seat and placed his head in Gus's lap. Will crawled in, and in seconds they were tearing out of the parking lot as fast as the vehicle could go in a foot and a half of water.

The Chevy stopped outside a rundown two-story house several blocks from the store. The neighborhood was filled with brightly painted homes and narrow streets. The front door of the house flew open as they pulled into the drive and a middle-aged woman wearing shorts and a spaghetti strap tank ran toward the car.

"My baby! My baby!" the woman cried as she yanked open the car door.

As they rushed Miquel inside, Will stood on the walkway shirtless. He stared down at his blood-soaked hands. He knew the kid wouldn't make it. Not with the amount of blood he'd lost. Another family would be grieving a senseless death that night. As a father, Will knew they were going to be living every parent's worst nightmare.

Will was rinsing the blood off in the floodwater when several young men stormed out of the house, rifles in hand. Will raised his hands in the air but they ran past him like he wasn't there. He exhaled and turned to watch them go. Miquel's relatives were going after the guys who'd shot him. They wanted blood, but they had no idea what they'd be walking into.

Will turned in a circle. He needed to get back to Isabella's apartment, but he had no idea where he was. He walked out into the middle of the street, trying to recall which way they'd come. After settling on a direction, he turned to his left and stepped between two abandoned cars.

"Will," Gus called out. "Wait up."

The shirt Gus was wearing was soaked in the kid's blood. He looked like he'd aged ten years in the last twenty minutes.

"How's the kid?" Will asked as Gus caught up to him.

Gus shook his head. "Died in his mother's arms. Thanks for helping me get him home."

"What really happened back there in the store? Why did Rudy run?

"Rudy's brother is in a rival crew. He knew he'd be blamed."

"But the Asian dudes shot Miquel. Do you think this relates to what happened to your friend on the interchange? I saw the military out in front of the store. I think we were just caught in the middle of their battle."

"Maybe. I overheard one of Miquel's cousins say they took something from them. I guess they wanted it back."

The last thing he needed was to get caught in some war between the kid's family, the military, and the insurgents.

"Our block is mostly college students and elderly folks. I hope that shit doesn't spill over to our complex," Gus said. "We'll try to stay out of it if it does."

"Let's hope that doesn't happen," Will said. That sealed Will's resolve to not wait for the water to go down to leave. Cayden had been through enough, and Will wasn't about to wait around and let them get trapped inside some battle that had nothing to do with them. Isabella's face flashed before him. She was sick. They'd run into the kid before he'd had a chance to find her medicine. He couldn't leave her sick and defenseless. Especially now, with this new threat.

"Where's the nearest pharmacy?" Will asked.

"There's one on the corner near the grocery store, but they hit that place before the storm came in. I doubt you'll find anything left in there."

"Isabella needs an antibiotic. I doubt that druggies took those. I need to have a look, at least," Will said.

Gus washed his hands in the floodwater and dried them on his jeans. "Okay. Let's go in the opposite direction to the fighting."

"Lead the way," Will said.

Will was surprised at how exhausted he was after only walking a few blocks in the knee-deep water. He tried not to think about all the cancer-causing chemicals soaking into his skin, not to mention the bacteria, E.coli, and everything else.

They stood outside the pharmacy staring at the busted windows and door. The store was on a slight incline and the water in the parking lot wasn't as deep. Will was hopeful that maybe inside the store was dry.

"They probably only took the good stuff," Gus said, stepping through the entrance.

"Let's hope they could read then," Will said.

The water inside was only ankle deep, but he could tell that it had made it to the top of the checkout counter, meaning any second shelf items would be ruined. Will grabbed a handbasket nearby and pushed through the debris on the floor. A display case full of cell phone cases floated by as they made their way back to where the prescription medication should be. Will wondered if they'd ever see working cell phones again.

He'd never been tethered to them like a lot of people and hadn't cared for social media or gaming apps. He did like streaming music though. It had been odd that the only music he'd heard in days was the live tunes from Kevin's band. Will perused the debris, looking for anything that Cayden or Isabella might need. Most everything was ruined by the putrid water, but the sunscreen and bug spray on the top shelf was still good. Will threw some in his basket and followed Gus to the medicine aisle.

Gus stopped, and Will nearly ran into him. He looked past Gus to see the empty prescription medicine shelves. There was nothing left. What hadn't been taken was floating in the water. Will left his basket on the prescription counter and rushed past Gus. He picked up the plastic pill bottles trying to find antibiotics, but all the labels had gotten wet and were unreadable.

Will cursed and threw a bottle across the store. How were they going to locate the meds Isabella needed? He'd hoped to at least find enough to treat her fever.

"How about a triple antibiotic?" Gus asked, holding up a tube of a topical cream.

"I don't know. If Isabella's burns are already infected, will that do any good now?" Will asked.

"It can't hurt," Gus said. "I'm taking it anyway. We'll likely need it at some point, I'm sure."

"I wish we could find clean gauze. She needs to keep the wound clean and wrapped," Will said.

Will pushed aside a floating dog toy and grabbed a large pill bottle. He twisted the lid and looked inside, hoping the pills themselves might have their name on them. They didn't.

"Here," Gus shouted. "This says it's for burn care."

Will grabbed it from him and read the factory-applied label. "Silver sulfadiazine antimicrobial wound gel. Use in the prevention and treatment of burns and wound infections."

"I had a vet prescribe that for my dog once. Buster decided to jump the fence and follow our car all the way to the mall. He was sitting by the car when we came out but his paws were burned to a crisp. They treated him with the same thing," Gus said.

"What she really needs is a doctor," Will said.

Guilt crept in. He should have taken her straight to the hospital instead of detouring to go get Kim's car. If they'd gone directly to get Isabella medical treatment, they would have avoided all the ugliness that came after. They might even be sitting at a Red Cross shelter right now instead of combing through a looted-out pharmacy for the lifesaving medication they needed.

"Let's grab as many of these bottles as we can. Who knows, we may find a doctor or nurse around nearby that would know what's inside. Someone might need their cholesterol-lowering drugs or thyroid medication," Gus said.

"Good idea. I'm going to look for trash bags," Will said, thinking that all the doctors and nurses would likely be at the hospitals. They would have been at work, preparing to receive casualties from the destructive storm. Taking Isabella there might still be an option. They'd have generators. FEMA usually brought in large ones after hurricanes to run things until the power company could get the electricity back up.

"Where is the nearest hospital?" Will asked.

Gus looked skyward, thinking. "There's one in the Third Ward, and there's one in Pasadena."

"Pasadena is at least ten miles away. I can't imagine us doing that on foot. What about the one in the Third Ward?"

"That's ten miles as well."

Will cursed under his breath. The risk of being exposed to toxins in the water was worse than just handling her burns at home. Will continued stuffing pill bottles into trash bags.

"That's too far to go on foot in this shit," Will said.

"I agree."

"Well, I think I've got all I can carry. Let's get back and see if we can figure out what to do with it all. Hopefully, we can find someone who can tell us which bottle contains the antibiotic Isabella needs," Will said, also hoping one of the bottles would contain sleep-aids to help him get some rest. He was beat.

SEVEN

Isabella

DAY SIX

Isabella reclined on the sofa with her arm propped on pillows. Cayden had wet a towel and placed it on her forehead. He was a good kid. Will was lucky. All the teens she knew were so self-absorbed they'd be useless in situations like these.

Cayden sat on a stool at the small kitchen island with the book they had found for him in his hands. He seemed small for his age, but what did she know about kids?

Her mother and father had been on at her to settle down and give them grandchildren. At thirty-two, most of her friends already had two or more. Isabella had come close to getting married a few times but she had rotten taste in men. Kevin was a perfect example. Selfish, lazy, jealous, and misogynistic. The overflowing trash can reminded her of their argument the night before. Kevin had opened several cans of food and was feeding his face even after they'd all agreed that they should ration.

The argument had quickly turned personal—as usual with him. He'd called her names—tried his best to make her feel small and stupid. This time it hadn't worked. Not after all she'd been through since the lights went out. The worst part was his attack on Will. He'd accused her of sleeping with him and claimed she was only on his case because of her new boyfriend. That had always been his way of gaslighting her. She prayed that Will and Cayden hadn't heard anything he'd said.

Their fight should have made her decision about whether to go with Will and Cayden easier, but it hadn't. She was finished with Kevin; that wasn't the issue but there were so many other things to consider. Mostly, it was the fear of the unknown. She'd been out there. She'd seen how ugly the world had become already. Isabella wasn't sure how much more brutality and desperation she could handle. What bothered her most was, she was afraid she'd be the one that messed up and caused Will, or God forbid, Cayden to get killed. She knew that Will would depend on her to help keep Cayden safe. He'd trusted her with his son's life back at the law office. She'd never forget him pleading with her to take care of his son if he didn't come back. What if something *had* happened to Will? How in the hell would she have protected Cayden?

On the other hand, life at Will's sister's sounded so much better than the one she faced here in her apartment. Isabella tried to imagine life without modern technology. How could one live long term scavenging from empty apartments and grocery stores? How long before they were looted out. Then what? She didn't have a clue about how to provide her own food. She couldn't hunt and there was no way she could rely on Kevin or any of their neighbors for her survival. Not really.

Did she have any choice? What was she really afraid of? She watched Cayden as he continued to read. She liked the kid. She couldn't bear the thought of something happening to him. Could she do it—for him? Could she leave her home and go back out there to help Will keep him safe? He needed an extra person to watch their backs. She was grateful that her dad had been a gun guy and had taught her to shoot at an early age. She'd never imagined how important the skill would become.

Isabella sighed, glad she had a little more time to decide. But, when the floodwater went away, she'd have to be prepared with an answer. She just prayed she would do the right thing.

"Do you like the book?" Isabella asked.

"Yeah. It's really good," Cayden said, bookmarking his page. "I know you picked it out."

"No. Your dad did. I found *Harry Potter*, but your dad picked *Ready Player One* for you. He said you used to read a lot with your mom."

Cayden's eyes fell to the book. "Yeah. She liked for me to read to her in the car when we took long trips."

Isabella's heart broke for him. She'd never lost anyone she'd cared about and even though her mother drove her crazy at times, Isabella couldn't imagine ever losing her.

"Your dad really loves you. I know it's tough being a teen. I hated my parents at your age and—"

"I don't hate him," Cayden interrupted. "I don't. I just…"

"You don't know what to say?" Isabella asked, finishing his sentence.

Cayden nodded.

"You two need each other. He needs you, Cayden," Isabella said. It was so sad to watch Cayden and his dad tiptoeing around each other instead of talking things out. They were both hurting. There had to be a way to get them to open up to one another. Will was too closed off. If it were going to happen, Cayden would need to initiate it.

A knock on the door startled her. Cayden stood and Isabella held up a hand to stop him from opening the door.

"Who is it?" she called.

"Lloyd. I'm looking for Kevin."

It surprised her that the bandleader had knocked on the door rather than use the key Kevin had given him. She rose and walked to the door, peering through the peephole. Lloyd was alone.

"He's not here," Isabella called through the door. "I thought he was with the band."

"We haven't seen him since last night. We need him. We want to practice our new song."

"He left after our fight. I assumed he'd followed you guys downstairs," Isabella said, opening the door a few inches.

"We went to a party at the apartments across the parking lot. We haven't seen him," Lloyd said through the crack.

"I don't know where he is then."

"Well, if you see him, will you tell him we're looking for him?"

"Yeah, but I doubt I'll see him."

"He didn't mean all that, you know. He just says shit when he's mad," Lloyd said.

Isabella's face flushed. It hadn't been the first time that the band had witnessed them fighting. Kevin seemed even more of a jerk when they were around, like he was trying to prove his dominance or something.

"Don't defend him." Isabella lowered her voice. "I'm done putting up with his drinking and cheating on me."

Lloyd was quiet for a moment. "Does that mean you'll give me a shot now?" He laughed.

"You drink even more than Kevin and I've seen you with the ladies."

"If you change your mind, I'm just downstairs."

Isabella waved her hand in the air. "If you leave the building, watch out for that gator."

"I'm not worried about that. I've been around gators all my life. Stuart is going to catch him and make gumbo for everyone," Lloyd said.

Isabella wrinkled her nose. She'd heard that alligator meat tasted good, but she wasn't about to eat anything that had been swimming around in that nasty water.

As Lloyd walked away, Isabella said, "When you see Kevin, will you tell him to come get his clothes."

The bandleader gave a thumbs up, and Isabella closed the door.

"I'm sorry you and your boyfriend broke up," Cayden said.

"I'm not," Isabella said, returning to her position on the sofa. She added another pillow to prop up her arm. It was throbbing now and she was afraid to look. The chills and fever told her that it was infected as Will suspected. It was a wonder that they weren't all sick after wading through the bacteria-laden water. Isabella pulled the fluffy blanket she kept on the back of the sofa over her and tried to sleep, but her mind wouldn't shut off. Images of all the dead people she'd seen in the last few days played on a loop in her mind. Gunshots rang out, and Isabella hit the floor.

"Cayden, get down!"

"Who's shooting? Is that my dad?" Cayden asked, crawling toward the open window.

"No, Cayden. Stay away from the windows and doors. We have to stay low. Bullets can easily penetrate these thin walls."

The gunfire continued. It sounded as if it were moving closer. Isabella wasn't sure what to do. She needed to protect Cayden. He was her responsibility. She crawled to the kitchen and reached onto the counter to retrieve her pistol. There wasn't anything she could do about the fighting outside without leaving Cayden alone. But if the battle came to them, she needed to be ready to defend them.

"We need to get to the bedroom and see if your dad left any ammo," Isabella said. Crawling with her injured arm down the short hall to the guest room was so painful she became light-headed. Sweat poured off her. *Hold on! Just hold on.*

"It's in the nightstand," Cayden said.

Isabella moved along the bed and pulled open the drawer. "There's only one 9mm magazine," she said, stuffing it into the back pocket of her jeans. She edged close to the window and peeked into the parking lot below. A young man was running between buildings on the opposite side, followed shortly by two other men. The first man turned and fired.

"That's Rudy," Isabella said, jumping to her feet.

"Who's that?"

Isabella stared at Cayden, unsure if she should tell him that Rudy had left with his dad and Gus.

"My neighbor," she said, opting to leave that information out for now. Isabella and Cayden moved back into the hall. "Stay here," she said. "I need to make sure there aren't people with guns coming up here."

"No. You said we should stay low."

"I'll only be a minute. One quick peek and I'll be right back." She gave his shoulder a little squeeze and headed for the door in a low crouch, her chest pounding, fearing what she might find on the other side of the door. If something happened to Will, it would crush Cayden.

Standing to the side of the door, Isabella turned the knob and eased it open. She peered through the crack but saw nothing but the empty landing. Relieved to not find a lifeless Will sprawled out on the stairs, Isabella puffed out a breath of air and reached to slide the chain across the door. She slowly opened the door and stepped outside.

"So much for the safety of a gated community," a familiar female voice said.

Isabella glanced to her right. Her neighbor stood in her doorway, a blunt in one hand and a bottle of beer in another. Isabella wasn't a bit surprised. Most of the building's residents had continued to party even after learning that there had been an attack on the country and that the lights weren't coming back on anytime soon.

"Did you see Will and Gus down there?" Isabella asked.

"No, just Rudy. He must have pissed off his dealer," the bikini-clad woman said.

Isabella glanced back inside her apartment. She needed to find out what had happened to Will. He could be out there, injured or…

"I'm sorry about Kevin," the woman said.

Isabella shook her head. "I'm not. It should have happened a long time ago."

As the young woman turned and closed her door, Isabella crept to the top of the stairs and scanned the green space between the buildings. She saw no one. She listened. The gunfire had stopped. She hoped Rudy had escaped and that Will and Gus were all right, but the not knowing was torture. She wanted to go check it out, but she couldn't leave Cayden. All she could do was wait. She sucked at waiting.

"Is it over?" Cayden called from the doorway.

She pivoted to face him and tried with all her might not to let the fear show.

"I think so," she said, waving for him to get back inside. "We should avoid going to the windows, though, just in case."

As Isabella closed and locked the door, she gave one last glance toward the stairs wishing she'd see Will finally ascending them. She didn't know what she and Cayden would do without him, and she hoped to never find out.

EIGHT

Savanah

DAY SIX

Jason wasn't a fan of Savanah's plan to spy on their neighbors in the gated community of Spring Hill. If she hadn't been convinced that they needed the information, she wouldn't have considered leaving her children with the Bertrands. But she wanted to see exactly what they were up against.

Trees lined the gully that ran behind all the properties between Savanah's farm and the gated community. They could remain hidden in the brush until they had to cross the road that led to the subdivision's south side. There, along the shorter side of the perimeter wall, they'd be able to see the front gate and be able to tell who was leaving and what they carried with them.

All was going to plan until the Jacksons' dog caught wind of them. At a different time, Savanah would have rolled on the ground laughing as Bruno yanked on Jason's pants leg as he hung from a branch.

"Bruno. Down!" Rod Jackson yelled as he approached. "What the hell?" he asked as Jason climbed down from the tree.

"What are you guys doing?"

Rod was tall and stocky. Even dressed in pajamas and slippers, he still looked intimidating. His jet-black hair was longer than he usually kept it, and it looked like he hadn't shaved since the lights went out.

Jason glanced at Savanah. She debated lying to Rob and saying they were looking for one of her goats. They escaped her fence regularly and made their way to Rod's garden, so it was a believable story. Instead, she decided to tell him the truth.

"Why on earth would you do that, Savanah?" Rod asked.

"They killed the Johnsons and attacked the Bertrands. I've got Mr. and Mrs. B at my house now. We need to know what we're up against. We have to find a way to stop them from picking us off one by one."

Rod shook his head. "It's a crazy idea."

"That's what I said," Jason agreed.

"If we know how many of them there are," Savanah said, "we can form a plan to stop them,"

"I can tell you how many. A whole neighborhood full. There's like thirty or forty houses back there."

She hadn't seen it since they started construction and hadn't been happy that a developer had purchased the property. She disliked all the trucks tearing up their road and the increased traffic with people speeding by her farm. But, other than the drunk teens plowing through her fence trying to do donuts in her field, she'd not had any trouble with anyone from the new community.

"I need to see it for myself," Savanah said.

"Well, shit. Let me grab my rifle, and I'll walk over there with you," Rod said.

At least ten minutes passed and Savanah thought Rod had changed his mind. She was just about to leave without him when he appeared at his back door. He was loaded down as if he were going into combat. Gone were his PJs and slippers. He had changed into tactical pants and a T-shirt topped with body armor, helmet, leg holster, and enough ammunition in pouches on a tactical vest to take on a whole army.

"All righty. Let's do this thing," Rod said as he pulled back the charging handle to his AR-15 rifle.

Savanah felt kind of naked compared to Rod. She clutched her AR-15 close to her chest and followed Jason and Rod across the field and over his neighbor's fence. Rod stopped and held a hand up. "Wait here. I'm going to tell August to keep an eye on my place."

Rod ran up and knocked on August Rubin's door. A moment later, the six-foot-four, three-hundred-pound man appeared. Savanah knew August to be a gruff but generous man. Keegan often earned extra cash helping him around his small hobby farm. He'd been good to her son, and Savanah appreciated it.

August looked around Rod and nodded to a greeting to Jason and Savanah before disappearing inside. Rod just stood there, holding the door open. A moment later, August exited his house dressed similarly to Rod. The two men joined Savanah and Jason.

"Once we cross the road, we should split up. Rod and I can make our way around to the other side near the golf course. From there, we can see anyone coming and going from the north," August said.

Savanah hadn't been aware the community had more than one entrance. August seemed much more familiar with the layout.

"That sounds like a good plan," Savanah said.

"Can someone explain what we hope to learn by spying on them?" Jason asked. "What good does it do to know how many people live there?"

"I'm more concerned with how many guns they have than how many people live there," August said. "They're targeting the elderly and defenseless folks along the road. They be afraid of getting into a gun battle, but I want to be sure what weapons they have available."

"Doesn't that mean that they know who lives in what houses?" Savannah said.

"Could be. Before the lights went out, a few folks had reported being broken into. They could have been casing the houses to see who to rob," August said.

"Still," Jason said. "We're risking them seeing us, for what?"

"I think it's about time we put a stop to their shenanigans before we lose any more neighbors. I waited, thinking the sheriff would be around soon, but evidently, that ain't about to happen. I'm not usually one for taking the law into my own hands, but enough is enough. Folks like the Bertrands worked hard for what they got, and they don't deserve to be gunned down in the driveway like dogs," August said.

"You really think there is something we can do about it?" Savannah asked.

"Won't know until we see what we're up against," August said.

Even before they crossed the road to the Spring Hill gated community, Savanah could see the high roofs peeking above the eight-foot wall surrounding the property. Savannah and the others stopped and crouched behind a row of bushes that lined the road and listened. Savanah heard voices, but they were too far away to make out what was being said.

"I'll go first. Savanah, you follow after me," August said as he straightened.

As Savanah stepped around the shrubbery, she spotted an older red truck in the ditch down the street to her left. Jason gasped. Savanah recalled seeing a similar truck filled with men chasing down rich kids when she'd first seen Jason after the lights went out. It looked like they'd followed them home. The bullet hole through the windshield was a good indication that the encounter hadn't ended well for the men in the truck.

As August and Savanah crossed the road, Jason ran to the truck. August dropped down beside the perimeter wall and pulled

Savanah down with him while Jason circled the vehicle. He shook his head and ran back to join Rod.

A knot formed in the pit of her stomach. The men had been someone's sons and fathers. How would their families make it without them? Would they ever even know what had happened to them? She thought how awful it must be for them not knowing.

August pulled a pair of binoculars from a pouch on his belt and scanned down the wall running along the road in front of the community. He lowered the binos and waved for Rod and Jason to join them.

Together they traveled west along the wall to where it dropped down to three feet. All Savanah could see from that point were the spacious lawns and the backs of the large southern French country-style homes. The tall, sloping, hipped rooflines with barrel-tiles, along with tall rectangular windows, and the natural stone facade of the exterior of French country architecture were common among the homes in the community.

Savanah didn't see a soul outside. Most of the windows were closed. That detail told her that the residents hadn't made it home before the lights went out. No one could bear to remain inside a closed-up house in south Louisiana without air conditioning.

At the back of the community, there were several houses with their windows open. Towels hung over the lounge chairs that flanked a large pool of one home.

"See the cooler?" Rob pointed. "Next to the grill. Someone's home there. You smell that. I bet it's steaks."

"Bastards," August said. "Probably from the Johnsons' cows."

"We're coming up on the golf course," Rob whispered. "The wall ends where the green begins."

"The back of the community is wooded," August said. "Past the trees is a chain-link fence."

Just before reaching the green of the golf course, Savanah spotted the community pool. Her heart flipped inside her chest. She recognized the half-dozen or so men lounging around it—and so did Jason.

"Isn't that...?" Rod said, turning to Jason.

Savanah was having a hard time reading Jason's face though he was definitely surprised to see his brother and cousins lounging around the pool of this exclusive community. It was bad. Very bad for all of them. It meant that they'd be going up against the Blanchard family. Were they behind the residents' crime spree? They had to be.

"I thought they'd set up in town," August said.

"I thought so too," Jason said.

NINE

Will

DAY SIX

Will and Gus had just entered the apartment complex before a paunchy man came running out, yelling something about Rudy.

"I told those fools he had nothing to do with the shooting. Why didn't they listen?" Gus said.

"Maybe they had their own agenda and used the kid as an excuse," Will said.

Gus handed his bags of medication to the man in front of him. "I gotta go find him."

"You probably shouldn't go alone," Will said.

"Don't tell Jaz," Gus called as he ran off.

Will had no intention of telling Jaz, but he wasn't going to lie to her if she asked.

"What is all this?" the paunchy man asked.

"Vitamins." Will lied. "He was afraid that if the man knew that he was possibly carrying prescription painkillers, he might not be so keen to hand them over."

"You heading to Gus and Jaz's place?"

"No, Isabella and Kevin's."

"They still together? I saw him with that chick Gus found in old man Hernandez's apartment," the man said.

"Last night?"

"No. This morning. They were coming out of an apartment on the back side of the complex. They've just about cleaned out every unit in here."

"Of food?" Will asked.

"No, man. Drugs. Prescription. Illegal. Don't matter to him."

"He's a druggie?"

The guy nodded. "Bad."

"Shit," Will said. "Does Isabella know?"

"I don't think so. I don't think she'd keep him around if she knew where he spent all his money," the guy said.

"You might want to hide these," he said, holding up one of the bags.

Will nodded. In light of this new information, he hoped that Isabella was through with the guy. She deserved much better.

As they approached Isabella's building, Will tried to think of a way to find out what was in the pill bottles. It would be useless to have them if they couldn't use them if someone got injured or sick.

"Do you know if there is anyone around here who's a nurse?" Will asked as they climbed the stairs.

The man pointed over his shoulder. "Candice works at a nursing home. I'm not sure if she's a nurse."

Nursing homes were filled with elderly people who took lots of medication.

"That's good to know. Thanks."

Cayden must have seen them coming from the window and opened the door before Will even knocked. The paunchy man dumped the bags of pills onto the floor and backed out the door. "I gotta go help, Gus. Jaz will have my ass if he doesn't make it home."

"Thanks for your help," Will said, closing the door.

Isabella sat up on the sofa. "What's up with Gus?"

No Other Choice

Will nodded toward the door. "Some guy told Gus there had been some issue with Rudy and he went to find him."

"Oh shit. We just saw some gangbangers chasing him through the complex."

Will was torn. He should go after Gus, but he had Cayden to think about. What would happen to his son if he got himself killed in the middle of Rudy's business?

"Don't even consider it," Isabella said. "Gus knew what he was getting himself into. He knows the people Rudy runs with."

"I know. It's just—he's got a kid on the way," Will said.

"I know. Jaz is going to kill him for being so stupid."

Will wouldn't want to be Gus when Jaz found out about the kid in the grocery store.

"What's in the bags?" Cayden asked.

"Medications," Will said. "Hopefully, there is at least one bottle of antibiotics, but all the labels are missing. But we do have this." He opened one of the trash sacks and rummaged around until he located the burn cream for Isabella's arm.

As he sat down to apply the ointment to her wound, he heard voices outside. He listened. None of them sounded like Gus or Rudy. He handed the medication to Isabella and rushed to the window.

Two of Kevin's bandmates were in the parking lot.

"What's up? Are Gus and Rudy all right?" Will called down.

"Don't know about them. We're looking for Kevin," one of the bandmates said.

Will thought about telling them what Gus had said about Kevin being with that other girl, but he decided he should mind his own business.

"What happened at the store?" Isabella asked.

Will turned away from the window, leaving Kevin's friends to worry about locating him on their own. "Some kid got shot. For some reason, Gus was afraid Rudy would be blamed since they're from rival groups.

"Is that where you lost your shirt?" Isabella asked.

Will glanced down and his face flushed at realizing he'd forgotten that he was shirtless. "I used it to control the kid's bleeding."

"Cayden, there are three trash bags on the floor by my bed. One of them should have a shirt your dad can wear," Isabella said.

As Cayden left to retrieve one of Kevin's shirts, Will turned his attention back to the parking lot below. More people were moving about now that the water was receding a little. He thought about heading back to the store and seeing if he could retrieve the shopping cart filled with supplies he'd been forced to abandon. There was a chance it might still be there. He'd sure feel much better heading out with those supplies, but it was risky. Maybe too risky.

Cayden returned with a small yellow and green striped polo style shirt. Will held it out in front of him.

"It might be a little tight on you," Isabella snickered.

Cayden pulled a second shirt from behind his back. "Here, I know you prefer black."

Will was pleased to see some of his son's old sense of humor returning. They'd used to razz on each other all the time. He suddenly realized that he'd seen more of Cayden's teeth in the last few days than in the past two years. He wasn't sure how he could be so light-hearted under the circumstances but suspected Isabella's presence had something to do with it. Either way, it was good to see.

Will was pulling the T-shirt over his head when he heard a woman scream. Isabella shot to her feet and sprinted to the window. "That was Jaz," she said.

"Gus!" Will said.

Regret flooded in. He knew he should have gone with him.

Isabella rushed to the door with Cayden on her heels.

"Wait. I'll go. You're in no shape," Will said, pushing past her.

"Jaz needs me," Isabella said.

Will grabbed his rifle and followed after her. "Hold on to my arm then. I don't want you falling down the stairs."

A crowd was gathered on the second-floor landing. Jaz was at the end of the walkway with her head hung over the railing, barfing.

"There's Izzy," someone in the crowd whispered, and everyone turned to stare at her.

"Jaz?" Isabella called over them. "Is everything all right?"

Jaz spun around wide-eyed. "Oh my God, Izzy." Jaz started toward her.

Isabella stepped around a man and a woman to move toward Jaz. The crowd parted between them.

"Izzy, stop!" Jaz yelled, holding out her hand, palm facing out.

"What? Jaz, what's wrong?" Isabella asked.

Will rushed toward her just as the crowd engulfed her. He pushed his way through and reached for her arm, but she turned toward the apartment door before he got to her. Isabella screamed. It was one of those blood-curdling screams like from the horror movies. Will had never before heard such a thing in real life. Her hand flew up to cover her mouth, and she dropped to her knees as Jaz reached her.

"No! No! No!" she cried out. She turned to Jaz. "Who would do such a thing?" she sobbed into Jaz's chest, her shoulders shuddering.

Jaz pulled Isabella to her feet, moved her out from the doorway. Will stepped up to see. The smell hit him first. It was like a mixture of vomit, piss, and feces. And then he saw him, splayed out on the floor like a butchered animal. Blood covered the floor and walls. There was hardly a surface that was clear of it. Blood even splattered the ceiling. Kevin looked as if he had been gutted. It was an inhuman sight. Will found it hard to accept that one human could be so brutal to another. And then he remembered Cayden.

Will spun around, grabbed Cayden by the arms, and pushed him back toward the stairs. "We have to go."

"What about Isabella?" Cayden asked.

Isabell was hysterical. She was in no shape to travel. Could he just leave her like that? Would Cayden leave her like that was the bigger question, and Will knew the answer was no.

"Let's get her back to the apartment," Will said.

"What's in there?" Cayden asked.

"Kevin. He's been killed." Will knew he couldn't sugarcoat it, but he wasn't about to describe the gruesome scene for his son.

"Isabella," Cayden said softly.

Will made his way through the crowd and walked up behind Isabella and Jaz. "Let's get her away from here. I'll take her back to her place."

"Okay," Jaz said, nodding. Mascara ran down her smooth cheeks. He feared she wasn't safe there without Gus. "You want to come with us?"

"I'm leaving. As soon as Gus gets back, we're getting the hell out of here."

Will nodded.

Cayden took Isabella's hand and led her toward the stairs. "Let's go back to your apartment."

Jaz grabbed Will's arms as he attempted to join them. "Where's Gus?"

Will knew she needed to know that her boyfriend was safe, and he hated to tell her where he'd gone. "He went after Rudy. There was trouble at the grocery store. A young man got shot."

"I'm going to kill him. He's the one that brought those two psychos over here and them in the apartment across from me. I told Gus that I thought they killed Mr. Hernandez. Now they've done gone and butchered Kevin. Any of us could be next."

"Has anyone seen them?"

"I saw them," a teenage boy said, stepping up beside Jaz. The scrawny kid stuck his chest out and glared at Will, trying to look more formidable than he was.

"Where? How long ago?"

"This morning. They were going into that apartment at the end of Building C."

"Someone should go check it out," Will said.

"You the one with the big-ass gun," the kid said, pointing at the rifle in Will's hand.

Will said nothing. He turned his back on the kid and made his way through the crowd to join Cayden and Isabella. He wasn't about to leave them alone to go on some wild goose chase. If Gus returned, he'd discuss it with him and they'd come up with a plan. In the meantime, he was getting them back to Isabella's apartment and barricading the door.

TEN

Savanah

DAY SIX

Savanah leaned against the stone wall that surrounded the exclusive subdivision feeling ill. The revelation that Jason's brother and cousins were behind the crime spree that had occurred on their road had knocked the wind out of her. Their situation was so much worse than she'd imagined. The Blanchards were a ruthless bunch and had previously only been kept in check by the sheriff of Calcasieu Parish and the major crimes task force assigned to investigate their criminal activities.

"So what do we do now?" she asked.

"We go home and protect our families," Rod said, jabbing a finger in the direction of their houses.

"What we need to do is organize folks to come back here and take those bastards out," August said.

"What do you think, Jason?" Savanah asked.

Jason looked at her with a blank expression. She knew what a difficult position this put him in. Some part of her worried that he'd leave them to join his family. It couldn't be easy to hear August contemplating killing them.

"August is right about organizing folks. Together, we can put up barricades at the ends of the road, post guards, and patrol the area. If we put up resistance, they'll likely move on to some easier target," Jason said.

"But they're using the residents of Sugar Hill to do their dirty work. They won't care if a few get killed," Rod said.

"A lot of us could be killed if we just charge up on them, guns blazing. They're entrenched in that community. They'll use the women and children as human shields. Could you live with that?" Jason asked.

Savanah hadn't thought much about the families in there. Up until that moment, she'd thought of them as the enemy—a threat to her children. But now she understood that they were as much the victims in all this as she was. She couldn't live with herself if her actions got children killed.

"I vote for barricading the road. We could use the tractors to move cars and trucks to block them," Savanah said. "Maybe we could build a wall even, like the one they have around their community.

"I think we're going to regret not taking the fight directly to them. They can just wait and pick us off one by one like they've been doing," August said.

"Maybe we should all just pull up stakes and leave—let them have the place," Rod said.

That was an option. They could load up everything they could carry and flee. But where would they go? She couldn't go into town even if the Blanchards didn't take over. Her ex-husband and the mayor's henchmen were there.

"I honestly don't think it will come to that. I'm telling you, if they see resistance, they'll move on," Jason said.

"Yeah?" August asked. He glared at Jason. "I guess you'd know better than anyone how your family operates."

Jason looked away. He'd left that life behind, but the shame appeared to follow him. It had to be very difficult for Jason now thought Savanah. He could get caught in the middle with neither side trusting him. Could that make her and her children targets? It was so difficult to know the right thing to do in these situations. They needed Jason and he needed them. She couldn't turn her back on him now though she did worry that it would make her an enemy to the rest of her neighbors if they saw Jason as a threat.

"Let's just go and talk to some of the other neighbors and see what they say. After that, we'll form a plan," Jason said.

Rod nodded. August turned and crossed the road.

Savanah took one last look over her shoulder as she stepped onto the blacktop to follow him. She prayed that her neighbors would get involved, otherwise, she'd be picking up her children and fleeing with no idea where they could go to be safe.

August chose to stay home, claiming they'd have better luck convincing residents to join them if he weren't there. Savanah wasn't sure why he felt that way, but if there was a chance it was true, she was grateful he recognized it and stayed away.

Savanah, Jason, and Rod stopped at the house closest to Sugar Hill. As they approached the walkway leading from the garage to the house, Savanah got the sense that no one was home. The side door stood open and clothes and papers were strewn about the porch as if someone had left in a hurry.

Jason stuck a hand out and halted Savanah. "Wait. This could have been them."

Savanah stopped in her tracks. She couldn't bear the thought that the Herberts could have become victims like the Robertsons. They had small children.

"Stay here. I'll go," Jason said. "Rod, you coming?"

Reluctantly, Rod joined him and the two cautiously entered the house through the side door. The waiting was torture.

So many horrible scenarios ran through Savanah's mind and she fought to rein in her imagination by trying to come up with ways to build a fortress around their community. She pictured medieval castles and wild west military forts.

A moment later, Jason poked his head out of an upstairs window.

"It's empty. It looks like they packed up and left on their own."

"How can you tell?" Savanah asked.

"All the family photos are missing from the walls and there are kids' toys in trash bags like the children wanted to take them all, and the parents said no."

That would be her daughter, Kylie. She would throw such a fit if they tried to leave without her toys. Savanah hoped to avoid that confrontation, but if other residents had fled, what hope was there of securing the neighborhood. She began contemplating how she could take the animals with them and then stopped herself. They hadn't lost yet. If it came to it, she'd find a way, but she needed to focus on saving her farm. That was their best hope.

Their second stop was the next homestead over. A young couple had just moved in a few months prior, and Savanah hadn't really got to know them yet. A split-rail fence surrounded the small single-story house where chickens roamed and scratched on the back lawn. Ducks swam in a small pond. A large garden was set out in rows filled with fall vegetables. Several unfinished building projects were in various stages of completion to the east of the house. They approached the door with caution, not wanting to be mistaken for Sugar Hill residents. Before they reached the house, the back door flew open.

"You're trespassing," a twenty-something man said. He was holding a shotgun, pointed at the ground.

Savanah was glad that he wasn't a shoot-first type of guy.

"Hi!" Jason said. "We're your neighbors. This is Savanah

Fontenot. She lives three farms over. This is Rod. He's two farms over."

"I know who you are," the man said as he set the shotgun in the crook of his elbow and leaned against the door jamb. His super skinny jeans and long beard gave off a hipster vibe. Part of his long blond hair had been pulled back into a Viking-style man braid, revealing large gauges in his ear lobes.

"We wanted to check in on you and make sure everyone was okay. There's been some trouble since the lights went out, and—" Jason said.

"We know about the trouble. We heard it," the man said.

"We've just come from the Sugar Hill neighborhood. We believe that armed thugs have moved in there and are forcing the residents to commit crimes for them," Rod said.

"Oh yeah? How are they doing that?"

"Holding their families as hostages," Savanah replied.

"You saw this?" a woman of a similar age to the man asked as she appeared beside him in the doorway. She was petite and attractive in her oversized prairie dress and white socks. Her hair was in pigtails.

"We did. The group holding them is from a local crime family. They're quite dangerous," Savanah said.

The couple looked at one another. "And we're all in danger?" the woman asked.

"Yes. That's why we stopped by today. We would like to get your help," Jason said.

"Help? How can we help? You need to get the cops," the man said.

"The cops aren't coming to help us. We need to look out for one another. If we work together, we can defend all our homes," Savanah said.

The couple was quiet for a long moment.

Savanah took in all the improvements they'd made to the place since moving in. Surely they wouldn't want to have to leave it all behind. They had to know that trouble would come for them eventually.

"What can we do?" the man finally responded.

"We want to barricade the road on the east and the west ends. We'll use cars and trucks to form a wall. We'll need people to guard them and do patrols," Jason said.

"That sounds too easy. What will stop them from shooting their way in?" the young woman asked.

"They won't. When they see we are willing to defend our property and it's too difficult, they'll go find someone easier to target."

"That doesn't seem right, just letting them do this to some other community," she said.

"Our only other choice is to do nothing and let them pick us off one by one. They've already killed several families."

The man whispered something then the woman nodded. "All right. We'll help. Just let us know what you need us to do," he said.

"Do you have any other weapons?" Jason asked.

"Yeah, a hunting rifle and a .38 caliber pistol," the man said.

"Ammo?" Rod asked.

The man nodded. "Some."

Savanah was relieved. She was hopeful that they could succeed if the other residents were as easy to convince.

"Good. We may need it if others don't have weapons," Jason said.

"How many others do you have?" the woman asked.

"Just you so far, but we're going from door to door, so hopefully a lot more by nightfall," Jason said.

"What if they come for us before then?"

Jason didn't answer her.

"You can come to my house. There's safety in numbers," Savanah said. She couldn't tell them her theory that the Blanchards might spare her place because they and Jason were family.

"We could do that," the man said. "I'm Luca. This is my girlfriend, June."

"I'm Savanah. I'm sorry we had to meet under these circumstances."

"We should go," Jason said.

"Can we grab our go-bags?" Luca asked.

"Of course," Savanah said.

Savanah took one last look over their garden and livestock. They were set up to make it long term. They appeared to be honest, hardworking people. She was happy to be adding them to their new little crew.

Savanah's four-year-old son, Karson, ran across the pasture to greet them. Kendra hadn't said anything, but she looked relieved that they were home. Savanah didn't want to worry them and wasn't keen to leave them again. If convincing the neighbors hadn't been so crucial to their safety, she would just stay behind with her four children and let the others handle rounding up the neighbors.

"Seeing a woman with us might disarm some folks who might otherwise not be inclined to open their doors," Jason had argued. He was right. It was just difficult to leave the kids.

"But why can't we come," Kylie whined, staring up at Savanah with her big brown eyes.

"Because you need to stay here and make sure the pigs don't get out and that your kitten behaves himself with the hens."

Kylie huffed and stomped off without a word.

Mrs. B handed Savanah a bundle of freshly made cookies. "She'll be fine. I'll keep her occupied."

The children seemed to be loving having a grandmother figure again. It had been five years since her mother had died and Kylie and Keegan didn't even remember her. Savanah regretted not getting to know her neighbors better before all this. There never seemed to be enough time in the day. There was always so much work to be done that visiting hadn't seemed possible.

"Thanks for looking after them," Savanah said.

Karson squealed loudly as June swung him in a circle by his arms. She seemed good with kids. Savanah took a quick glance around at the little community that was forming. She'd always heard that it took a village to raise kids and knew there was no way she could manage now without one, not and protect them from the evil that had descended upon them.

"You ready?" Jason asked.

Savanah lifted the rifle that dangled from the sling hung around her neck and fell in behind him. "Ready as I'll ever be."

ELEVEN

Will

DAY SIX

Will knew he should say something. Isabella had just discovered her boyfriend had been heinously murdered. There just weren't any words that could fix that. As soon as they returned to her apartment, she retreated to her bedroom and locked the door. Will understood. He'd done the same after Melanie died. It was horrific what those psychos had done to Kevin. All he could do was be there for her.

Thirty minutes later, Jaz arrived and stood outside Isabella's bedroom door. "Please, Izzy, let me in." She tried the knob, but the door was locked. Jaz threw her hands in the air and walked to the front door. "Please tell her that I'll be downstairs if she needs me."

Will nodded.

The young woman from across the hall followed after her. "You sure you should go back down there? What if they come back?" she asked.

"I'm packing my shit. As soon as Gus gets back, we're getting the hell out of here," Jaz said.

"What? Where are you going to go?" the woman asked.

"My mom's in Liberty. That's where we should have gone

when they called for an evacuation. But Gus felt he had an obligation as the manager of the complex."

"That's a long way. How on earth are you going to get there without a vehicle?"

"Walk if I have to. I'm not staying here," Jaz said as she exited the apartment.

Three of Kevin's bandmates lined the sofa. Two more leaned against the wall by the door. They all looked devastated.

Cayden sat across from Will at the kitchen island, chewing his thumbnail. Will's first thought was to grab his son and get the hell out of there. They could be in Deer Park by nightfall if they left now, putting him closer to his sister in Vincent, Louisiana. They could stay the night at the high school's football stadium. They'd find a dry spot to sleep in the bleachers.

"We should go too," Cayden said.

Will did a double-take. He couldn't believe what he'd heard.

"We're safe in here, Cayden. We have guns, and there's too many of us for them to break in. They can't hurt you."

"I'm not worried about me," Cayden said. "It's Isabella. We need to get her away from here. She can't stay here like this."

"We can't make her come with us," Will said.

"She might want to go. She might want to leave behind the memory."

"Now isn't the time to ask her. Besides, she's locked herself in her room."

"Maybe I should ask her?"

It was as Will suspected. He wasn't going to get Cayden to leave without Isabella.

"We should wait until the morning. You can ask her then," Will conceded.

"Okay," Cayden said. "What do we need to do to be ready?"

Will stared at him for a long moment. Cayden was such a bright and kind person. Melanie would be so proud. "We should gather all the food and water we can find. I'll inventory my pack and see what else we need. I know we could use more flashlights, matches, or a lighter. I'd like to put as much as we can of that medication Gus and I found in a bag and take it. We may never find more."

"We need a shopping cart to carry everything," Cayden said.

"It's too dangerous to go back to the grocery store. It would be great to find a bicycle with a trailer like your mom had. Remembe- Cayden shook his head. He'd been too young to recall it.

Tears stung Will's eyes as he pictured Melanie pedaling down their street with Cayden seated in the bike trailer. "She used to take you to the park on her bike. She had this cart thing that attached to the rear tire,"

"I've seen those. Our neighbor had one," Cayden said. "I bet we could find one. How much weight would it hold?"

"I think it was rated to like eighty pounds, maybe. We'd be able to carry almost ten gallons of water if we found one like that."

"We should go look for one," Cayden said.

"Not a good idea."

"Why not? You have a gun."

"What if Isabella needs us?" Will asked.

Cayden glanced around the room. "We won't go far."

"It's just not a good idea. Not until the killers are found."

"You think they stuck around? That's kind of dumb. They had to know everyone would know they did it."

"It's not a chance I'm willing to take and no one's looking for them," he said, pointing to the band. After making a quick stroll through the neighborhood, Kevin's bandmates had returned to Isabella's. From the looks of the bedrolls, it seemed they intended to stay awhile. "When Gus gets back, I'll have a talk with him. He may know which apartment might have that bike we're looking for," Will said.

Will reached across the island and rested a hand on Cayden's shoulder. "Listen, Cayden, it's going to be hard out there. It may be worse than what we encountered on our way to the storage facility.

People will be even more desperate now. They'll be hungry and willing to fight for even a small amount of food."

Cayden looked him in the eyes. "I know. I can handle it. We'll be all right."

"I know you can. I just don't want to take unnecessary risks. We'll do what we need to do to get to Aunt Savanah's, but we have to be smart about it."

"I'm looking forward to seeing them."

Will smiled. "Me too!"

"What do you think it's like there?"

Will's shoulder lifted in a half shrug. "I imagine things are pretty much normal for them. They have solar for their well and refrigerator. They have a garden and animals."

"How long will it take to get there?"

Will ran a hand over his stubbled face and did the calculation in his head.

"A week. Maybe more."

Cayden wrinkled his nose. "A week? It's gonna suck, isn't it?"

"I'm afraid so. It's over a hundred miles. We can't travel very far in a day on foot."

"We need a car. I wish we still hand Granddad's Jeep."

"Me too. Sorry about that."

"It's not your fault."

Will believed it was. He thought every bit of it was his fault. If only they'd left sooner, they would have arrived at the lake house before the EMP strike. They would have been away from all the chaos here in the city. It was comforting to hear that Cayden didn't blame him—at least for losing the Jeep.

While Cayden retreated to the guest room to read, Will searched the drawers for a pen and paper. He was seated at the island, making notes about what they needed for the road, when one of the bandmates shouted, "It's Gus. He's back."

Will lowered his pen and crossed the room. Flanking the opposite side of the window, Will spotted Gus in the parking lot below.

"Hey, Gus. Did you find Rudy?" someone yelled.

Will couldn't hear his reply.

Jaz greeted Gus in the parking lot. He opened his arms out to greet her but Jaz flew at him and beat her hands against his chest, screaming in his face before throwing her arms around him. He held her tight and allowed her to sob into his neck then looked up and gestured for Will to join him downstairs. Will held up one finger to indicate he'd be down in a moment.

Will walked down the hall to the guest room where Cayden was seated on the floor, going through their bags. He had things in piles and was organizing them into groups.

"Gus just returned. He wants me downstairs. I'll be right back."

"Don't forget to ask him about the bike. We're going to need a lot of stuff to make it to Aunt Savanah's."

"I'll ask," Will said as he backed out of the room. He was shutting the door when he heard Isabella behind him.

"Gus is back?" Her eyes were red and swollen from crying. She had changed clothes and looked like she was going for a hike with her running tights, long-sleeve shirt, and hiking boots.

"He's downstairs. He asked me to go down."

"I'm coming with you," she said, pulling her hair into a ponytail.

What could he say to that? It was a free country. At least it had been.

The bandmates all gathered around her as she attempted to walk through the living room. She politely stepped around them and continued out the door. Gus met them on the stairs and stopped, but Jaz rushed past, entered their apartment, and slammed the door behind her. Isabella turned to watch her go but quickly spun to look away. Will was unsure if Kevin's body was still inside the apartment across from Gus and Jaz's. Isabella hadn't asked. It wasn't like you could call the morgue and have his body transported to the funeral home. It sounded callous, but right then, they had to take care of the living.

"Jaz told me. I'm so very sorry, Izzy."

"We have to find their asses before they do this to someone else," Isabella said.

Will blinked several times, her words taking him by surprise. He'd never thought of her as a vigilante but he could understand her reaction. When someone you love is taken, you want to blame someone. You want them to pay. When it had happened to him, he'd had no one to blame but himself. It was hard to go on.

"I don't know. Jaz wants to take off for her mother's. If I go off again, she'll kill me," Gus said.

"But no one is safe with them still out there," Isabella said, tears filling her eyes.

"I know, Izzy. That's what I told Jaz, but we got a kid coming. I have to think about Jaz and the baby," Gus said.

Isabella turned to Will. "I guess you're going to use Cayden as an excuse."

Will understood that it was the pain talking, but he still didn't like it.

"It's too dangerous. We should just pack up and go too," Will said.

Isabella turned and stomped back up the stairs. She flung open the door and yelled back, "If you're not going to go find them, I will."

"Shit," Gus said. "I can't."

"I understand," Will said.

Hey, do you know if anyone around here has a bike with one of the kid's trailers attached to it? Will asked as they climbed the steps.

Gus stopped at the landing then looked out across the parking lot, his eyes scanning apartment buildings. "Two forty-two used to have one."

"Thanks," Will said. "Good luck out there."

"You too. I hope you make it to Louisiana okay," Gus said before disappearing inside his apartment.

Will descended the stairs and took in the buildings across the parking lot. He had to talk Isabella out of searching for the couple. It would serve no useful purpose at the moment except to exact revenge. It wasn't as if they could call the cops and have them arrested. The only thing they could do was shoot them. What if they were innocent? He had enough on his conscience. Could he live with that too?

Isabella's door opened, and she stomped down the stairs with the bandmates trailing behind her. Over her shoulder hung the AR-15 Betley had given her. This was not good. She was in no emotional state to confront anyone. She wasn't thinking clearly. Isabella wanted revenge, but she could get herself killed by seeking it.

Isabella was going, and there was nothing he could say to stop her. He could see that all over her face.

"Isabella!" Cayden yelled from the top of the stairs. "Please!"

Cayden too was aware of what that type of grief could do to a person. He'd been only eleven at the time, but he was old enough to remember.

She stopped and turned then stared at him for a long moment. "I have to, Cayden. I have to."

"Then I'm coming too," Cayden said. He held a pistol in his hand as he descended the stairs.

"Oh hell no," Will said, jabbing his finger toward the door. "You get your ass back up those stairs. You're not going anywhere." Will grabbed Isabella's arm as she passed him on the stairs. "We should just leave here. This won't make you feel better."

"I'm going, Will."

"Shit, Isabella. Don't do this," Will pleaded.

"Just go. Take Cayden and go."

She was taking her anger out on him. He could handle it. But could Cayden?

"Don't go, Izzy," Jaz called down. She was hanging over the railing at the top of the second-floor landing.

Her face was contorted with fear. Isabella was lucky to have such caring friends and Will wondered if she realized it at that moment. He hadn't back then. He'd pushed everyone away, and soon they'd all stopped calling, stopped dropping off food, and stopped taking Cayden out for ice cream to get him out of the house. Gus and Jaz were leaving. If Isabella chose to stay, would she be alone? Will's gaze scanned the bandmates. Would they stay and support her? From what he'd seen, she didn't respect them. It was a bad situation. Isabella would likely not survive if she didn't leave with Will and Cayden. But in her current frame of mind, would she prove to be unsafe out there on the road?

Isabella stared up at Jaz. "I have to do this. Just go to your mom's. Take care of the baby."

"Okay. Okay. Gus will help find them. One condition, though, you have to come to help me pack."

Isabella stepped down one step of the stairs, not backing down.

"We'll bring them here—if we find them," the pudgy bandmate said.

"Yeah. We'll let you decide what to do with them. Just help Jaz," another bandmate said.

Isabella turned slightly.

Will didn't think that was a good idea. What purpose would that serve? Feeding Isabella's thirst for revenge would only make things worse in the long run and lead her down a path from which there was no return. Justice, on the other hand, might serve a purpose. In Will's mind, it should be swift and intended to prevent future violence. The idea of a mock trial came to mind. If Isabella could hear the accusations against the couple, be presented with the evidence, and then have a say in the punishment, maybe, just maybe, she might not forever regret her actions. Justice would honor the memory of her boyfriend. Revenge might forever taint it.

Will stepped down next to Isabella and took her free hand. "I know why you want to see them pay, I do." Isabella's face contorted. Her mouth opened and closed as if she wanted to say something and then thought better of it. "If they're still in this area, we'll find them," Will said, gesturing to Gus and the bandmates. "And we'll bring them back here to stand trial. They should have the right to defend themselves. If we all agree that they did this horrific thing, we'll vote on a sentence." Will scanned the group. Some nodded in agreement. "All right?" he said, giving her hand a gentle squeeze.

Isabella was silent a long moment before nodding. "Find them, Will."

"We'll do our best. Will you look after Cayden?"

She lowered her head. The tears began to flow again, and she wiped them away with the back of her hand. "Go find those assholes," she said.

"Cayden, stay with Isabella and Jaz. I'm going to go find that bike we talked about," Will said.

"Okay, Dad. Be careful."

"I will." As Gus joined them at the bottom of the stairs, Will waved goodbye to Cayden. "I love you, son."

Cayden nodded.

Will watched as Cayden greeted Isabella at the top of the stairs. He took her hand and led her to Jaz's apartment, and closed the door. A moment later, he appeared at the window.

"I locked the door," he called down.

"Don't open it for anyone but one of us."

"I won't," Cayden said.

TWELVE

Will

DAY SIX

"I think we should post guards at each of these four buildings in case they spot us and run out," Gus said.

"Should we split up like that?" Lloyd asked.

"We're going from door to door. They're going to hear us and take off. If we're all over at building two hundred and they are at building four hundred, they could slip out, and we'd never see them. I don't want to be at this all day and still not find those psychos."

"Okay."

"Lloyd, you and Paul take building three hundred, Stuart and Marcus, you take four hundred while Will and I go door to door in two hundred. If you see anything, call out," Gus said.

As the bandmates went off to their posts, Gus and Will crossed the parking lot toward building two hundred. Gus unlocked the doors without knocking, hoping to surprise the couple. He did surprise a couple, just not the one they were looking for.

"You two should get back to your families. Psycho killers are roaming the complex. They butchered Kevin."

"What the hell. Was it that couple from Mr. Hernandez's apartment?" the middle-aged man asked.

The twenty-something woman threw back the covers and began pulling on clothes. She ran from the room without a word, only taking a fleeting glance back over her shoulder as she went through the doorway.

"We believe it was that couple. Have you seen them today?" Will asked.

The man threw his legs over the bed and pulled on his pants. "I saw the guy. He was headed across the parking lot toward building three hundred. Jerrod Blake found oxy and Xanax in a house a couple of blocks over that he was trading for food."

"You haven't seen the girl?" Gus asked.

"No. The last I saw of her, she and Kevin were heading up the stairs to your building."

"What time was that?"

"Shit, I don't know, man. I don't got no watch or nothing. I don't really pay attention to the time of day anymore. I'd say an hour or so after sunrise. We'd all been partying all night, and I was just heading back to my place to go to bed."

"You partied with the couple and Kevin?" Will asked.

"Yeah. We all hung out here. Someone found one of those old school MP3 players with some retro music on it."

"Were Kevin's bandmates with you guys?" Will asked.

"Not all night. They hooked up with those chicks that live across from Izzy and Kevin."

"We should check with them," Will said.

"You're not suspecting the band, are you? They were tight, bro. They wouldn't have anything to do with hurting Kevin," the man said.

Will turned to Gus. "We should still ask the women if they saw or heard anything."

Gus tilted his head slightly. "Why? You really looking to do a trial for those scumbags? I ain't got time for that. Jaz is going to want to get to her mom's as soon as I get back."

"I would just like to know where the band was when Kevin was killed, is all."

"Whatever. I agreed to find Kevin's killers and bring them back. You do what you want after," Gus said. He headed for the door. "Let's head on over to building three hundred. I have a feeling we'll find them there."

"You should plan on getting you and your family out of here. It's going to get very bad, very quickly," Will told the man as he followed Gus from the room.

Gus stopped at the landing of the second floor and leaned over the railing. Will joined him, taking in the green belt separating the complex from the houses next door. The killer couple could have gone anywhere. It would be like finding a needle in a haystack. Will imagined that if they could have called the police, they too would have had to go door to door questioning each resident on what they might have seen or heard. They might also search outbuildings and cars looking for the couple. They could be hiding inside an RV, or even a boat like the Boston Bomber had. He just hoped this wasn't a total waste of energy because time was running out to get away from the city.

"Hey, Gus, what happened with Rudy? Did you find him?" Will asked.

"Nah, but I ran into one of his homies. He told me that Rudy took off to his baby momma's house to hide out. She lives twenty miles north of here." He shook his head. "It's rough out there. I sure hope he makes it."

"Me too," Will said. "

"I saw something out there. Something troubling."

"What now?"

"I saw some military dudes pulling this Asian guy out of a house full of Mexicans. The Mexicans came out, guns blasting.

The military opened up on them with automatic weapons and mowed them all down. It was a bloodbath. We got the hell out of there quick like."

"You were close enough to see that the guy they took was Asian and not Mexican? Could you be mistaken?" Will asked.

"Nah. I was close enough. I saw the dude around here before. He and a few other Asians came and went from there. Never thought much of it. They run drugs together sometimes. No biggie."

Will stopped at the bottom of the stairs to building three hundred. "And the military got this Asian dude and took him?"

"Yeah."

The military must be rounding up the people from Kim's list, he thought. That means there is a list, and insurgents really have infiltrated Houston.

It was concerning that it was occurring so close to where he and his son were staying. Will hoped that they would be able to get away before any of it spilled over into their area.

"That is a worry," Will said. "Are there any other places these Asians hang out around here?"

"Why are you so concerned about the Asians? I'm more concerned that the military is operating as law enforcement in the streets of the United States. Doesn't that violate some law? The Posse Comitatus or some shit like that?"

Will wondered if the law still applied considering that they'd been attacked by foreign powers. Posse Comitatus was a federal law that limited the use of federal military personnel to enforce domestic policies on US soil. They were going after foreign fighters.

"The law doesn't stop the National Guard," Will said.

"Really? So they can just roll on up on a house and drag someone off, and that's legal?" Gus asked.

"I don't know, man. It's hard to judge with all the crazy shit going on. Someone has to do it. I haven't seen a single police officer since I was carjacked on the first day," Will said.

"Damn, you were carjacked?"

"The cops were chasing some dude, and he yanked me out of my ride and took off with one of the officers hanging onto the steering wheel."

"Crazy!" Gus said.

Will couldn't tell him everything that happened that day. He wasn't sure why? It wasn't like he could get into trouble for giving out classified secrets or anything. He just didn't think Gus would believe him.

Starting with the ground-level apartments, Gus unlocked the first door and eased it open. Will burst through, trying to mimic how he'd seen Betley clear a room back at the law office. His heart pounded in his chest as he scanned the room from corner to corner. The living room was clear. Will repeated the maneuver throughout the one-bedroom apartment, and they moved to the next three units. There was no sign of the couple.

"What apartment was it that you said might have that bike with a trailer I'm looking for?" Will asked.

"Three fifty," Gus said.

"Great. I hope it's there."

"You planning on riding bikes all the way to Louisiana?" Gus asked.

"As much as possible. I'm thinking with the trailer, I can haul enough water to at least make it halfway. That's my biggest concern really. Uncontaminated water will be hard to come by, and in this heat, we'd die without it."

"I hadn't really thought about how much water me and Jaz would need. I was going to try to pay Miquel's brother to take us over to Jaz's mom's. I just wasn't thinking about what it would take to go on foot. After you saying you were carjacked, now I'm kinda concerned. We ain't prepared to be on foot," Gus said.

"It might be difficult for Jaz—being pregnant and all," Will said.

"I need to rethink some things before we head out, that's for sure."

Gus inserted the key into the lock of apartment three hundred fifty. He turned the knob and shoved open the door. Will ran through and scanned the corner to the left of the door. A sofa lined one wall. On it sat a man and woman. The man and woman for whom they were looking. The man shot to his feet. He raised his hand as if to shield himself from an incoming bullet. Will's rage threatened to overwhelm him and his finger twitched inside the trigger guard. It would have been so easy to just squeeze and end it all right there.

The woman slowly rose from the sofa, brushing crumbs or something from her short skirt as she stood. She didn't show the same fear the man did. Her dark brown eyes bored through Will. She was deviant to the point of almost daring Will to shoot her. Will looked her up and down. She wasn't covered in Kevin's blood as he'd expected. He knew it wouldn't be that easy to prove their guilt.

"What's up, guys?" the man said, his hands still out in front of him, palms out.

"Kevin's dead," Gus said.

The woman's expression never changed. She lowered herself back onto the sofa. The guy slowly took a seat beside her. Neither of them asked what had happened to Kevin.

"We're going to need you to come with us," Gus said, hiking a thumb over his shoulder.

The woman batted her eyes a few times and cocked her head to one side. "I don't think so. You aren't law enforcement. I don't have to go anywhere with you."

No Other Choice

Gus took two steps toward her, but Will blocked him with an outstretched arm. "Don't fall into her trap."

"You're both coming with us, or you're never leaving this room alive. Take your pick 'cause I got places to be and I ain't got no patience for this shit today," Gus said, stepping back.

"We need you two to come over to Isabella's until we can clear up a few things. We just have a few questions, and then you're free to go on about your day," Will added, trying to get the pair to come with them willingly.

The woman turned to her boyfriend. "You ready to die today?"

His mouth dropped open, and his eyes widened. His skin turned two shades lighter. He wasn't ready to die.

"That's not necessary. We just need to ask you about the last time you saw Kevin."

"I didn't do anything. I wasn't any part of that, man. I'm not covering for you this time, Reba," the man said.

Reba threw her head back and laughed. Will saw the glint of the knife two seconds before she thrust it into her boyfriend's throat. The scream she emitted was unearthly and evil. Will raised his rifle and almost took the shot, but he knew Isabella needed her alive. She needed to hear the woman say she'd done it so she could have closure.

"On your feet!" Will yelled. "Get to your feet, or I will shoot!"

The man's hands were around his throat. Blood spurted through his fingers. Reba casually sat back and crossed her legs, daring them to come to take her.

"Drop the knife!" Gus yelled, holding his baseball bat high in the air.

Will aimed for her chest, ready to drop her if she came off that sofa. Her gaze went from Gus to Will, and she held the knife out, palm down, with the blade pointing down. She smiled as she let it drop to the floor.

"Stand up and turn around," Will said, channeling every cop movie he'd ever watched.

She stood, not taking her eyes off him. A cold chill ran down his spine. The woman before him was pure evil. She'd butchered Kevin and stabbed her boyfriend in cold blood and had zero remorse. If she were allowed to live now, there was no telling how many lives she would take without law enforcement to stop her. An image of Isabella splayed out on the floor covered in blood flashed before him. His blood boiled at the thought. He wanted to drop her right there. He went back and forth over his decision, agonizing over it, knowing even small mistakes could cost people their lives.

"Gus, do you have a knife?"

Gus reached into his front pocket and produced a small, folding pocketknife. He opened it and held it out for Will to see.

"Cut the cord off that lamp and then tie her hands," Will said.

Gus wrapped the electric cord around the woman's hands several times before tying the knots to secure them.

"Okay. Put her on the floor, face down. We're going to tie her feet," Will said.

"Are we hog-tying her?" Gus asked. "We'll have to carry her if we do that."

"I think that's the safest. Unless you want to end up like her boyfriend there," Will said.

Gus glanced at the man and quickly turned away. He'd slumped down on the sofa, his glazed eyes staring up at the ceiling. He'd stopped breathing.

"I'm too tired for this shit. I can't wait to get to my mother-in-law's and get some rest," Gus said.

Will didn't want to burst the man's bubble, but he doubted anyone would be getting much rest from then on. Life had been hard years ago when, without technology, even the simplest tasks would take back-breaking work. He'd had a glimpse of that life as a kid on his grandpa's farm. They'd been old school and didn't have many of the modern conveniences. His grandmother washed clothes in an older wringer washer and hung them to dry on a clothesline outback. His grandpa used a scythe to cut the tall grass for hay and then stacked it loosely in the barn loft to feed the animals. Now, with the looks of things, Will was grateful that they'd taught him and his sister those old ways of living. It might just give them a chance to survive this thing. Heaven help the others without a clue how to do such basic things.

Will and Gus dragged Reba to the door and out onto the landing. Will had no concern about being gentle. She was no lady. He wasn't even sure she was human.

"Lloyd, Paul," Will called out. We found them. Come help us get the girl back to Isabella."

Isabella and Jaz stood over Reba as she lay on the landing just outside the apartment where she'd killed Kevin. Isabella's jaw was set as her eyes bored into the back of the woman's head.

"Roll her over," Isabella said. "I want to see her face."

Will looked over his shoulder, making sure Cayden had obeyed him and remained inside Jaz's apartment. Lloyd and Paul grabbed the woman's feet and hands and rolled her onto her back. She scowled at Isabella. When the corners of Reba's mouth began to turn upward, Will lunged for Isabella. He grabbed her from behind, wrapping his arms around hers, preventing her from raising the rifle she held.

The three young women who lived across from Isabella gasped. Some stepped back and covered their mouths with their hands.

"Don't let her goad you into doing something you'll regret," Will whispered in Isabella's ear.

Isabella turned her head to one side. "Oh, I won't regret it, I can assure you of that."

"Please, Isabella. You want to be sure, right?" Will said.

After witnessing the woman murder her boyfriend in front of him, he was certain she was guilty of killing Kevin, but Isabella needed to be positive as well or what she was about to do could eat her up later in life. He knew that, before all this, she'd been a kind and loving person and hoped that someday soon, she could find her way back there. Killing this woman could make that journey much more difficult. If she heard it from the woman's mouth, at least she wouldn't wonder if she'd killed an innocent person.

Maybe I'm projecting, he thought, knowing all too well how guilt could eat a person alive. He just didn't want that for her.

"Sit her up," Isabella said.

Will eased his grip on Isabella and stepped back as Lloyd and Paul pulled Reba over to the wall and pulled her into a seated position. Will wanted to beat the smug look off the woman's face as she scanned the crowd gathered to judge her.

"Tell her what you did," Gus said.

She stared directly at Isabella then dropped one shoulder and blinked. She had to know what fate awaited her. She was toying with them, enjoying torturing Isabella.

"We were all getting high across the way. Brad passed out and Kevin began making moves on me. He said the two of you'd had a fight—that he was through with you. He called you the 'C' word. I hate that word. It's so disrespectful, don't you agree? That's when I decided to do it. That's when I knew."

Tears were streaming down Isabella's cheeks. Her jaw clenched, and she gripped the rifle so tight her knuckles turned white. Will wanted to stop this before there was too much description. He didn't want Isabella to have that in her head forever. She'd already been traumatized by seeing the body.

He stepped around Isabella and raised his rifle.

"No!" Isabella yelled.

Will turned toward her to reason with her that he should be the one. As he did, he caught movement from the corner of his eye. Jaz screamed, and Will spun back around to find Gus and the woman in a struggle on the ground. Will couldn't make sense of what had happened. Her hands were free. Somehow, she'd gotten them untied, and now she and Gus were struggling for control of a knife. She must have taken one from Lloyd or Paul when they moved her. There wasn't any other explanation.

Jaz ran toward them, but Paul grabbed her and hauled her off her feet. He spun her around and pushed her back a safe distance. Stuart and Marcus rushed over and grabbed the woman, yanking with all their might. She twisted and dropped under Stuart's arm and broke free. Will and Isabella fired simultaneously. Several rounds struck the woman in the chest and abdomen and her mouth formed an O as she realized what had happened and dropped to the ground. Isabella took two steps toward her as Reba gasped for air. She coughed and spat before keeling over and taking her last breath. Will threw his arms around Isabella and led her toward the stairs. Their job there was done. Kevin's killer was dead. There was no reason to linger.

"Let's get the hell out of here. You ready?" Will asked.

Isabella nodded and she melted in his arms as they descended the stairs. It had been a horrific day in a string of horrific days. But she was tough. She'd get through this. They'd all get through it.

THIRTEEN

Will

DAY SIX

Isabella placed a backpack on the sofa next to Cayden. "There are a few pairs of socks and a couple of my old T-shirts in there. They're not too girly—one's red, the other's blue. I gave you a new toothbrush and some wet wipes."

She looked too calm after what had just transpired. Will knew that it would eventually all catch up with her and when it did, he and Cayden would be there for her. Hopefully, so would Savanah and her kids. If they made it that far by then. Will was pretty confident that Isabella had what it took to hold it together until they reached Calcasieu Parish.

Will was checking his ammo supply when he thought he heard an engine in the distance. He stopped what he was doing and listened. A moment later, four military vehicles pulled into the apartment complex and drove up to Isabella's building.

The three of them crowded in front of the window overlooking the parking lot.

"What the hell?" Isabella said.

Doors opened, and soldiers quickly exited the vehicles, pointing rifles at Lloyd and the other men outside. They yelled and ordered them to raise their hands. Will thought of what Gus had said about them taking the Asians and firing on the men they were with.

"Where is apartment one hundred nine?" a soldier barked.

"That's my apartment," Isabella whispered as she backed away from the window.

Will turned and ran to the door. He turned the deadbolt and slid the chain across.

"What are you doing?"

"We can't be sure what side they're on," Will said.

"Whose side they're on? They're with our military."

A loud bang on the door startled them and Isabella jumped, bumping into Cayden.

"You two go hide in the bedroom," Will whispered. He picked up Isabella's rifle and handed it to Cayden. "Take this."

"But…"

"Please, Isabella. Do this for me," Will said, his gaze turning to Cayden.

She nodded and took Cayden's hand. "Let's just hang back and see what they want, Cayden."

The banging continued as they disappeared down the short hall. "Isabella D'Angelo?" a gruff male voice called through the door.

They knew her name. This had to have something to do with Kim and Betley. He knew Isabella shouldn't have given him her address.

Will turned the lock and cracked open the door, leaving the chain across.

"We're looking for Isabella D'Angelo. Is she home?"

"What do you want with her?"

"Is she home?"

"I'm not telling you until you tell me what this is about," Will said.

"What's your name?" the soldier demanded.

It dawned on him that they hadn't asked for him and Cayden. They might believe that they'd gone already. He was debating whether to give an alias when the man gave the order to kick in the door.

Will jumped back just in time. But the soldiers were on him in seconds.

"What is this all about?" Will repeated as they applied flex cuffs to his wrists.

"Will!" Isabella yelled as she ran into the room.

"Why are you cuffing him?"

"Are you Isabella D'Angelo?" the soldier asked.

"Dad," Cayden said as he ran to him.

"It's okay, Cayden. We'll get this straightened out."

Another soldier grabbed Isabella and spun her around.

"Isabella!" Cayden screamed and stepped toward her.

"It's okay, Cayden."

"Are you Cayden Fontenot?" the soldier asked.

"Yes."

"And you're Will Fontenot?"

"Yes. Will you please just tell us what is going on?" Will asked.

"I'm not authorized to say. You'll all have to come with us," the soldier said.

Will knew they were in trouble when they were put into three different Humvees. If Betley had been pulling some strings to get them moved to a shelter, they wouldn't have split them up like common criminals. But he couldn't panic, even though they'd separated him from his son. They'd done nothing wrong—except defend themselves. Unless the military was rounding up looters. If they were going to attempt to do that, they'd likely have very full jails.

The events since the lights went out played in his mind. He was trying to recall details of the incidents that might get them in trouble with the law, but the only thing that made sense is that they wanted to speak with them about Kim and what was on that thumb drive. He wasn't sure what help they could be. They knew less about it than Betley and had spent most of their time with Kim either fighting or running for their lives.

They passed through a series of military checkpoints just before the Sam Houston Freeway. Will leaned forward in an attempt to see if the petroleum fuel tank farm on their left had been one of the fires he'd seen. The soldier to his left stuck out an arm and pushed him back. Shortly after, the Humvee slowed and pulled into a turning lane. Will watched the two vehicles in front of them make the left-hand turn and proceed across the railroad tracks. The sign ahead indicated that they'd arrived at their destination—the Ellington Field Joint Reserve Base.

Ellington was located less than ten miles from Will's home in Friendswood. He didn't recognize the base now and was surprised at how much work the military had been able to accomplish in such a short period. Hesco barriers similar to the ones used for flood control had been installed along the road for as far as the eye could see. The ten-foot wall, topped with razor wire, made it nearly impossible to see movement inside. Will wanted to ask how they'd managed such a feat since the EMP knocked out most vehicles. Then he spotted an old excavator dumping sand into the open top of the Hesco unit.

After proceeding through another checkpoint, the three military vehicles in front of them zigzagged around the concrete barriers and rolled to a third checkpoint. Sandbags were stacked waist high all around the buildings and in various places on the lawn. Dozens of military trucks filled the parking lot.

A moment later, the Humvee stopped. The lettering on the multistory building read United States Coast Guard. Will, Cayden, and Isabella were led in by a side door.

"Dad, what's happening?" Cayden said as he was taken down the hall to Will's left.

"Where are you taking my son?" Will protested.

"We just need to have a little talk," a female voice said behind him. "You can release him, private."

The soldier eased his grip on Will's forearm and removed the flex cuffs from his wrist.

"I'm Analyst Rachel Stephens. I just need to ask you a few questions. I'll start with you, Mr. Fontenot. Sergeant Hollingsworth will take Ms. D'Angelo down the hall to the conference room to wait.

"Will?" Isabella was frightened.

"Should we have a lawyer?" Will asked. He didn't know why he'd said that. It made him sound guilty.

Stephens chuckled, "No. It's not that kind of questioning."

"Is this about Kim?" Isabella called back over her shoulder.

The sergeant didn't stop and wait for her to receive a reply. Stephens wanted to act like none of this was a big deal, but their treatment by the soldiers told another story.

"Have a seat, Mr. Fontenot," Stephens said, pointing to the chair on the opposite side of a small table flanked by three other chairs. On it was a notepad and pen. The room was small. He doubted there'd be room for two more people. As he took his seat, he looked for the two-way mirror, typical for interrogation rooms, at least Hollywood's version. He found none. Will checked the ceiling for cameras. If they were there, he couldn't see them.

"Can I get you anything? A cup of coffee, soda, ice tea?"

"You have ice tea?" Will exclaimed.

She smiled and nodded. Stephens knocked once on the door, and a soldier appeared. "Get Mr. Fontenot a glass of ice tea." She turned back to Will. "Sweet or unsweet?"

"Sweet," Will said. She must not be from around here. He'd almost resigned himself to never having southern sweet ice tea again. The thought of it now made his mouth water.

Stephens closed the door and took a seat across from him. She scooted her chair in, causing their knees to touch. Tilting her head to the side, her scrutiny was intense, but he didn't look away. She shifted her weight in the chair and pulled the notepad closer then picked up the pen and wrote his name and the date at the top of the page.

After asking him for his full name, date of birth, and current address, she got right into the meat of the interview. He appreciated that she didn't take time trying to build a rapport or waste his time lying about what this was truly about.

"How did you know Kim Yang?"

"I didn't. Not really. I only met her the day of the EMP," Will said.

"EMP?"

"The electromagnetic pulse that fried our electric grid and took out all the electronics."

"What leads you to believe that was the result of an electromagnetic pulse?" she said in a way that had him questioning himself. All he knew was what Betley had told him. He'd known very little about them before meeting him. "Agent Betley told me."

"How long have you known him?"

"The same amount of time I knew Kim. We met the day that whatever happened, happened," Will said, doubt firmly setting in.

"And you met Kim Yang where exactly?" Stephens asked.

"At the convenience store near downtown. She plowed her car into a line of vehicles fueling at the pumps."

"What do you do for a living, Mr. Fontenot?"

Her calling him by his last name made him even more nervous for some reason. No one ever called him that. Mr. Fontenot had been his grandfather. "I am..." He corrected himself. "Was an instrumentation technician with Preston Chemical in Pasadena. I turned valves."

Will watched her write it down. She looked up, her head tilted to one side, her gaze lasering in on him.

"And you were conveniently there at the same time as a Chinese spy who had information about plots to destroy refineries, including the one where you work as an instrumentation engineer.

"No... I mean, yes. I'd never met her before. I was there with my son. We were evacuating the storm like two hundred thousand other people." He acting overly defensive, he knew, but she was accusing him of treason or something.

"You have inside knowledge of how your refinery operates."

"Not really. I'm a technician. I know the area I am responsible for monitoring. Mostly, I handle shutdowns." His tongue felt thick. Will ran a hand across his Adam's apple.

"You were working with Kim Yang to sabotage the refinery in advance of an invasion. Isn't that the truth?"

Will shot to his feet, causing his chair to bang against the wall. The door popped open, and two soldiers stepped in.

Stephens raised her hand, and they stopped. "Mr. Fontenot was just stretching his legs." She smiled. "Take a seat, Will."

"I was not working with Kim Yang or anyone else. I had my kid with me. We almost died. Multiple times. I would never—"

She stopped him. Her tone softened. The corners of her mouth curled up.

"Just take a seat, Will, and tell me everything that's happened from the time you met Kim Yang until you met the soldiers on the bridge."

He lowered his voice. "I had nothing to do with whatever Kim did."

"What do you think she did?" Stephens asked.

Wordlessly, Will waved his hand.

"The EMP?" she asked.

"Yeah, and whatever else they have planned."

"They who?"

"I don't know. All I know is I tried to help some people and me and my boy almost died because of it."

Will's legs were shaking under the table, causing their knees to knock together. He pushed his chair back and placed his hands in his lap.

"Tell me again how you were introduced to Kim Yang," Stephens said.

They were going around and around covering the same ground. She was now wasting his time. Anger simmered just below the surface. Will's shoulders and wrists were burning from being cuffed behind his back, but all Will could think about was Cayden and Isabella. He had to get to them—somehow—they had to escape this place.

"I told you. She plowed her car into a bunch of vehicles waiting to fuel up at the gas station. I told Betley all this. Why are you questioning me about it? Betley knows everything."

"I need to hear it from you," she said calmly.

Will exhaled hard and started at the beginning. "A car jumped the curb and plowed into vehicles at the fueling island. I pulled Isabella from her burning car. I was giving her first aid when Kim Yang, the Asian lady, approached us." He took her through the entire story as best he recalled it. By the time he'd finished, he was worn out by having to relive it all. It sounded crazy, even to him.

Stephens picked up her pen and drew a circle around his name. "You're asking me to believe that you just happened to be in an accident with a Chinese spy and show up with her at the safe house of an FBI agent.

"She took us there."

"Why?" Stephens asked.

"The hurricane. She said he had a safe place to ride out the storm."

"So she lied to get you and your son to go along with her? Why? Why would she want you to tag along to meet up with her contact from the FBI?"

Will tried to recall her exact words. Was there something he'd missed at the time? Something that would have indicated what she was dragging them into. If there was, he hadn't caught it.

"I don't know. I... I think she really did want to save us. It was a good location—she didn't lie about that. She gave her life to protect my son. I don't know what else she was, but I know that in the end, she sacrificed herself for him."

"That makes no sense. You can see that, right? Why would she sacrifice herself for a kid she didn't know?"

Will stared her down. "Maybe because some part of her was a human being, and maybe she felt guilty for dragging him into this mess. I don't know why. I just know that she did."

"What did she tell you about what was on the thumb drive?"

"Nothing. I didn't even know there was a thumb drive until Betley told me. I knew that there was something important in her duffle by the way she clung onto it, but I swear, I had no idea what was in it until after I met Betley."

Stephens leaned forward. "You never met Agent James Betley before that day in the storage locker?"

"No."

"Yet he involved you in a mission to retrieve something he believed contained classified information?"

"We were trapped because of the storm, and outnumbered. We had no idea how many gunmen were in the building."

"You had your son with you, yet you left him to engage with the men with guns?"

Is she implying I'm an unfit parent?

"I did what I had to do to protect my son. It wasn't like I could call the police."

Someone knocked on the door and Stephens excused herself. A moment later, two guards came and escorted Will out. He was led through a maze of hallways before the soldiers stopped at a closed door and knocked. "Where's my son? Can we leave now?"

"Not yet," one of the soldiers said as he opened the door.

FOURTEEN

Will

DAY SIX

Will sat in the dimly lit and sparsely furnished office for over an hour without hearing a sound other than the noise of military vehicles outside. The small south-facing window was closed tight and the sun shining through heated the room to unbearable temperatures. His clothes were soaked, and sweat dripped from his brow. If someone didn't come for him soon, he could die of heatstroke.

He tried the door handle for the hundredth time and yelled as loud as he could. There was no response. Were they planning on leaving him in here to die? Wasn't there some rule or law about cruel and unusual treatment? He still had constitutional rights, didn't he? Or did he? What happened to the rule of law when there wasn't anyone around to enforce it? A knot formed in his throat. He was screwed. Stephens could keep him there indefinitely and what recourse would he have? It wasn't like he could call a lawyer or alert the media to his mistreatment.

While attempting to count the military personnel and vehicles that he could see from his window, he spotted a crowd of eight or ten civilians forming outside the gate. They were likely desperate and had come seeking assistance from the government. The fact that they weren't let in concerned Will. That meant that the military had no intentions of helping—not in that way.

Keys jingled outside the door, and Will spun around. The same soldier from earlier appeared and motioned for him to turn around.

"What's going on?" Will asked.

"Just turn around, sir. I need to cuff you. Lieutenant Sharp has asked to see you," the soldier said.

"But why the cuffs? I'm not a danger to anyone."

"It's protocol, sir."

Protocol?

Will suspected nothing that was going on there was protocol. Being offered a lawyer would be protocol. Not being locked in a hundred-degree room without water would be protocol. Anger seethed and threatened to surface. He held it in and turned, placing his hands behind his back. He'd needed to play nice for now. They had his son—somewhere. If he had any hope of finding him and getting the hell out of there, he'd have to rein in his temper. Through gritted teeth, he said, "Let's go then."

The window in Lieutenant Ryan Sharp's office was open, and a fan blew the hot, humid air around the small office. He gestured for Will to take a seat in one of the two chairs in front of his desk. Will sat on the cushion's edge as sitting back made the plastic cuffs dig into his wrists.

"What is this about, Lieutenant?"

"Analyst Stephens tells me that you were at the scene when Kim Yang crashed her car."

"Yes. Her vehicle died when everyone else's did. It jumped the curb, plowing into vehicles at the gas station."

"You told Analyst Stephens that you found the way she clutched her bag odd. Why?"

Will thought back to the moment he first saw Kim. "I don't

know. It was just an impression. Everyone was upset. I really don't know."

"But you did learn later on that there was something inside that duffle that was very important to her."

"Yes. I told all this to Stephens already. Why do I have to keep repeating everything?"

Sharp's gaze narrowed. He leaned forward and placed his hands on his desk. He had perfectly manicured nails. He looked like he'd showered and shaved. The apocalypse hadn't hit him like the rest of Houston. Not like the folks outside the gate, and not like him and Cayden. He wasn't scavenging people's homes and looting stores to eat.

"Stephens thinks you were working with Kim Yang."

"What? No. I never met her before that day. I told her that."

They were accusing him of committing treason. What the hell had Betley told them?

Will stood. "I want a lawyer. I have a right to counsel if I'm being accused of something."

"Sit down," Sharp said, gesturing toward the chair. "I said that is what Stephens thinks. I'm able to make up my own mind."

Sharp pushed away from his desk and rose. He walked over to a cabinet by the window, poured a glass of water, and placed it on the desk in front of Will. Even though he was so dehydrated that his tongue cleaved to the roof of his mouth, he would have thrown it at the man had his hands been free.

Sharp reached into a pocket of his combat uniform pants and pulled out a small knife. He opened it and moved around behind Will. "Stand. Let me get those off you," he said. "Frankly, I think it is pretty farfetched. I don't think you are spy material."

"Thanks," Will said. "I won't take that as an insult."

"It wasn't meant as one. I need your help to prove to Stephens that she's barking up the wrong tree."

"Help? With what?" Will asked.

Sharp retook his seat and leaned back in his chair. He

pretended to be relaxed. Will could tell from the tension in his shoulders that he was anything but. "I need you to talk to Agent Betley."

"Betley?"

"I need you to see what he knows about the other items in that duffle. The ones he didn't turn in."

"But he gave you the file and the thumb drive," Will said.

"I need to know if there was something in Kim Yang's bag that he is not telling us about. Can you do that? Can you help me clear your name?"

"As you said, I'm no spy. He will know what's up immediately. He's way too smart to fall for that trick," Will said.

"You may be right, but are you willing to try—for your son?"

Will wanted to fly across the desk and pummel the man. For him to use his son like that proved these people had no soul. He couldn't trust any of them. The sooner he found Cayden and got the hell away from there, the better.

"First answer me this," Will said.

"I'll try."

"Why do you think Betley isn't telling you the truth? He's FBI. He's on your side."

Sharp just stared back at him. After a long, tense minute, he leaned forward and placed his hands back on his desk, steepling his fingers. "The same way you knew something was off with Kim the moment you met her."

That shouldn't have been a good enough answer, but Will couldn't argue with it. Sometimes you have to trust your gut. If he had, he and Cayden wouldn't have gotten sucked up into any of this.

Will shook his head. "I don't like it, but I'll do whatever I need to do to get my son and get the hell away from here."

Another soldier led Will down a series of dark hallways to a locked room at the corridor's end. The soldier stationed outside the door pulled keys from his belt and unlocked the door. Will was shoved inside, and the door slammed shut behind him. Against the far wall of the tiny space was the only chair in the room. He found Betley leaning on the wall beside the window that let the only light into the room.

"Will, fancy seeing you here," Betley said sarcastically.

He was dressed in what looked to be workout clothes. Will could see bandages protruding from just below his shorts. His arms and legs were bruised and scraped, revealing the injuries received in the fight of his life. Will had some to match. This was the same man he'd fought next to and had trusted with his life—with his son's life. *Did he really believe Betley was anything but what he said he was? Not for a minute.*

"Are they listening?" Will asked.

"Probably," Betley said, turning to face him. "How's Cayden and Isabella?"

"Good. They're here..." He raised his eyebrows. "Somewhere."

Betley gave a tiny bob of the head. He chewed his bottom lip as his gaze fell to the floor.

"Do you believe them—that I was working with Kim against my own country?"

Will shook his head.

"They blaming you too?" Betley asked.

"It appears so, yes."

"They're just paranoid. Stephens isn't taking any chances. Not under the circumstances."

"You're defending them?" Will said. "They are accusing you of treason."

"I know I didn't do that. They'll investigate and discover the same thing."

"But how do you prove you didn't do something? They're not even letting us have lawyers."

"Stephens is good at what she does, and Sharp—well, he's…"

"Sharp?" Will pulled the chair into the middle of the room and took a seat. He was feeling light-headed, and standing wasn't helping. "I don't have the same faith in the system as you do, I guess."

"They want you to get me to tell you there was something more in the duffle than I gave them. There wasn't. You saw it at the same time I did, remember?"

"I didn't see inside it," Will said. Was Betley trying to get him to testify to something he didn't see? Why? Could he be wrong about the man? The lack of food and sleep was affecting his brain. He was having trouble processing everything.

"Are you sure? Think. You and Kim had taken a walk. You came back alone, looking for her. I was seated at the table, going through the bag. You saw what was in it."

"Not really."

"What did you see?"

"The cash," Will said. "A lot of cash."

A loud boom startled Will and he jumped, nearly falling off his chair. Will leaped to his feet as Betley dove away from the window. When seconds passed without another explosion, Betley ran back to the window.

"What is it?" Will asked as he came up beside him.

"My guess is that was the Texas Department of Public Safety building across the highway," Betley said.

Smoke rose in the north. "It could have been the freeway interchange. I spoke to someone this morning that had witnessed Asian men attempting to blow up an interchange near Isabella's apartment."

"It could be that. They'll want to interfere with our ability to get resupplied and block reinforcements. It is typical guerrilla warfare."

Will's eyes widened.

"Are we safe here? Is Cayden safe? I need to get to him. We need to get the hell away from here." Will paced the room, walking in circles like a caged animal. "Dammit. I knew I should have left right away. But no. I had to overthink things like always. I wanted to wait until the water receded and gather supplies." He turned to Betley. "I should have listened to you. I would have been halfway to my sister's by now."

As Will passed him, Betley reached and grabbed Will's arm. "Stop beating yourself up over things you can't change. It won't help you get out of this." Betley walked over and righted the chair. "Sit. Let's figure a way out of this."

Will curled his arms over the top of his head. "I can't just sit here. I need to get my boy."

"Sit!" Betley snapped.

Will studied him. He needed his help. He was his only ally on that base. Right then, he was Will's only hope. Will rubbed his hands over his stubbled face and took a seat. "You didn't answer me. Are we safe here?"

"As safe as anywhere," Betley said, returning to his spot next to the window.

"That is not comforting."

"It's not my job to coddle you, Will. We all want the same thing. You want to keep your kid safe. Stephens and I want to find that list and stop the insurgents before they do irreparable harm."

"I thought you had the list," Will said.

"I thought I did too. I think Kim played me. I think she held out, just in case I backed out of our deal."

"What deal?" He stood. "Were you two working together?"

"No. Not like that. She was my informant. I'd promised her a green card and a new identity in exchange for providing proof of illegal theft of corporate secrets. She brought me something bigger. Bigger than even she knew. But when those men came after it, she knew she needed to hold out until she got her safety secured. She was very mistrusting."

"So she hid it somewhere?" Will said.

"That's my guess."

"Why didn't you tell Stephens that?"

"I did. That got me locked up in here. They think I know something that I don't. How am I supposed to prove that?"

Will sighed. "You can't."

FIFTEEN

Cayden

DAY SIX

The soldier standing in the turret turned from left to right as the Humvee exited the apartment complex behind the two other military vehicles. Cayden didn't quite understand what was happening. It was pretty clear to him that it was something significant. The soldiers had cuffed his dad and Isabella like they were criminals. He hadn't been cuffed, but he'd been separated them. After being placed into the Humvee, he got distracted by the soldier standing in the Humvee's turret.

"I ain't going to lie, this ride is sweet," Cayden said. "How does it still work after the EMP?"

"There aren't any electronic engine controls, electronic braking, or circuitry that could fry with the electromagnetic pulse," the soldier seated to his left said.

"Awesome," Cayden said. "Does the other stuff up there work too?" Cayden pointed to the screens and other high-tech equipment attached to the dash.

"Nah. The EMP wiped those out," the soldier said.

Cayden thought about his computer and gaming console. It was hard for him to imagine a life without them. As they drove through the neighborhood, Cayden saw people pulling furniture and household items from their flooded homes and piling them at the curb as if everything was normal and someone would be around to pick them up soon. Did they not understand that life wasn't returning to normal? He wondered if they even knew that the country had been attacked and the lights weren't coming back on.

When the Humvee pulled onto the road leading to the retailer outlets, Cayden got a real sense of the devastation. Other than the vehicles that had been shoved out of the roadway, nothing had been cleaned up. Electric lines and metal sheeting littered the sides of the road and nearby parking lots. Cayden gasped as they passed a body half-buried in the debris near the intersection.

"You might want to cover your eyes, kid. It's pretty bad out there," the soldier to his left said.

Cayden tried to imagine what their lives would be like now without modern technology. If they weren't able to get the lights back on soon, it would look a lot worse because all the people who'd survived the storm would start starving to death.

If the military weren't able to fight back the insurgents, they might not live long enough to starve. Cayden wasn't sure how they'd fight back without their modern equipment. The soldiers looked like they could handle themselves. The soldier to his left looked young, maybe only eighteen. A mere five years older than him. He wasn't as muscular as the two soldiers in the front. Cayden couldn't tell how old the soldier in the turret was, but the man had arms bigger than Cayden's thighs.

Cayden glanced at his own skinny arms, wondering how much he'd have to work out to have muscles like that. He'd gone to the gym a few times, back when his dad still cared what he looked like. He'd stopped going after Cayden's mom died though, recently, he'd bought a stationary bike and some weights and started again. Although he still looked depressed most of the time, Cayden thought it was a good sign that his dad was exercising.

The Humvee weaved back and forth through stranded vehicles as they approached the freeway. At the on-ramp, Cayden spotted the blackened shells of military vehicles. "Those are yours, right?" he asked.

No one answered him.

"What happened to them? Was it the insurgents?" Cayden asked.

The soldier in the seat to his left glanced his way but said nothing. Cayden wasn't sure if they just didn't know or weren't allowed to discuss it.

"Is that what this is about? Is that why you came for us? Did Agent Betley send you?"

No response.

The Humvee turned south, and within minutes, they arrived at Ellington Field Joint Reserve Base. Cayden watched from the rear passenger seat as his dad and Isabella exited separate vehicles and were led inside.

"Why can't I go with my dad?" Cayden asked.

"I can't say," the soldier said.

The soldier from the front passenger seat climbed out of the Humvee and motioned for Cayden to exit the vehicle.

"It's going to be all right, Cayden," his dad yelled as he was pushed through the door of the building.

Cayden wasn't afraid, but it concerned him that his dad was. It seemed like he didn't trust the military. But they were the good guys, right?

Inside, the soldiers took his dad one way and him another. He didn't see where they took Isabella.

Cayden followed the four soldiers through the building to a small coffee shop alcove. The soldier from the turret pointed to a small sofa. "Take a seat. You want something to eat or drink? We got sodas, chips, and cookies."

"I'll take a Dr. Pepper and some Doritos," Cayden said.

No Other Choice

The soldier went behind the small counter and opened the floor to ceiling cooler. That's when it dawned on Cayden that the base had electricity. The cool air and overhead lights should have been a clue. They were such everyday things, but he'd totally missed the fact that they shouldn't be on.

"How do you guys have electricity?" he asked.

"Generators," one of the soldiers said, plopping into a chair opposite Cayden.

"Don't get too comfortable. Sergeant Rawls said our replacement will be here in a few minutes," the soldier from the turret said.

He handed Cayden his drink and snacks before dropping into a chair to the right of Cayden.

"So, what now?" Cayden asked.

The stocky soldier shrugged. It was clear that they were just his babysitters and weren't going to tell him anything. Cayden observed them as he sipped his drink. He tried to drink his soda slowly, knowing that it might well be the last cold one he had for a very long time.

The soldiers seated next to Cayden looked relaxed and as though they were relishing the downtime in air conditioning as much as he was. Each of them was dressed in a military uniform loaded down with gear. He didn't know how in the world they could stand to have all that on in the heat.

The third soldier, a skinny guy with a scar on his cheek, paced in front of the counter. Either he knew something the others didn't, or he was more anxious to get on with something else. Minutes passed and the soldiers grew bored. They were throwing half-full water bottles at one another when their replacement arrived.

She was just a little taller than Cayden and dressed in a different patterned uniform than the other soldiers. Cayden thought she must be someone important since the soldiers all stood and saluted her.

"Cayden Fontenot?" she asked.

"Yes."

"I'm Lieutenant McKinney. Would you come with me, please?"

She wore her blonde hair in a tight bun. Cayden guessed she was older than the soldiers but younger than his dad. She was pretty. He couldn't see her figure much under the baggy uniform, but she appeared fit.

"This way," she said, pointing down the dimly lit corridor.

"When can I see my dad and Isabella?" Cayden asked.

"In a little while. I just need to ask you a few questions first," Lieutenant McKinney said.

She led him into an office and gestured for him to take a seat. The room was small and contained no windows. The furnishing was sparse. A small desk and two chairs sat in one corner. Two more chairs lined the opposite wall. Nothing hung on the walls, and there were no framed photos or certificates. Cayden selected a chair in the corner with a view of the door. Lieutenant McKinney sat opposite him on the other side of the desk, pulled a notepad and pen from a pocket in her pants, and leaned back.

"Okay, Cayden. I need to ask you about the day that you and your dad met a woman named Kim Yang. Do you know who that is?"

He nodded.

"Can you tell me where exactly you were when you first saw her?"

Cayden described the scene at the gas station and how he'd first come in contact with Kim. He walked Lieutenant McKinney through the carjacking and their time at Fahima's. Cayden didn't understand why she wanted to know Kim's every movement before they got to Betley's storage unit. He did his best to recall, but she didn't seem to believe him as she repeated the same question over and over.

"When your dad and Isabella were in the bar, you said that you and Kim were outside waiting for them. Did she step away from you at any time?"

"No. Not that I can recall. I wasn't all that focused on her, though. I was watching for fire in the skyrises. A lot of the buildings were on fire, and I was concerned that—"

"So you can't be sure that Kim didn't, say, get into one of the vehicles or step into an alcove of a nearby shop?" McKinney asked, interrupting him.

"If she did, it would have only been for a few seconds. She mostly stood right beside me. I think she thought she was responsible for me or something."

"And what happened after that?"

Cayden told her about hearing gunshots and rushing toward the bar. "Kim wouldn't let me go in."

"Did she go inside?"

"Yes."

Cayden told her everything that he remembered until they were picked up by the soldier on the bridge. By the third time of being asked the same questions, he was bored and frustrated and wanted out of the tiny room. He needed to see his dad and know that he and Isabella were all right. Cayden yawned. He couldn't help himself. They hadn't been able to sleep much in the last few days. His dad had been up and down all night after the explosions started.

"Would you like something to drink? Maybe something with caffeine?" McKinney asked.

Although Cayden did want something to drink, her offering one with caffeine made him nervous. That meant that they weren't finishing up anytime soon. He was tired of repeating the same answers over and over. If she had nothing new to ask, he wasn't in the mood to cooperate any further.

"Nah. I don't need caffeine. I'd like to see my dad now."

"Just a few more questions—"

"No. I think I'm done answering your questions until I see my dad."

Her eyes narrowed and then softened. She slowly pushed her chair back and walked toward the door. "I'll see about getting you that caffeine."

SIXTEEN

Isabella

DAY SIX

Between the heat and the pain in her arm, Isabella was quite irritable as she sat across from Stephens. She couldn't help but notice her nails were neat and trimmed, nothing like the mess hers had become. The woman's hair was clean, and there weren't dark circles and bags under her eyes. Isabella hadn't bothered to look in a mirror in days. Her vision was a little blurry due to her swollen eyelids. It seemed that once she'd allowed the tears to begin to flow, the pain and grief over everything that had occurred during the last few days had all come rushing out at once.

She'd been numb for the first few days. It was too much to process, all the death and the fear for her safety. Isabella had just started accepting the fact that things may take time to get back to normal but certainly hadn't yet reached the point that she could begin looking toward the future. She'd seemed stuck in a moment-by-moment survival mode. Witnessing the brutality that had taken Kevin's life had been her wake-up call. If she was to survive, she had to snap out of her fog and do something. She refused to be a victim. She refused to let anything like that happen to anyone else she cared about either.

Isabella studied the CIA analyst as she shuffled papers from one folder to another. She imagined she'd had a rough time in the male-dominated CIA. She must be fairly important to be working on such a crucial investigation. Thwarting a foreign insurgency and invasion couldn't be easy. They'd want their best on the job, right?

After several hours of answering the woman's questions, Isabella started getting pissed. She understood that Stephens was just trying to understand the incident with Kim, but how was answering the same questions twenty times remotely helpful? Isabella could smell the woman's fear. That is what had her so freaked out. She was with the government. She was here, surrounded by sexy soldiers carrying guns. Yet Stephens was more afraid than Isabella had been out there on the streets. Stephens had to know something awful to have her so rattled.

"You can ask me a hundred times and I'll still have the same answer. I never saw Kim hide anything. She didn't tell me anything. I know nothing that can help you. I never for a moment suspected her and Betley of working together. I want to help you, Ms. Stephens. I do. But I can't."

"Let's retrace your steps one more time," Stephens said.

"No!" Isabella spat. "No. I've told you all I remember."

"I keep asking to jog your memory. You could recall something new."

She didn't want to recall any more details about their time out there. She tried to forget the look in the crazy woman's eyes as she lunged for her and sank her hands into Isabella's hair. She needed to forget about the girl and her brother from the bar and the man they'd left dying in the middle of the street. It was all so damn senseless. If they'd just been able to call an ambulance, those three lives might have been saved. Trying to recall their every move was too painful. Isabella's brain wanted to shut down. It was too much.

As Stephens stood and paced the floor, she chewed her thumbnail. It only served to make Isabella more nervous and drove home the seriousness of the situation. If this calm, cool, and collected

CIA analyst was on the verge of losing her shit, what hope did Houston's residents have?

"Why don't you just go out there and look in the places I told you?" Isabella asked.

"That's a great idea. You'll just have to come with me."

"Excuse me?" Isabella asked, not believing her ears. She didn't know what the woman was smoking, but she must be crazy if she thought Isabella was going back downtown. That would be the epicenter of chaos for hundreds of thousands of refugees who'd become stranded on the freeways when the EMP took out the electronics in their cars.

"You and Will need to come with me to retrace your steps. Maybe something out there will jog your memories."

Isabella was just about to protest when a loud boom reverberated outside. Stephens spun and dropped to the floor, pulling Isabella down with her. "What's happening? Are we under attack? Is this the invasion?" Isabella cried.

"Just be calm," Stephens said. She straightened, then sat up. "I don't think it was that close."

"That close? Any explosion is too close for me."

"Do you want to get out of here?" Stephens asked.

"Yes, please."

"Then help me, Isabella. Help me stop these people. I need that list."

"It's too dangerous. It's bad out there, and not just the insurgents. People are desperate, and people are doing stupid things. I saw one of my neighbors chased down by a gang this morning. Will saw someone get shot."

"I know, but that is only going to get worse until we can restore law and order and get people the help they need. We can't do that if we are dealing with attacks like that." Stephens pointed over her shoulder toward the explosion.

"I can't," Isabella said.

"If you won't do it for your country, do it for Will and Cayden.

You care about them, don't you?"

That was a low blow. Of course she cared about her country. And Will and Cayden. She'd help if she could.

"How does me going out there with you help Will and Cayden?"

"If you and Will help us locate what we're looking for, I will have them escorted to his sister's in Louisiana away from all this. You too if you want to go with them. Otherwise, we can take you somewhere else."

Isabella thought of her family. The thought of them struggling to survive as she had hurt her heart. "My family is in Oklahoma." Somehow she imagined a nine-hour trip was out of the question.

"We can get you to the shelter in Huntsville. From there…"

Isabella interrupted her. "No. I'm not going to a shelter."

"Well, you decide where you'd like to go, and I'll see what I can do."

Isabella lowered her head. The thought of going back to her apartment, knowing the danger everyone in the city was in, scared her to death. She had no other choice. She had to help this woman. And then she'd decide where to go from there. The last week had shown her that she was tougher than she thought. She would come up with something. At least Will and Cayden would be safe. That would make it worth the risk.

She looked Stephens in the eyes. "Tell me there's help on the way. Tell me that the Army, Marines, Navy, Coast Guard, Air Force, and even the Space Force is coming to rescue us."

Stephens' gaze fell to the floor. "I can't. The EMP disrupted communications. We're doing our best to get them reestablished in order to communicate with the Pentagon, but it takes time."

"But they're coming, right?"

"The forces that were pre-positioned to provide aid following the hurricane are on their way. We have sent for them. They'll be in position soon."

"Is it enough? To prevent an invasion?" Isabella asked.

"I believe so."

She didn't sound all that convincing.

"But we still have planes, ships, and tanks, right?"

"Some. The US military has been working to harden its equipment for decades, but technology changes rapidly, and so much of our military equipment is electronic. No one knew what would and would not operate after an EMP. We have some assets. The Humvees start and run but a lot of the gadgets used for navigation and communications are dead. It's things like that. As far as planes, the ones on the ground here are inoperable."

Isabella's hand came up to cover her mouth. She knew they were screwed without planes. The United States had won wars due to its air superiority.

"We have planes on aircraft carriers and around the world that won't have been impacted by the EMP. They'll return to the US."

"And the ships?"

"Of course."

She relaxed a little, knowing that they wouldn't be left on their own to fight off foreign enemies.

"We just have to do what we can until they all get here. In order to do that, I need the information that Kim was carrying."

"But Betley gave you the thumb drive."

"There had to have been a second one. The one he gave us only contained corporate plans for another chemical plant in Pasadena. We believe that the man Kim Yang was working with had a list of his contacts and potential targets. If we can find it, we can stop them. So you can see how important this is," Stephens said.

Isabella's legs were bouncing up and down uncontrollably now. She pushed her hair back from her sweaty face and tightened her ponytail. She absolutely did not want to go back down memory lane, but there was so much at stake, how could she not. Not just for Will and Cayden, but possibly for the country. Could she live with herself if she refused just because she was scared? She dabbed sweat from her eyes and stood. "When do we leave?"

SEVENTEEN

Will

DAY SIX

An hour after learning of Stephens' proposal, Will and Isabella sat in a government vehicle in the flooded parking lot of the convenience store where the whole mess began. Isabella stared at her burned-out car, now half underwater.

Retracing their steps was going to be much more complicated than Will had thought. To bring them out there told Will that Houston was in deeper trouble than he'd thought, and the likelihood of a ground war was that much more likely. With all that was going on, why else take the risk. A thumb drive, it could be anywhere. But none of that made sense to Will. Why would Kim hide it if she took it to use as leverage to get Betley to keep her safe?

Will was greatly relieved that they'd insisted Cayden remain behind with Betley but he did find it suspicious that they *hadn't* brought Betley along as he'd been there for the ordeal at the storage facility.

Lieutenant Sharp looked straight ahead, his hands still gripping the steering wheel of the older SUV. Will wondered how many more old vehicles like that the military had around. Had they known they would be the only ones operable? Or had they acquired them after the EMP?

Stephens turned in her seat to face them. "Was there a moment when Kim Yang was out of your sight before you all got into your Jeep?"

"I can't say," Will said. "So much was happening. Isabella was injured, and I was attempting to give her first aid. We were just learning that the grid was down and that the phones and cars weren't working. We were all in shock."

"What about you, Isabella?"

"No. Kim stayed by our side the whole time here at the gas station."

"Did she speak to anyone besides the two of you?"

"No. She seemed very nervous. I remember that. She kept watching over her shoulder like she expected someone to jump her at any minute." Isabella turned to Will. "Now we know why she was so jumpy."

"She never went inside the store or went to help any of the other injured drivers?" Stephens asked.

"No," Isabella said.

"All right. Which way did you go from here?"

Will tried his best to recall the route they'd taken before the carjacker stole his Jeep, but the names of streets failed him.

"We had to zigzag a lot due to stalled traffic and people in the roadway. But we never stopped except for when the Jeep was stolen."

"And that was where?"

"Take that next right, I have to show you."

Sharp weaved through the parking lot, heading for the intersection. Will spotted movement down the street. Someone stepped between cars—a man. There was something in his hands.

"Watch out!" Will yelled.

Sharp spotted the man and yelled, "RPG!" He stomped on the gas, bumped the car in front of them, and did his best to accelerate toward the freeway underpass where they'd be shielded from the blast. Will grabbed Isabella and shoved her toward the footwell, covering her head and upper body with his own just before the concussive rumble of the explosion hit as the rocket-propelled grenade slammed into the vehicle two cars back, sending a ball of smoke into the air and metal fragments raining down on their SUV.

"Oh, my God. Oh, my God," Isabella repeated as Sharp sped away from the scene.

He made a sharp left turn at the next intersection and accelerated. Will turned in his seat and looked out the back glass. They hadn't been followed. Sharp turned right at the following street and slowed. Water was coming in at the bottom of the SUV's door. The flooding was too deep in that spot. Will was afraid they'd kill the engine and be stranded on foot again.

"Who the hell was that back there?" Isabella asked.

"Are we close?" Stephens asked, ignoring her question.

"Who was shooting at us?" Isabella barked.

"We need to stay focused. Where did you get out of the Jeep?"

"How did the insurgents know we would be at that gas station today?" Will demanded. There was much more to the story than they'd been told. He and Isabella were out there, risking their lives, and had been kept in the dark. What were they keeping from them?

"Can we just keep on task so we can find what we're looking for and get back to the base?" Stephens asked.

"We didn't sign on to get killed out here. I've got a kid. I can't leave him an orphan for some wild goose chase."

"There might be someone on the inside working with the Chinese," Sharp said, looking at Will in the rear-view mirror.

Will's mouth fell open. That changed everything. Cayden could be in danger back at the base. If they knew that Will was helping to uncover their identity, they could go after his son to stop him.

"Take me back to the base," Will demanded.

"I can't do that," Stephens said. "We have to complete the mission.

Stop whining and concentrate." She adjusted herself where she was twisted around in her seat. The veins in her forehead protruded. Will thought she was about to fly into the back seat to attack him. Where did your Jeep get stolen?" she asked through clenched teeth.

"Two blocks over," Isabella said. She pointed south.

Stephens turned and faced the front, scanning the street and side roads. No doubt looking for more men with RPGs.

As they approached the side road where Will's Jeep had been carjacked, Isabella reached over and took Will's hand. More bodies were lodged up against cars in the intersection. That might have been them if Kim hadn't taken them to see Betley. Why had these people not sought shelter inside one of the skyrises that hadn't burned? It had been hours before the flooding began. They'd had time.

Stephens glanced over at the tragic sight and quickly turned away.

"They must have been afraid the rest of the buildings would burn," Will whispered. He hated to think about their last moments and how frightened they must have been when the storm hit downtown.

"Where did you go after you exited the vehicle?" Stephens said, sadness lacing her voice.

Isabella pointed to the road to their left, and Sharp turned in that direction.

"Was there any time that Kim was out of your sight as you walked?"

"No. I was holding her arm. She'd hit her head in the crash, and she was unsteady on her feet," Isabella said.

"What about you, Will? Did you have eyes on her the whole time?"

Will thought back. "I walked ahead of them most of the time. The streets were crowded. We had to weave back and forth across the street to get around people."

"You didn't stop and rest at any point?" Sharp asked. His tone conveyed more of an accusation than a question.

"Our first stop was at Fahima's," Isabella said. Her eyes brightened, and the corners of her mouth curled up slightly. "We can find her and bring her with us to the base," she whispered.

Will nodded, though if Fahima had survived and they could find her, Will doubted that she'd agree to leave with them.

He smiled. "Yeah. That's great."

Will instructed Sharp on how to get to the alley where they'd first met Fahima while Isabella recounted how she'd been attacked out of nowhere by a naked woman.

"Fahima came to my aid. She knew the woman."

"So you didn't have eyes on Kim during this period," Stephens asked.

"Um... no."

"What about you, Will?"

"I lost sight of Isabella and Kim for a few seconds. When I ran into the alley, Kim was trying to get the woman off Isabella, so I don't think she had time to stash anything."

"Where was the duffle while she was fighting with the naked woman?" Stephens asked.

"Slung over her back. She never let it out of her sight," Will said.

Stephens nodded and scanned the alley.

"Where did you go after you were rescued from the crazy woman?" Stephens asked.

Isabella pointed down the blind alley to her left. "To Fahima's."

"Okay. Let's go," Stephens said, opening her car door.

EIGHTEEN

Will

DAY SIX

Sharp went first with his rifle raised as they entered the blind alley leading to the mechanical room that Fahima called home. Will was relieved that the water only came to mid-calf near the door. As they approached the door, Sharp stepped to one side and tried the knob. It was locked.

Will stepped up and knocked. "Fahima. It's Will and Isabella. We've come to check on you."

No answer.

Isabella's smile faded. She stepped in front of Will and pounded on the door. "Fahima. Fahima. It's Isabella. Please open the door. I need to know that you're all right."

Sharp stepped back and spoke into the radio microphone attached to his tactical vest. "Hollingsworth, find me another way into this building."

Isabella continued knocking on the door and calling Fahima's name as the soldiers escorting them went around the building searching for an alternate way in. A few minutes later, Sharp's radio crackled, "We're in. You can make entry through the double doors on the north side. The first floor is clear."

"Let's move that way," Stephens said.

As they made their way around to the front of the building, Will scanned the balcony overhead. The bicycles were still there. It was hard to imagine that they were now more valuable than a car since most vehicles were now as useless as a pile of scrap metal.

At the front of the building, they waited for the all-clear so they could enter. Isabella chewed her thumbnail and tapped her foot on the sidewalk out in front of the building. "She's probably in one of the apartments. She wouldn't have stayed in the flooded basement," Will said, trying to reassure her.

"I know. You're right. She's smart and stronger than all of us."

"It'll be good to see her again," Will said.

"All clear, Lieutenant," a soldier called from the open doorway.

"All right. We're going to make our way down to the door you say you entered and walk through every step Kim took," Stephens said.

There were six inches of water in the entryway of the apartment building. The brown line on the wall indicated that the water had been much higher. A soldier led them past the stairs for the upper floors to a door leading to the basement. Will and Isabella walked Stephens and Sharp through their movements in the building. The soldiers fanned out and searched every nook and crevice, looking for anything Kim might have hidden there.

"You're sure Kim didn't enter any apartment without you?" Stephens asked.

"I don't think so." Will strained to recall that day. It was difficult. His mind wanted to forget. "No. She didn't. We stayed together after we left the area by the loading bay."

As they made their way up the steps toward the roof, soldiers escorted the few remaining residents downstairs. Isabella scanned each face. She was looking for Fahima.

"I didn't come up to the roof with them. I can't help you. I never left the mechanical room. I want to find my friend. She's still here somewhere. I want to go down and see if she's among those the soldiers have rounded up," Isabella said.

"Not an option," Sharp said.

Isabella huffed and spun around on the stairs. "I wasn't asking permission."

Sharp reached to grab her, but Stephens stopped him. "Baker, escort Ms. D'Angelo down to the first floor."

Will wasn't comfortable splitting up. It was apparent, though, that Isabella was determined, and Stephens wasn't going to let Will follow her. All he could do was hurry them along with searching the roof so they could get the hell out of there.

"I'll meet you down there, Isabella," Will called to her.

"I'll find her," she replied.

There wasn't much to search on the roof. Stephens looked disappointed.

"Stephens, what makes you think that Kim would hide something along our trek to the storage facility? That just doesn't make any sense. She needed that information to trade with Betley."

"That's what he said but we can't rule anything out."

"I heard her tell him that she'd provided the information, and now he had to fulfill his end," Will said.

"But Betley couldn't verify what was on the flash drive. She knew that. She could say anything."

"But why would she hold back?"

"For leverage with the Chinese mafia if they captured her," Sharp said.

"They didn't want to capture her. They wanted her dead. They tried numerous times."

"Didn't she try to use the flash drive as a bargaining chip when they captured her at the storage facility?" Stephens asked.

That was true. Will had forgotten that fact.

"And you've searched all the lockers at the storage facility? I just can't imagine that she'd stash something that important so far away."

"We searched every inch."

Will stared at the western sky. He was beginning to believe they were out there on a wild goose chase. There never was a second flash drive. Kim likely never had a list of insurgents and their targets. How stupid of them to put that type of information on something that could be so easily stolen and then not lock it up more safely.

"All right, let's get Isabella and continue on the path you took to the next stop," Stephens said.

Isabella was standing in the corner with her back to Will. When he called her name, she turned with a huge grin across her face. "I found her, Will."

Fahima stepped into view. "Fahima. It's so good to see you," Will said, walking over to her. She hugged him and kissed his cheek.

"It's good to see you too. How is your son?" Fahima said.

"He's well. Are you doing okay? Did you find a safe place to stay?" Will asked.

"Yes, I did. Those sweet children over there invited me into their apartment. They're great kids."

"We have to go," Stephens said, walking toward the busted door.

Isabella spun around and rushed toward Stephens and Sharp. "We have to take her with us."

"Not an option," Sharp said, glancing back at the other residents. "FEMA and the Red Cross will be along shortly."

Will knew Sharp had lied to avoid a panic, but it was cruel not to tell them that help wasn't coming. They needed to know so they could do what they had to in order to survive.

"No. Fahima needs to come with us." Isabella grabbed

Stephens' arm. "You know she won't make it out here. We have to help her."

"What do you think we can do for her?" Stephens whispered. "We are under attack from insurgents. We aren't equipped for refugees. She's better off here." Isabella started to protest, but Will slid his arm around her waist and moved her away from Stephens. "She's right. The military is a target. She is safer here—at least for now."

"She can come with us," Isabella said. She wiped tears from her cheeks.

That's when Will noticed. Her face was flushed. He reached out and placed the back of his hand on Isabella's forehead. The topical medication wasn't working. Her wound was infected, and she was burning up with fever. He reached for her injured arm. She pulled away. "She has to come with us, Will."

"Let me see your arm, Isabella," Will insisted.

She held out her arm. "Fine."

"What's the problem?" Stephens asked.

"She's burning up. Her arm is infected," Will said, peeling back the bandage.

Sharp stepped over, took a look at Isabella's wound, and motioned for one of the soldiers.

"Hollingsworth is a medic. He's going to take you to the Humvee and get that cleaned up."

"No!" Isabella said, yanking her arm away. "I'm not going anywhere without Fahima."

"Now, now, child. You go with them and take care of that nasty wound. You can't mess around with stuff now," Fahima said, stroking Isabella's hair.

"But I can't leave you here, Fahima. You don't understand. No matter what they say, no one is coming to help these people. You'll die here."

"Oh, baby, I been on my own out here for years. I'll be fine. You go. These folks need you."

"Please, Fahima," Isabella cried, reaching for her as two soldiers pulled her toward the door.

Will wanted to stop them, but he knew she wouldn't go on her own. As bad as it was, Fahima was better off there. He had no idea what they were going to face on their way to Louisiana, but he doubted she would be able to handle the physical demands of over a hundred miles on foot.

Will turned to Fahima. "I wish there was something I could do for you."

"I'll be fine. Don't you worry about me," Fahima said, pulling Will into a hug.

There was a deafening sound as an explosion rocked the side of the building, sending dust and debris raining down on them. Will pulled Fahima toward the door. They needed to get out in case it collapsed or caught on fire. People were screaming and running toward the exit. All Will could think about was Isabella.

The soldiers were firing back at someone. Will couldn't see the battle from where he was hunkered down behind a car shielding Fahima. He had no idea where Sharp and Stephens were and all but two of the apartment residents had fled the scene. A twenty-something couple crouched beside an SUV that had been shoved against the building across the street.

"Fahima, are you okay?" the young woman called.

"I'm all right. You go on and save yourselves," Fahima said.

"No. We won't leave you," the young man said.

Fahima looked up. "I should go with them. I don't want to be responsible for them getting hurt."

Will nodded. "You take care, Fahima."

"I will. You look after Isabella and Cayden," she said as Will helped her to her feet. The young couple ran over, and each took one of Fahima's arms. "You hold on to that woman, Will. You two deserve love and happiness," she called as they hurried away.

Will waved as they disappeared around the corner of a building. He searched the street to his left. The sound of gunfire seemed to be coming from that direction. The military vehicles were parked in the alley at the back of the building. That was where Isabella should be. Will moved to his right and stayed close to the east side of the apartment building. When he reached the loading bay, he crouched behind the large dumpster. He listened. It was hard to make out the direction of the gunfire reverberating between the buildings. He had to risk it and cross the distance to the back of the building. If gunmen were out there, they could fire on him, and there would be nowhere to hide. He wished he'd insisted on having a weapon but he'd never anticipated being in this situation.

At the back corner of the building, Will pressed himself against the wall and peered around to where the vehicles should be. He gasped. His knees almost gave out at the sight of the mangled Humvee. The RPG had found its target, and Isabella and the soldiers were nowhere to be seen.

"Will," Stephens yelled. "Over here." Stephens was crouched behind a dumpster

Will looked to his left, unsure about crossing the alley without a weapon.

"I'll cover you," Stephens said.

What choice did he have? He couldn't stay there. Will sprinted toward the dumpster and dropped down next to Stephens. "Where's Isabella? Where's Sharp?"

NINETEEN

Will

DAY SIX

Stephens led Will to the building on their left. They entered through the broken door and raced down a short hall. "Durant. Hollingsworth," Stephens yelled.

"Back here, ma'am," one of the soldiers called.

Will and Stephens rushed into the room. "Isabella?" Will called out.

She was on the floor and he couldn't see her face. His stomach lurched. He wasn't prepared to lose Isabella. Hollingsworth, the medic, was wiping blood from a gash on her cheek that was small but actively bleeding. He dropped down beside her. The soldier lying next to her hadn't fared as well. A piece of metal protruded from his jaw. Somehow, he was conscious. He stared at the ceiling, wild-eyed. His skin was pale.

"How you doing, Durant? We're going to get you out of here in just a minute and back to base so the docs can get you fixed up," Stephens said, standing over the man.

With all of the experience military doctors had gained over the last twenty or so years of war in Iraq, Afghanistan, and other war-torn places, Will thought she was possibly right, and they might be able to not only save this man but fix his face so that it didn't leave him horribly disfigured.

"Where's Fahima?" were Isabella's first words to him. How was he to explain that he'd let her go off with those college kids?

"She took off," Will said. "The kids seem to be taking good care of her. She trusts them."

"Better than us?" Isabella asked.

"Better than them," Will said, pointing to Stephens.

Isabella glared at Stephens. "You're going to get us all killed, and for what? Something that likely doesn't even exist."

Even if Kim had had the information Stephens was searching for, it was like trying to find a needle in a haystack. Someone knew they were looking and would do whatever it took to make sure they didn't find it.

"They know you don't have it, don't they?" Will asked.

Stephens shrugged one shoulder.

"Why would they come after you if they didn't want whatever it is?" Will asked.

Isabella waved the medic's hand away and sat up. "So, Kim really did have something important?"

"We think so," Stephens said.

"Wait. They knew where we were going. They had time to set up ambushes," Will said. "They have someone not only on the inside but close to you, don't they?"

Stephens said nothing.

"Can we move him, Hollingsworth?" Stephens said, ignoring Will's question.

"Stephens. Someone inside your sphere knows we're here looking for the damn thing, don't they? Tell me. We have a right to know the danger we're in."

It was so much worse than Will had imagined. Insurgents were one thing, but a traitor on the inside put everyone at risk, including his son. A hollow feeling had settled into the space below his rib cage.

"Take me back to base. I need to get to my son. I'm not doing this," Will insisted.

"I can't do that," Stephens said. "We can't fail. If we fail, we might as well lie down and let them take over. Don't you see? We can't fight an enemy we can't see coming."

A muscle in her jaw twitched. "I know this looks crazy and may not seem worth the risk to you, but we have to try. There's too much at stake. We need all the help we can get. Finding out who is in the sleeper cells and where they may be operating from is crucial, but most importantly, I need to know who on the inside is feeding them information."

"My son, Stephens. I don't know if you've got a kid, but he's not safe, and it's my job to protect him."

"We have him guarded. Trust me. They're not getting near him," Stephens said.

"How can I trust you to protect him? You don't even know who they are," Will said, a bitter edge to his voice.

"I trust the people guarding him. I'd trust them with my life."

Will ran a hand across his chin stubble as he fought back the string of woulda, coulda, shoulda that began to play in his mind. That wasn't helpful. It would do nothing to get him back to Cayden.

Will turned to Isabella. "When you and Kim first encountered the Chinese mafia where Kim kept her car, you ran into the building across the street."

"Yeah," Isabella said.

"Could Kim have stashed something in there?" Will asked. He was determined to help Stephens find what she was looking for and get back to base—alive.

A soldier burst through the door, startling Will. He spun around, ready to fight.

"Stephens, we need to move," the soldier said.

"Where's Sharp?" Stephens asked.

"He's pinned down. He said to get you guys back to base."

No Other Choice

"No. I'm not going back until I find what I'm looking for."

Hollingsworth stepped around Stephens. "Will you...?" He pointed to Durant. "Will you stay with him until I return?"

Stephens nodded, and the two soldiers disappeared out of the doorway. Durant began crying and thrashing in pain. Stephens pushed another syringe of morphine into his leg, and the man went silent. His eyes closed, and his breathing slowed—and then stopped. Was Stephens an angel of mercy or Doctor Kevorkian? Maybe she knew the soldier wouldn't have wanted to lived messed up like that.

"Let's get you ready to travel," Stephens said, helping Isabella to her feet.

Isabella swayed and stumbled back, unsteady on her feet. Will wrapped his arm around her waist. "She can't walk. We need to go back to base. She needs a doctor," Will said.

"Hollingsworth gave her antibiotics. She'll be fine. We need to move the vehicle and get to where Kim stored her car."

Stephens was dedicated, he'd give her that, but at what cost? She didn't seem concerned about Sharp in the least. Will held no illusions about whether she would sacrifice him and Isabella to achieve her goal. He supposed that was what made her a good intelligence officer. Her goal was to save the country. Will's goal was to save Isabella and his son. It appeared those two goals were incompatible at the moment.

"We're not going. Whatever it takes, I'm getting Isabella back to base, getting my son, and getting the hell away from Houston," Will said.

Stephens' jaw clenched. She raised the pistol and pointed it at Isabella's forehead. "You're going to help me find that flash drive, or you will not live to see your son. Do we understand one another?" She tilted her head back slightly and glared at Will. "Let's get this straight right here and now. This is not a democracy. You don't get a vote. You are not free to come and go as you please. If you aren't going to help me save this country, then I have to believe that maybe I was right, and you were working with Kim and the Chinese."

Rage boiled in Will's gut. His gaze fell to Isabella. Alarm flashed across her face, and he could feel her shaking in his arms.

"Stephens, let's go." It was Sharp. He'd extricated himself from the insurgents somehow.

Stephens twitched the barrel of her pistol toward the door. "Hurry."

"Is he…?" Sharp asked nodding to Durant's lifeless body.

Stephens nodded and moved toward the door.

Sharp held the passenger side door of the old SUV open. Hollingsworth was in the driver's seat. The second soldier was in the back seat. "Let's go. Let's go. We need to get the hell out of here," Sharp barked.

"Put her in the front," Stephens instructed. She raced to the SUV and yanked the rear door open. "Johnson, climb in the back." The soldier jumped out, ran around, and hopped into the back of the SUV. "Get in, Will."

Will climbed in and scooted across the bench seat. Sharp crawled in beside him, followed by Stephens. Will was pinned between Sharp and the door. He could open it and maybe jump out before Sharp could grab him, but what good would that do him? If he somehow found his way back to the military base, would they let him back in without Sharp and Stephens? What would become of Isabella? He could do nothing but cooperate with their crazy, suicidal plan, and he hated the sense of helplessness that gave him.

Isabella glanced back. Her eyes were pleading. Will leaned forward and placed a hand on her shoulder. "Hang in there. I'll get you back to your apartment. I promise."

The husks of the high-rise buildings that had burned punctuated just how devastating the EMP had been on the city's infrastructure.

Even if the government thwarted the insurgency and stopped the invasion, it would take years, maybe even decades, for Houston to recover. It could take months just to restore electricity. It was too difficult to think about. Somehow, it was easier for Will to imagine learning to live without modern technology than how they would rebuild the city.

The SUV stopped at the corner where Will had first seen the Chinese mafia pursuing Kim. Just days ago, everything had been so normal. Will had taken so much in his life for granted. He'd wasted time feeling sorry for himself for things he'd caused. Now he wished he could turn back the clock and do everything differently.

"Which building did you and Kim enter?" Stephens asked.

Isabella pointed to the property on the opposite side of the street. The two soldiers exited the vehicle and disappeared inside the building. A long minute later, they reappeared at the side of the SUV. "It's clear. It's just a lobby, mostly bare. There are not many places to hide things," Hollingsworth said.

"Watch them," Stephens said as she exited the vehicle.

The two soldiers stood guard outside the SUV as Sharp and Stephens hurried across the street and slipped inside the building.

"You okay?" Will asked Isabella.

"I'm scared."

"I know. We'll make it," Will said.

Will heard the sound of an engine and spun in his seat. One of the vehicles filled with soldiers came roaring up.

"Where's the lieutenant?" a soldier asked as he ran up.

"Inside with Stephens." Hollingsworth pointed.

Three soldiers raced toward the building.

"What's going on?" Isabella asked.

"I don't know." Will stuck his head out and asked Hollingsworth.

"Everything's fine. Just stay in the car."

Isabella's head swiveled, searching the street behind them. "It's not fine. None of this is fine. What the hell have we gotten ourselves into here, Will? Why do things just keep getting worse and worse? It's like some freaking nightmare that I just can't wake up from."

"I know. It'll be over soon," Will said and then realized how patronizing he sounded. She wasn't a child. She was smart enough to know that they could very well die out there. He agreed. It was a waking nightmare. One he was growing tired of, and it only served to increase the rage he felt boiling to the surface.

Stephens exited the building flanked by soldiers. Sharp brought up the rear. "Get that SUV running," Sharp called as they crossed the street. A soldier pulled the Humvee up, and Sharp and Stephens jumped inside. Hollingsworth was just putting the vehicle in gear as the Humvee sped up and disappeared around the corner of Main Street. Hollingsworth weaved back and forth around cars trying his best to catch up.

"What's going on?" Isabella asked.

Hollingsworth said nothing.

When they reached the freeway, it became clear to Will that Stephens had found what she'd been looking for inside that building, or else she wouldn't have given up the search. Kim must have hidden it there when they encountered the Chinese enforcers. Relief washed over him. Now they could get back to the military base. He could get Cayden and leave the area before the shit really hit the fan. He was more convinced than ever that the city was no place to survive this.

"Will," Isabella said. "When we get back…"

An explosion rocked the vehicle. An RPG had slammed into a pickup two lanes over. Hollingsworth yanked the wheel and raced between a mid-sized sedan and a box van. Will lost sight of the Humvee.

"Can you see Stephens and Sharp's vehicle?" Will asked.

"They just pulled down the exit ramp," Hollingsworth said.

Out the front glass, Will spotted two Humvees racing toward

them. They stopped fifty feet away and began firing off to Will's right. Will looked back as Hollingsworth pushed the SUV as fast as it would go past them.

"They're ours?" Will asked.

"Yep!"

A moment later, the SUV pulled through all the military checkpoints before coming to a stop outside the building. Will threw open the door, rushed up the walk, and entered the building. Stephens and Sharp were at the end of the corridor.

"Stephens, where is my son?" Will yelled.

She didn't answer him. Instead, she and Sharp disappeared into one of the offices. Will and Isabella raced up and down the corridor, pulling and banging on every door trying to locate where they were holding Cayden. All the doors were locked. Will pounded on each one and called Cayden's name. He received no reply.

He wasn't there.

"I have to find Stephens," Will said, turning back toward the lobby.

TWENTY

Will

DAY SIX

Two soldiers stood outside the door of the room where Will had last seen Stephens. As Will and Isabella approached, two of them blocked their way.

"You are in an unauthorized area," one of the soldiers said, holding a hand out in front of him. His other hand was on a pistol holstered on his hip.

Would they shoot him? Will wasn't sure, but he couldn't risk it. He shifted from one foot to the other. "Stephens!" he yelled, fear stretching his voice high and tight. "Stephens. Where is my son?"

The second soldier grabbed Will, twisting his arm behind his back and slamming him against the wall. He drew his lower lip between his teeth and attempted to pull away. It didn't work. In seconds, he again was in flex cuffs and being led through the maze of corridors. Thankfully, they were more gentle with Isabella and allowed them to remain together. His eyes bored into the soldier as they were shoved into the room. Will heard the door being locked from the outside. They were trapped.

Banging his fist against the door in the windowless room did nothing to free them, but it gave an outlet for his rage. When he'd exhausted himself, he dropped onto the chair and placed his head in his hands. He looked around for something to break the window or smash through the wall. All he saw was the plain steel desk with a laminate top typical of government office furniture. Metal filing cabinets took up the wall behind it. A framed photo of a man in military uniform hung on the wall on one side of the door. Will rushed around the desk and pulled open drawers, looking for a letter opener or anything he could use to pry open the door. He found nothing useful.

Isabella put a hand on his shoulder.

"We'll find him. Stephens said she had someone guarding him that she trusted. When she's finished with whatever she's doing in there, she'll tell them to let us go."

"You trust her? She could be the mole for all we know. We're screwed, Isabella. We're trapped in here, and I have no idea what they've done with Cayden."

"You have to calm down, Will. If they see you as a threat, we may never get out of here."

"A threat. Did you not see what was happening out there? We were targeted by someone. They knew where we were. How? Phones aren't working. The only people with radios that I've seen are the military. One of them is communicating with the people with the bombs."

"All the more reason for you to calm down. Sit. Let's talk this about this and find a way out of here," Isabella said.

He couldn't sit. His insides were a bundle of nerves. If he'd just hit the road the minute the military dropped them off at Isabella's apartment, they'd be miles away from here by now. They could have found resources along the way. Sure, they'd have been wading through the toxic floodwater, but they'd have been much safer than the situation they now found themselves in.

Will paced the floor in front of the door. Every few minutes, he stopped and pressed his ear against it, listening for anyone in the corridor. After an hour or so, he heard keys jingle and a door open and close.

"Hello, I need to speak to someone. I need to find my son," Will called through the door.

No one answered.

Desperation was about to overtake him when he heard a familiar voice on the other side of the office wall.

"Will? Is that you, Will?"

"Betley?" Will rushed over, pressing his ear against the wall to the adjoining office.

"Will. It's Betley. Did Stephens find anything?"

"Betley, is Cayden with you? Have you seen him?"

"No. Not since they separated us. I'm sure he's safe. Don't worry."

"Don't worry. Why are they keeping him from me?"

"I don't know. Most everyone is on perimeter defense, I think. There was an attack south of the base somewhere. I could hear it."

"You sure it wasn't to the north. We were attacked. First at the gas station and then at an apartment building."

"By gunmen?" Betley asked.

"No. Rocket-propelled grenades," Isabella said.

"Was anyone injured? Are you both all right?" Betley asked.

"A soldier dove on top of me. I caught some glass in my cheek. He died." Tears streamed down her cheeks as she spoke.

"I'm sorry, Izzy," Betley said. "Did Stephens find what she was looking for?"

"I don't know. I think so. She went inside a building, and when she came out, we rushed back here," Will said.

"That sounds like she did. She didn't say anything?"

"No. We didn't get a chance to talk to her. When we got back, they locked us in here," Will said.

"What's going to happen, Betley?" Isabella said.

"It's going to be all right. Reinforcements are on their way from the north of the city. There were thousands of troops positioned to come in to help after the hurricane passed. Soldiers from

Fort Hood will get here soon too. We just have to hold on until they arrive," Betley said.

"Betley, Stephens said there could be someone on the inside working with the Chinese. If that's the case, none of us are safe until they're stopped," Will said through the wall.

"Did Stephens know who it was?" Betley said.

"No. She was hoping the information on the flash drive would lead her to them."

"If it has anything useful on it," Betley said.

"Can't you get us out of here, Betley? If they have what they want, they don't need us anymore," Will asked.

"I'm not really in any position to request anything, Will. I'm locked in here too."

"They can't still think you were working with Kim," Isabella said.

"They're being cautious. They need to isolate anyone that could be a threat right now and sort out the truth later."

"You sure sound awful understanding for someone being accused of treason," Will said.

"I know the truth, and right now, there's nothing more I can do to clear my name. I have to trust Stephens and Sharp to figure it all out. If they don't, it won't matter."

"Why are they keeping me from my son?" Will asked. "I've done nothing but cooperate."

"Stephens is using him to gain your cooperation. If she has what she wants, then there is no reason to hold any of you now. As soon as they can, they'll reunite you."

A loud bang rattled windows around the complex. Will grabbed Isabella and dove to the ground, covering her with his body. It was followed by the sound of automatic gunfire. Will could hear yelling but couldn't make out what was being said. He couldn't be sure how close the explosion was to them, but he wasn't just going to sit around and wait for bombs to drop on them. He had to find a way out of that room.

Will pushed himself off the floor and grabbed the straight-backed metal chair. He flung it against the wall, attempting to bust through the sheetrock. It barely dented the drywall. Unperturbed, Will gripped the seat back and jammed the metal legs into the hole over and over, trying to chip away and break through.

Isabella appeared beside him, a heavy-duty tape dispenser in hand. She repeatedly smashed it against the wall, widening the hole, but they were still no closer to getting out. Will turned and began kicking with the back of his boot.

The door opened, and Hollingsworth appeared. "Let's move."

"What's happening out there?" Isabella asked.

"We have to move you," Hollingsworth repeated as they stepped into the corridor.

"I need to find my son," Will said, grabbing the soldier by the arm. "Tell me where my son is."

"I don't know, sir," Hollingsworth said

"Find me someone who does then," Will demanded.

"Everyone's a little busy at the moment, sir. We'll get you reunited with your son as soon as possible, but right now, we need to move to the interior of the base."

"Where's Stephens?"

"I can't say."

"I'm not going anywhere until I speak with Stephens," Will insisted.

"That is not going to happen."

"We had a deal. We helped her find what she was looking for. Now she needs to get us the hell out of Houston before it's too late," Will said.

Hollingsworth unlocked the door to where Betley was being held and gestured for him to follow.

What appeared to be automatic gunfire echoed through the corridor. A voice sounded over Hollingsworth's radio, and he turned back. "I need you to go back inside for a moment."

"Like hell," Will said.

"Let's go, Will," Betley said, backing into the office. "It's all right. Trust me."

The soldier didn't even wait to secure the door. As he ran off, Betley pushed open the door and stepped out.

"I have to find Cayden. Do you know your way around here, Betley?"

"They may have taken him over to the flight museum. He was pretty excited when they told him about it."

"Show me," Will said.

TWENTY-ONE

Will

DAY SIX

Betley stopped at a single glass door on the south side of the building. He pushed it open slightly. "We're going to take that walkway there on the west side of that single-story building. If the gate is closed near the road, you may have to jump it. Are you up to that, Isabella?" Betley asked.

She nodded, but her blank expression said she wasn't all that sure.

"Are you not coming?" Isabella asked.

Betley pointed to his leg. "I'll have to go around. I can't climb a fence."

"You'll need to hurry across the street and through the parking lot to that building on the other side." He pointed to the Lone Star Flight Museum.

Will had never been there. He'd always meant to take Cayden but had never taken the time. According to Cayden, the flight museum was home to some forty historic aircraft. He'd been particularly interested in the Aviation Learning Center's simulator bay. Melanie had discussed allowing him to take one of the warbird flights they offered. Will had complained that it would be too expensive. He could still recall the disappointment on both their faces. He'd made so many mistakes in his marriage and with Cayden. He'd give anything to be able to go back to that moment and do things differently, but he couldn't. All he could do is try to do right by Cayden now. At the moment, Will was failing him.

"Are you sure they took him to the museum?" Will asked.

"Not for certain. He asked if he could go."

Another round of guilt surface. He should have taken him instead of spending so much time working.

"The soldiers said they didn't have permission to leave the building, but if they moved him, my bet it would there," Betley said.

"I guess it is a place to start."

"All right. Will, you're going to go first? If the gate is open, hurry on across the street. If it isn't, wait for me. I'll help you both over."

Will stepped in front of Betley and peered around the door frame. He looked to his left and then right, surprised no one was out there. Sandbags had been stacked in a U-shape about ten feet from the door. He expected to see soldiers guarding all the exits, but there were none at this door. Will looked back and gave a nod to Isabella before taking off toward the walkway. He was five feet away from the Maritime Safety and Security Team (MSST) building when an explosion in the distance sent him scrambling for cover. An enormous cloud of black smoke erupted to the north. Someone was attacking the checkpoint at the Sam Houston Freeway.

Will was just getting to his feet when Isabella and Betley appeared. Betley grimaced as he grabbed Will under the arm and hauled him to his feet. None of them were in any condition to be running for their lives, but Will couldn't let that stop him.

"They're getting closer," Isabella said.

Will took her hand. "We need to go before all hell breaks loose."

They took off down the walkway, heading for the museum. As

they walked by the MSST, Will noticed that the bays where the twenty-five-foot response boats were usually kept were empty. They might have been deployed to aid in search and rescue efforts, but Will hadn't seen any of that near Isabella's apartment.

Will glanced back. Betley was lagging behind. Will weighed the risk of him slowing them down against not knowing his way around the base. That one detail could mean the difference between getting out or not. Will released Isabella's hand and ran back to Betley. He wrapped his arm around the man's waist and helped him to the fence bordering the street. Automatic rifle fire could be heard plainly now. It was some way off, but still too close for Will.

Isabella ran ahead and pushed open an unlocked gate. She waited, and when they reached her, she took Betley's arm, and the two of them helped him across the street. The parking lot was full of rather old looking, olive drab-colored army trucks and desert sand-colored containers.

"We need a vehicle," she said as they reached the parking lot. "Stephens promised a vehicle to get you and Cayden to your sister's."

"I don't think that's going to happen now. We can't risk going back to find her," Will said.

She released her grip on Betley's arm and stopped walking. "But she promised. She said if I helped her, she'd make sure you got there."

"It's okay, Isabella. We'll find another way. I'll find one somewhere. Right now, we just need to get out of here," Will said.

"Why can't we just take one of these?" she asked.

"Because they would make us a target. In case you haven't noticed, those assholes are going after military assets. We want to stay under the radar, at least until we can score some weapons," Betley said.

By the time they reached the museum, the gunfire and explosions had stopped. Will glanced back at the ball of smoke to their north as he moved around another stack of sandbags, pushed open the double doors, and stepped into the flight museum's arrival hall. The nearly three-story ceiling made the space feel enormous. The circular welcome desk that once greeted guests now sat empty. To their right was the gift shop filled with plane memorabilia, and on the left was a café devoid of tourists. At the end of the long hall, the orientation theater ticket booth was empty. They searched exhibit rooms and galleries lined with photos of several Apollo astronauts, both Presidents Bush forty-one and Bush forty-three, Gene Autry, Bessie Coleman—the first African-American female to receive a pilot's license—and other Texans. Next, they checked classrooms, the flight academy, and both hangars filled with vintage airplanes without finding Cayden. The building had been completely evacuated.

They moved through the hanger filled with vintage aircraft and out the east side door without seeing anyone. He took in the area outside the hangar. He was beyond frantic. Will pressed his fists against his temples. "Where would they have taken him?"

Betley rubbed his forehead and looked across the runway where old and new planes sat uselessly. "We have to go back, Will. We have to find Stephens. She'll be in communication with McKinney, Lieutenant McKinney, the one who is guarding Cayden."

"Damn! Damn! Damn!" We don't have time for this." Will pounded his fists against his head in frustration. Isabella grabbed his arm and turned him toward the front the MTTS building. "We have to find Stephens."

Will pulled his arm back and stared at her. "You should go. You and Betley should take off, get far away from here," he said, pulling open the door stepping back inside the museum.

Isabella grabbed the door and held it open. "I'm not leaving you. I'm going to help you find Cayden. We'll all leave here together, right, Betley?"

Betley gave a slight nod. He didn't owe Will anything but he doubted the man could make it very far on his own. He'd taken quite a beating and lost a lot of blood from the stab wound to his thigh.

If Will was honest with himself, he had to admit he needed them. He knew that he stood little chance to find Cayden and make it away from the city without help.

"Okay. Let's hurry," Will said, taking hold of Betley's arm.

Will listened for the sound of gunfire, relieved when he heard none. Maybe it had been a small attack on the checkpoint that they'd been able to quickly repel. Maybe he wasn't out of time, but the pressure of the ticking clock had been building ever since the moment the lights went out. He wondered when, if ever, he would be safe enough that he didn't feel that time was running out.

Will heard it seconds before he felt it and turned his head slightly, listening at first to what sounded like the whine of a jet coming in hot and then the concussive boom when whatever it was hit the building. He grabbed Isabella's hand and pulled her to the floor. The ground shook. Smoke bellowed from the gaping hole in the side of the building. Fragments of concrete and metal rained down around them. It was pitch black, and thick smoke choked Will's lungs.

"We have to get out of here," Will yelled.

He could barely see Betley. Isabella stood and grabbed Betley's arm. The three moved toward the arrival hall and the exit doors, but the smoke was too thick. "This way," Will said, taking Betley from her and leading them toward the Waltrip hangar and out the doors and making it out onto the walkway just as a second explosion rocked the building. Will was now desperate to find Cayden. Panic was clouding his judgment. Not knowing where his son was the most excruciating experience of his life.

"Where the hell is my son?!" Will screamed.

"We have to find Stephens," Betley said, taking off across the parking lot.

Will's stomach tightened. Stephens could be anywhere. Cayden could be anywhere. He prayed he got to him in time. Will prayed.

He prayed like he'd done that night as he held Melanie's hand. He begged God to help him find his son before it was too late.

Will ran back to the Coast Guard building and flung back the door. "Hurry!" he yelled, fighting the urge to leave them both behind. Isabella's face was black with dust from the explosion except where the tears streamed down her cheeks. He was grateful they'd made it this far. Cayden had experienced enough loss in his short life.

"This way," Betley said as he led them down a hall to their right.

Two soldiers ran past them, and a second later, Stephens appeared in the doorway down the corridor. "Down here," she called.

A lone laptop still sat on the table, open and booted up with a spreadsheet displayed. Betley slid into the chair in front of the computer and ran his finger over the screen. "I knew it," he said. "I knew they were planning something and not running drugs up across the border."

Will stared over Betley's shoulder at the screen. "It's an inventory?"

"Yes," Stephens said as she walked up behind him. She slammed the laptop closed. "It's classified."

"How is that working? I thought all electronics were fried," Isabella said, pointing to the computer.

"EMP hardening. Lots of technical stuff you wouldn't understand," Stephens said.

Isabella put her hands on her hips. "Really?"

Stephens' facial expression softened. She tossed her head back slightly. "These are special EMP shielded rooms." Stephens pointed over her shoulder. "That door is an EMP protected double door entry. No cables or lines come into this room. The walls are like a giant Faraday cage."

"A what?"

"It's a six-millimeter-thick steel box, basically."

Will was relieved to know that the government wasn't totally in the dark and some technological capabilities still existed, but all he cared about at the moment was finding Cayden.

"That's fascinating. I just want my son, Stephens. Where's Cayden?" Will said.

"He's safe." She picked up the laptop and stuffed it into a black metal case.

The two soldiers returned and stood in the doorway. "Staff Sergeant Woodward is missing, but someone saw Colonel Edwards about five minutes ago. He was headed to the TOC," one of the soldiers said.

Stephens slid the computer case off the table and clutched it to her chest. "We have to find him before he gets away."

The soldiers stepped into the hall, and the taller of the two said something into a mic attached to his shirt's collar. He stepped back and said, "He never made it. He's in the wind."

"Get hold of Lieutenant Sharp. Tell him I need his team to stop Colonel Edwards and Staff Sergeant Woodward."

Betley leaned with both hands on the table. He was in pain. It was written all over his face.

"Were their names on the list?" Betley asked.

"You know I can't tell you that," Stephens said.

"I'm on your team. I've been working on these issues. Kim Yang was my informant."

"That's nice, Betley, but this is not the same."

"Where's Special Agent in Charge Rybeck? He can tell you."

"He's dead. They hit FBI headquarters that first day. They tried to infiltrate this base, but they underestimated the number of military personnel there would be."

"You're CIA. This is an FBI investigation. I should be read in," Betley said.

"I've been working on this case for over two years, Betley. I'd just returned from southern Mexico. I've been down there for two months tracking down the cartel members that have been helping the Chinese nationals sneak across the border."

"And what did they tell you?"

"I received a list of names. My team spent the better part of a month verifying the names on the list with Mexican Immigration and Customs and attempting to track them down within Mexico."

"How many did you round up?" Betley asked.

"Not enough."

"Weren't you able to track them through their communications? You guys have a big database that stores every phone call, email, and text. How'd you miss this one?" Isabella asked.

"They weren't communicating via those methods."

"How were they coordinating things then? You don't pull this off without being able to talk to your people," Will said.

"They used apps to coordinate things and running all communications through the Chinese and Mexican consulates. That is why we had to shut down the Chinese Consulate last month. It was the second time in the last few years that we caught them moving CCP spy information in diplomatic pouches between consulates and Beijing."

Will heard footsteps outside the room. Stephens stepped through the doorway. "Sharp said to get the case to the hangar."

"Is he meeting us there?" Stephens asked.

"They went after Colonel Edwards."

"I'm going to need your help, Private First Class Johnson."

"Yes, ma'am. We'll be your escort," the soldier said.

"Stephens, what about my son?" Will said, stepping through the doorway.

"He's safe. I'll take you to him. Come with us," Stephens said.

"No. I want you to tell me where to find Cayden. Now!"

"Help me get this to the hangar, and I'll tell you where he is."

Will lost it. He grabbed Stephens by the throat and shoved her against the wall. "You will tell me now or so help me—"

"Will, stop!" Isabella yelled, pulling on his arm. "Stop. That won't help."

The two soldiers grabbed him from behind and shoved him to the floor followed by a boot slamming into the middle of his back. He struggled to breathe under the soldier's weight.

"You have no right to hold my son. He's a damn kid. You're going to get us all killed."

"Just help me, Will. Help me get this case to the hangar, and I will get you and Cayden away from here, I promise."

He didn't trust the woman as far as he could throw her, but what choice did she leave him. It would take days for him to search every building and hangar on the base.

"Okay. Okay. Where the hell is the hangar?"

TWENTY-TWO

Will

DAY SIX

Stephens and the two soldiers led them to an office at the end of the corridor, where she retrieved a pistol from a locked box in a desk drawer.

"I need a weapon, Stephens," Betley said. "They took mine when I arrived."

Stephens glanced at Hollingsworth. "Can we get him a weapon?"

"I'm not authorized to arm civilians, ma'am."

"I'm not a civilian, private. I'm a federal agent."

"I'm sorry, sir. I'm not authorized to provide weapons to none military personnel."

"How am I supposed to defend myself," Betley said.

"We've got you, sir," Hollingsworth said.

"Stephens?"

"I'm sorry, Betley. Stay close. We need to move quickly."

Will was as pissed as Betley. He and Isabella hadn't asked to be there. Stephens and the military had an obligation to arm them or protect them and he didn't feel two soldiers could provide adequate protection against armed insurgents.

Stephens turned right and was headed toward the front of the building.

"We can't go out the front. A sniper has zeroed in on those doors," Wallace said.

"How many insurgents are we dealing with?" Betley asked.

"Fifty, maybe more. They're hitting and then disappearing into the neighborhoods on the west side of the freeway. One will strike with RPGs and rifle fire, then drop back, allowing another group to advance. Without eyes in the sky, it's impossible to track them."

The soldiers rushed them through the maze of corridors toward the exit leading to the MSST building.

"None of our drones are operating?" Betley asked.

"Very few. The ones that are working are monitoring the Gulf of Mexico," Stephens said.

Wallace craned his neck and shot Stephens a dirty look.

"Wait, you have drones here?" Isabella asked.

"The 147th Reconnaissance Wing is stationed here, and they have MQ-1B Predator Unmanned Aerial Systems and MQ-9 Reapers. I don't know if any of them are operable. That's classified. I can't say more," Hollingsworth said.

"So some stuff survived the EMP?" Will asked.

"Some," Stephens said.

"You can't or won't elaborate?"

"I can't. I'm not involved with that aspect of the mission. My job is to find and eliminate the insurgency. The military's role is to protect our borders. I do pray that enough of their equipment survived for them to do their jobs."

The soldiers didn't chime in. Maybe they didn't know, or they were more tight-lipped than Stephens.

"EMP-proof hangars. All metal with no outside lines penetrating the building?" Betley asked.

"I just don't know. That's not my area."

They paused at the end of the hall and checked for intruders. Thankfully, the corridor was empty.

The soldiers stopped at the door. "Stack up. We need to make it down the walkway and across the street in front of the flight museum before stopping. Is everyone ready?"

If the military hadn't taken his rifle and gear, Will would be ready, but going out there without it, he felt naked. He sure hoped Stephens and the two soldiers were good marksmen.

"All right, let's go." Hollingsworth threw back the door and turned to his left. The others followed close behind him, running down a short walkway between the buildings. The soldiers made a right at the corner of the MSST building and proceeded along its east side where a line of newer-model Ford trucks sat useless due to the EMP. Stephens, clutching the black case containing the computer to her chest, quickly passed Betley and took off down the walkway behind the soldiers. Will thought they were going to leave them all behind. They weren't injured like Will, Isabella, and Betley. There was no way for them to keep up.

The lawn between the MSST and the single-story brick building next to it was filled with a mix of old and new army vehicles and equipment. Some were the old olive drab, and others the desert sand-colored. Small Conex shipping containers were interspersed throughout. Will wondered if any of them contained weapons or ammunition.

Stephens slowed before stepping between the last two trucks in the row. "Hurry!" she yelled over her shoulder. She and the soldiers sprinted across the open lawn separating the MSST building from the street. The sound of small arms fire could be heard in the distance, followed by bursts of automatic gunfire. Will hoped that the insurgents stayed away, but he knew things could quickly turn, and they could be caught in the fight. The wind shifted, and black smoke drifted their way. The entire fuel farm along the road had to be on fire for there to be that much smoke. As Will grew closer to the road, a gaping hole was evident in the front of the museum.

"Stephens, stop. I need a second," Betley said, bending and

placing his hands on his knees although he wasn't gasping for air nearly as much as Will. None of them were. Will was regretting letting himself get so out of shape. He'd never been so keenly aware of how important being able to move quickly was. He needed to take better care of his body.

"We need to keep going, Betley. It's not safe out here in the open," Stephens said.

"I'll help you, Betley," Isabella said, dropping back and sliding an arm under his.

"I'll get him, Isabella. You're not a hundred percent yourself," Will said.

Betley shot him the stink eye like they were in some type of competition for her attention, but he wasn't aware that she'd just learned her boyfriend had been brutally murdered, so Will dismissed it.

As Will and Betley stepped off the sidewalk, several rounds ripped up the grass in front of them. Stephens ducked and Isabella dropped down with her hands over her head as the two soldiers began returning fire. Will turned to run toward the empty bay of the MSST but Betley was dragging his foot, making it difficult to move quickly.

"Isabella, move! Hurry!" Will yelled.

Isabella passed them and held open a door as round after round peppered the side of the building. The insurgents were either terrible shots or they were too far away to be very accurate. Either way, Will was grateful. Stephens remained behind with the soldiers, returning fire as Will, Betley, and Isabella retreated inside.

"Stephens!" Betley yelled.

Stephens and the soldiers began backing toward the building. While the soldiers guarded the door, the others looked for another way out.

Will stomped back and forth near the rear of the bay. "Damn, I need a weapon. This is bullshit."

"He's right, Stephens. We aren't going to make it to the hangars without weapons," Betley said.

"Well, look around, Betley. Where the hell would I get a rifle?" she snapped.

"What are we going to do? We can't just sit here and wait for them to blow us up. We need to get the hell out of here and away from the city," Isabella said.

"How far away is an armory?" Betley asked.

"How the hell am I supposed to know. I've never been here before," Stephens said.

"There's an ASP on the other side of the guard station there," Hollingsworth said. Will followed his finger, hoping it was nearby. It wasn't. It was at least a couple hundred feet. Not that far really, unless you're trying to avoid getting shot.

"Where are Sharp and the other soldiers?" Isabella asked.

"They went to help hold the gates."

"Maybe we can go another way," Isabella said. "Can't we head north until we are far enough away and then head east."

"They've overrun the north perimeter," Stephens said.

"Wallace and I will have to hold them off while the four of you make a run for the museum," Hollingsworth said.

"I don't like that idea," Will said.

"Neither do I, but we don't have much choice."

"Betley, you're going to have to run like hell," Stephens said.

"I'll do my best," he replied.

Hollingsworth went first. He moved to the end of the building and raised his rifle. "I've got at least four hostiles," he said.

"Where?" Wallace asked, coming up beside him.

"In the aerospace building, side parking lot. Two behind that white SUV and two more behind the sign near the road."

"You take the sign. I'll take the SUV," Wallace said.

"Ma'am. We're going to go through the bays here and draw their fire away from the road. We'll join you after we've taken out the trash. Wait for us on the east side of the museum," Hollingsworth said. He and Wallace ducked into the bay that usually contained Coast Guard watercraft and disappeared from Will's view.

TWENTY-THREE

Will

DAY SIX

As soon as Will heard shots being fired, Stephens took off across the grass toward the museum. The tall military vehicles in the parking lot obscured Will's view, making it impossible to tell if any insurgents were waiting for them there. The near-constant sound of automatic rifle fire told Will there were a significant number of them infiltrating the base. How long before they were overrun? He ran a hand over the top of his close cropped hair and tried to remain focused.

Isabella followed closely behind Stephens, with Will and Betley bringing up the rear. It was all so unreal. How could this be happening on American soil? Every muscle in his body tensed as he anticipated getting shot in the back as they ran across the street. He quickened his stride. That wasn't how he wanted to go out.

Stephens dropped down behind an army truck and waved for them to hurry. Isabella ran and crouched beside her. Will looked back as he and Betley neared them. Hollingsworth was firing over the top of the hood of a mid-sized sedan. Will tried to see where the enemy was located, but they must have been well concealed. When they reached the truck, Will leaned Betley against the fender while he tried to catch his breath. It hadn't been that far to run, but he'd held his breath the whole time.

"Where are they?" Isabella asked, craning her neck above the hood to see.

Betley grabbed her arm and pulled her backward, causing her to fall on her butt. "Keep your head down."

Her brow knit tight, and her jaw clenched as she got to her knees. "I thought he said there were only four of them. What the hell is taking so long?"

"It's not a video game," Stephens said sarcastically.

That statement earned her a dirty look from Isabella. He wasn't sure what Stephens' problem was, but Will wanted no part of their bickering. His focus remained on finding Cayden. As the gunfire slowed to just a few shots here and there, Will resisted moving to get a look, not wanting to risk taking a bullet. A moment later, Will heard footfalls on concrete and stiffened until he saw Hollingsworth running toward them.

"Where's Wallace?" Stephens asked.

"Right behind me. Be ready to move," he said.

A few more shots and Wallace rounded the back of the truck and joined them. "Enemy eliminated. Let's move out," he said.

The soldiers moved in a crouch down the row of vehicles and stopped, holding a fist in the air to halt Will and the others. Hollingsworth rose slightly and pulled his rifle to his cheek. He scanned back and forth before declaring the space between the vehicles and the building safe.

When he reached the end of the row of trucks, Will was hesitant to step out into the open. Not knowing how many insurgents were out there or where they were located had every nerve in his body on edge. He didn't know how the soldiers did this for a living. It took a kind of bravery he didn't possess. The soldiers were putting their lives on the line for them. All he was doing was trying to survive so he could find his son. He prayed he didn't fail.

"You ready?" Betley asked.

Will nodded. It was a lie. He was far from ready. He'd never been so ill-prepared in his life. Right then, he vowed to himself that if he somehow made it out of this mess, he'd get prepared, somehow, someway. He'd get armed. It was Texas. There were millions of guns out there. He'd find a way to be ready when trouble found him again, and he knew it would.

"Okay, try not to drag your foot," Will said.

"I'm trying, man. The damn thing just ain't cooperating."

"We need to get you a wheelchair, old man," Will said as he pushed away from the truck and took off after the others.

"Old man? Look who's talking. You sound like an eighty-year-old, huffing and puffing like that."

Will chuckled. "Bro, I'm feeling it today."

Hollingsworth and Wallace took off toward the next row of vehicles. When they reached them, they surveyed the scene looking for more gunmen before waving for Will and the others to follow. Isabella went first, followed by Will and Betley. Stephens covered them until they were safely across.

Will's shoulder and ribs were screaming from carrying most of Betley's weight. He was beginning to feel the effects of the heat and dehydration. A headache was forming behind his eyes, but he had to concentrate on making it safely to the building. He just had to keep putting one foot in front of the other and tune out the pain. Isabella's face was flushed. He worried for her. She was fighting a wound infection, and pushing too hard could be costly to her, but with gunmen waiting to mow them down, they couldn't afford to stop and take it slow.

When everyone had safely reached the second row of vehicles, the soldiers took off toward another. The high beds on the military trucks made it impossible to see what or who was on the other side. Hollingsworth stopped, pressed his shoulder against the vehicle, and peered around the back toward the front of the museum. A second later, he gestured for them to move again. As soon as he stepped from behind the truck, a bullet cracked somewhere to their right, sending Wallace diving back behind the vehicle. More rounds peppered the vehicles to their right.

Will and the others squatted, trying to keep the truck's engine and tires between them and the bullets flying.

"Keep your heads down!" Hollingsworth shouted as he stuck his head up and returned fire overtop the hood. He dropped down and grabbed his head with both hands. "Shit! Shit! I'm fucking hit!" he yelled.

Wallace moved forward and returned fire, shooting around the front of the vehicle. After a few rounds of automatic fire, he stopped and helped Hollingsworth remove his helmet. He held it up to him to see. "Your helmet saved your ass." The side of the helmet had a small hole, and blood spotted the interior. "Are you bleeding?"

Hollingsworth touched the side of his head. His fingers came away damp.

"Let me see," Wallace said. He probed the wound with tactical gloved fingers. "Just a scratch," he declared.

Hollingsworth strapped the helmet back on, grabbed his rifle, and moved to the rear of the truck. As he disappeared, Will's heart flipped in his chest. A moment later, the gunfire concentrated on the back end of the vehicle. It was terrifying being pinned down with rounds striking nearby and not having a weapon with which to defend himself. He prayed nothing happened to Hollingsworth and hated that he and Wallace were Will's only hope of making it to find his son.

The shooting stopped, and Hollingsworth reappeared. "Let's move!" he said as he took off for the next row of vehicles.

Stephens tapped Isabella on the shoulder. "Follow him."

Isabella's head pivoted to face Stephens. Tears welled in her eyes and spilled down her cheeks. She looked like a deer caught in headlights.

"I got her," Wallace said, taking hold of her by the shoulder. He stepped in front of her. "Stay on my left." The two took off for the next row.

Pop! Pop! A cacophony of gunfire erupted.

Wallace dropped to the ground in a heap, his helmet bouncing off the pavement. Isabella froze, staring down at him. She looked up in the direction of the gunfire and screamed.

Will ran to her. "Get his arm," he said, grabbing hold of the soldier's vest. Isabella stared blankly at him for a second before sliding her arm under Wallace's armpit. As they struggled to pull the soldier out of the line of fire, Stephens and Betley ran past and dove beside a shipping container at the end of the next row.

"Isabella, I got him," Hollingsworth yelled as he ran up.

He quickly grabbed hold, and they dragged him to the cover of the twenty-foot container. Hollingsworth immediately began ripping the man's vest off to find the wound. Will picked up Wallace's rifle and moved to the end of the storage container. Stephens was there, returning fire.

"I'm out," she said, dropping back.

Will stepped around her, pulled the soldier's M4 up, and began firing to his left in the direction he thought the insurgents were firing from. Rounds bounced off the heavily armored vehicles. Will didn't believe any of them had found their target, but the enemy stopped shooting.

"I'm hit, man. I'm hit," Wallace cried out.

Will stole a glance to see how bad the wound looked. Hollingsworth was applying tourniquets.

"Am I going to die, Hollingsworth? Oh, man, I'm going to die, ain't I," Wallace said, lifting his head and staring at the wound in his side. The round must have struck under his arm where the vest didn't cover.

"You're going to die an old man, at home in bed with a twenty-year-old above you, remember?" Hollingsworth said.

Will returned his attention to the military transport truck about fifty feet from their position. He couldn't see anyone, but he was reasonably sure that was where the rounds had come from. A moment later, he spotted the barrel of a rifle on the top of one of the hoods. Will watched through his scope and waited for a head to appear. When it finally did, he squeezed the trigger. The pink mist he saw was confirmation that he'd hit his target. He felt relief and then guilt. He'd shot a man. It wasn't something he wanted to celebrate.

"Let's move out," Hollingsworth said.

Isabella pointed to Wallace. "What about him."

"He's gone. We have to go," Hollingsworth said.

As Hollingsworth checked the next aisle for insurgents, Will rushed to Wallace's side, removed the man's vest and tactical belt, and then grabbed the ammo from his pockets. It was like robbing from the dead, but he no longer needed them, and Will did. It was about self-preservation at that point. Will was keenly aware of how much they'd abandoned civilized behavior already.

"How many mags did he have left?" Betley asked as he leaned against the container.

Will pulled three empty thirty round magazines from a pouch from the belt and then counted the full mags remaining in the tactical vest. "Four mags."

"Grab his knife," Betley said, pointing to a thigh holster.

Will removed it and handed it to Betley. It wasn't much, but it was better than nothing.

Will scanned the distance between the containers and the northeast corner of the museum as he pulled on the vest and adjusted it to fit his smaller frame.

"It's clear," Hollingsworth said, taking off toward the building.

Isabella stood with her arms across her chest, holding herself. He wished he had a weapon to give her. She'd shown so much more confidence when they'd battled the Chinese mafia, but he understood the vulnerable feeling of being in this situation without a means of defending oneself.

Will tapped Isabella on the shoulder. "We'll go first. You stay close behind me." Will let his rifle dangle on its sling and grabbed Betley's arm, lifting him to his feet.

"I got him," Stephens said. "You get her."

Will released his grip on Betley and reached out to Isabella. "Take my hand. We'll go together." Slowly, Isabella extended her hand. Will wrapped his arm around her shoulders, and they took off behind Hollingsworth. The gunfire came from the left this time. The insurgents had either moved around the museum to flank them, or these had come from somewhere else. An unknown number of hostiles were firing from the cover of vehicles in the parking lot of a building to the left of the museum.

Will returned fire as he and Isabella ran. As they approached the building, Isabella broke free from Will and raced ahead. Stephens and Betley appeared in Will's peripheral vision. The three of them reached the corner of the museum simultaneously and dropped down behind the four-foot wall of sandbags for cover. Hollingsworth returned fire, emptying a magazine before stopping. While he reloaded, Will poked his head up and fired until he was out of rounds. It slowed the enemy's return fire, but only temporarily. When a bullet hit the sandbag in front of his face and kicked debris into his eyes, Will was forced to stop firing and drop back down.

"We can't stay here. There are too many of them. We have to get inside and make it around to the west side of the building," Stephens said. She still clutched the computer case in her arms. She'd abandoned her empty pistol.

Hollingsworth sprinted to the door and yanked on the handle. It didn't open. He fired, and the glass shattered. "Hurry!" he yelled.

Rounds slammed into the steel walls to the left of him as he flung open the door.

Will fired on full automatic as Stephens and Isabella helped Betley reached the doorway. Will felt a tap on his shoulder, and then Hollingsworth dropped down beside him. "Go with them. I'll hold them back."

"No!" Will said. "We need you to get us to the hangar."

The soldier glanced back toward the museum. "Okay. I'll cover you while you get to the door. You cover me when you get there."

"Deal," Will said, moving toward the door.

TWENTY-FOUR

Will

DAY SIX

Once they'd made it inside the building, Hollingsworth spoke into a radio attached to his vest.

"Bravo one-niner. This is Bravo two-three."

Will and Hollingsworth ran to catch up with the others as he waited for a reply.

"Bravo one-niner. This is Bravo two-three," he repeated.

A knot formed in the pit of Will's stomach. What did it mean that there was no answer? Was the base overrun? Were they doomed? His pulse pounded in his ears as he ran. He was like he was going in slow motion. It was all so unreal. Was this really happening?

While Stephens helped Betley onto the floor just outside a bathroom, Isabella paced back and forth in front of the elevator, chewing on her thumbnail. She was breathing hard. Will hoped it was from the running and not the infection getting worse.

"Bravo two-three. This is Bravo one-niner." The next words were drowned out by heavy gunfire, and then "sitrep" crackled through the radio.

"Bravo one-niner. This is Bravo two-three. We're in the northeast corner of Building F. We're taking heavy fire from two teams of six to ten hostiles. Requesting additional support. Over."

"Bravo two-three. Hold your current position. Sending Alpha two-six to your location. Over."

"Roger that. Holding current position. Bravo two-three out."

Will felt a rush of relief at hearing that help was on the way. He hoped they'd be able to hold out until they arrived. Stephens didn't look all that relieved though.

"How long, Hollingsworth?" Stephens asked.

"They were at the checkpoint at the freeway. Ten. Fifteen minutes."

"Ten or fifteen minutes?" Isabella asked, her voice pitching high.

"They're on foot and have to fight hostiles to get here."

Isabella's face contorted. She opened her mouth to say more but didn't, then she pivoted and stomped down the hall. Will understood her concern. They were trapped like cornered animals. But all he could think about was Cayden and what would become of him if he didn't make it out.

"How much ammo do you have left?" Hollingsworth asked as he ejected a magazine from his rifle and replaced it with a fresh one.

Will counted the magazines in the pouch on the vest. "One."

"We'll have to make each shot count, conserve ammo. Don't shoot unless you see someone, okay?"

"Got it," Will said. He hoped it wouldn't come to that. He prayed the hostiles wouldn't try to get inside. The minutes crawled by as they waited for Sharp and his team.

"You watch that door there," Hollingsworth said, pointing to the door they'd just come through. "I'm going to check the other doors on this side of the building."

"What? No. What if they break in?" Isabella asked, stepping in front of him.

"I won't go far. I'll be right back."

Isabella slid down the wall and sat on the floor beside Betley who reached over and took her hand. She winced and pulled away. She needed to see a doctor, not be running around being shot at.

"Maybe we should find something to barricade the door," Will said, remembering when they'd been able to use a barricade to escape from the Chinese mafia. But the museum had multiple entrances and a big hole in the front of the building.

"Hollingsworth will find a way out, and Sharp and his team will be here shortly," Stephens said. Will heard her confident words, but her face said something else entirely. He could see the tension in her entire body.

Will found it hard to resist stealing quick glances over at Isabella and Betley. When he tried to put his arm around her shoulder, Isabella removed it and stood. If that didn't cause Betley to get the message, nothing would. She was obviously pissed that he'd given them her address.

"I'm going to use the restroom. Will, please don't let me get shot on the potty," she said.

"Make it quick," Stephens said. "We need to be ready to move when Hollingsworth returns."

Isabella acknowledged Stephens' statement with a thumbs-up gesture and slipped inside the restroom.

"What happens when we reach the hangar, Stephens?" Betley asked. "Do you expect to hop on a plane and fly that computer out of here?"

Stephens said nothing.

"What do Colonel Edwards and Staff Sergeant Woodward have to do with the insurgency?" Betley pressed.

Stephens pivoted slightly as if about to say something and then shifted her weight to the opposite foot. Her focus returned to the door.

After a long silence, she said, "I think they're being run by an army general by the name of Dempsey. His name has been on all the intelligence briefings regarding the Chinese Consulate here in

Houston. We intercepted a call between Dempsey and Edwards. You and I both know how unusual that is. Colonel Edwards isn't in Dempsey's chain of command.

"Wait. You think a four-star general is working with the Chinese?" Will asked.

"Until I received the thumb drive that Kim Yang took, I didn't have proof."

"Now you do?" Will asked.

"Won't do any good. They won't find him. If he's involved, he knew this was coming. He's likely on some beach somewhere with a generator and a well-stocked bunker," Betley said.

"I don't believe that's the case. Dempsey had been working hard with the president's advisors to get him to adopt a new continuity of government plan. One that would benefit Dempsey. Fortunately, the president didn't take that advice, and Dempsey has no authority outside of taking orders from his military superiors, but it shows me where his aspirations are."

"This continuity of government plan, that was for in case the president and vice president are killed or unable to serve? Isn't that spelled out in the constitution? I mean, the speaker of the house becomes president in that case, right?" Will said.

"Can't you just contact the Pentagon?" Isabella asked.

Stephens' face flushed. She glanced away.

"What aren't you telling us, Stephens?" Betley asked.

Stephens said nothing.

"Stephens?" Betley repeated.

"Everyone was there."

"Who was where?" Will asked.

"All of them. The entire government was in DC. The president, vice president, both the house and senate as well as all nine justices of the Supreme Court."

"So, what happened?" Will asked.

Slowly, she turned to face them. Her back straightened and her shoulders stiffened. "Washington's gone. The East Coast is gone," she said matter-of-factly.

"Gone? Nuked gone?" Betley asked.

She nodded.

"What do you mean Washington is gone? You can't reach them?" Will asked.

Stephens' gaze fell to the floor. "After they launched the nukes into the atmosphere causing the EMP, they launched nuclear strikes on D.C. and New York City."

It was too horrible to contemplate. The idea that their entire government could be wiped out in an instant was unfathomable. What would that mean for the country and its ability to recover? Was it even possible?

"What about radiation and fallout? Are we all going to die?" Isabella was nearing hysteria.

Will's mind went blank. It didn't feel real. None of it felt real. This couldn't be happening. America could not have been brought to her knees like this. Not like this. Not this easily

"How do you know?" Isabella asked. "How can you be sure?"

"One of our Coast Guard cutters in the Gulf received word from the Fourth Fleet off the coast of Latin America," Stephens said.

"Was South America affected by the EMP? Were we the only ones?" Isabella asked.

"As far as I know, Central and South America weren't hit," Stephens said.

"Well, that means that our military down there wasn't either, right?" Will asked.

"That's correct. They are on their way home now, but they will be concentrating most of their attention on the West Coast, I'm told."

"Why? Don't they know about the insurgents here?" Isabella asked.

"I'm not sure. I wasn't part of the briefing to them," Stephens said.

"You have to get word to them," Will said.

"So, back to my original question, what good is the information contained on that thumb drive? Even if you have proof that this General Dempsey is collaborating with the colonel to aid the insurgency, what can be done about it under the circumstances?" Betley asked.

"I need to alert the military commanders in the Midwest. Right now, that is the biggest threat outside the insurgency. I believe that the forces here can get this situation under control soon. After over twenty years of fighting insurgents in Iraq and Afghanistan, our military knows how to eliminate them."

Will wasn't sure what difference any of it made now. No one was in control. Will pictured mass chaos—the wild, wild west—if they weren't invaded first, that is.

"How can you do that with comms being down?" Betley said.

"Comms aren't down everywhere," Stephens said. "I need to get to Fort Hood."

"You're going to fly?" Betley asked.

"If one of those old vintage planes can take off," she said.

Some of the older vehicles still worked. It was plausible the older planes would as well. There were several on display around the base, but that didn't mean they were operable. Even if she could fly somewhere, how could she get a message out to the rest of the country? Will knew nothing about electromagnetic pulses or what damage they could do. It was clear that some vehicles still worked. Older ones, maybe some new ones too, but he had no clue why. Hollingsworth was able to communicate with someone on the base, so some short-range radios worked. It was the United States military, and they supposedly prepared for something like this. No doubt they'd planned for alternative communications.

Will hoped Stephens was right, but he wasn't willing to stick around and find out. "I understand you need to do what you need to do, Stephens, but I need to protect my son. Tell me where he is."

"He's at NASA."

Relief washed over Will. He knew where to find his son. All he had to do now was get there and get him the hell away from the city.

"Are the buildings secured? How can you be sure he's safe?" Will asked.

"It has a heavy security presence. I didn't think it would be a target of the insurgents."

Will attempted to plan the route in his mind. He'd never taken back streets to get there. It could take an hour to walk it.

"I'll help you to the hangar, but you need to get me a vehicle to go for my son," Will said.

"Deal."

TWENTY-FIVE

Will

DAY SIX

"Bravo two-three. This is Alpha two-six. How copy? Over," crackled over Hollingsworth's radio.

"Alpha two-six. I read you, Lima Charlie. Over."

"We're moving around to the southeast side of the building. Can you make it to that southeast exit by the restaurant? Over."

"Alpha two-six, affirmative. We'll meet you at the southeast exit. Bravo two-three out."

"Will, grab Betley's left arm. I'll get his right," Stephens said. "We're going to be moving quickly, so try your best to lift your feet, Betley."

In order to reach the rendezvous point, the group had to pass through the Waltrip Hangar with its displays of the B-17 Flying Fortress, a North American B-25, and P-47 Thunderbolt, all relics of a bygone era. Will wondered if their modern cars, planes, and ships would become no more than junk heaps sitting idle for years with nature claiming them like in the dystopian movies he'd seen.

How closely would this apocalypse resemble the fictitious ones depicted in books and movies? Would their lives now be like the *Walking Dead*, but without the zombies? The thought of his son growing up in a world like that renewed the boiling rage inside him. He hated the people who had brought this down on the city and the nation. It was hard to stay positive when he thought about the struggle they would face even after escaping the city. He questioned whether he was even up to the task. He knew one thing for sure, he'd fight until his last breath to give Cayden the life he deserved and make sure he had a fighting chance at something resembling normalcy. Was he kidding himself? Anything resembling normal was a long way off.

They exited near the Aviation Learning Center and made their way down the corridor toward the orientation hall. As they passed the arrival hall, Will got a view of the interior damage to the front of the building made by the RPGs and mortar fire. The multi-story building's glass windows were gone. In its place was a pile of twisted metal and glass.

The gunfire sounded closer now. Will hoped that the team that had been sent to collect them had enough ammo to resupply him. He didn't like the prospect of crossing the open ground to the hangars without being able to defend himself. Not that he could do much while holding on to Betley.

As the group hurried past the Heritage Hangar and headed toward the flight academy, the sound of the gunfire faded. Will spotted soldiers standing in the doorway of the southeast exit—only two. He didn't think that would be near enough to take on the group of insurgents. Will's stomach tightened. He just wanted all this to be over. He'd had enough of fighting and death. He tried not to think about what they'd face after leaving Houston. He could only hope that things weren't as bad away from the city.

Texans were generally good people. The rest of Texas, away from the big cities, was filled with hardworking, salt of the earth folks that loved their country and helped their neighbors. Those were the people he hoped they'd find on the journey. It was also those people he believed they'd find in Louisiana. Will tried to imagine building a life there instead of focusing on the horrors that awaited them outside the museum.

"It took you long enough," Hollingsworth said as he lined up behind the new soldiers.

"You should be grateful that Lieutenant Sharp ordered us to come to save your ass," the stockier of the two soldiers said.

Will noticed he wore a different uniform to Hollingsworth and recalled that Ellington was home to all the military branches. This man's blue uniform with USCG written across his vest told Will he was with the United States Coast Guard. Even though they were in different branches, their familiarity with one another made it obvious they'd met and worked together before all this.

"How's it going along the wall, Bardonkey?" Hollingsworth asked.

"My name is Bordonski, and it's a damn shit show out there. They're lobbing Molotovs and shit at us as well as RPGs and mortars."

"Let's go, puddle pirate," the second soldier said.

Bordonski flipped him the bird and pivoted to face the door. "Eat shit, Santos."

"What's the condition of the southern perimeter?" Stephens asked as they approached.

"They seem to be concentrating their efforts on the north and west sides of the base at the moment. Company B took out a group of four heading south," Bordonski said over his shoulder.

"We need to move," Santos barked.

"We need more ammo," Hollingsworth said.

"Santos, you got any 5.56?" Bordonski called out.

Santos stepped into the doorway. "I've got two mags," he said, holding the ammunition out to Hollingsworth.

"Can I get one of those?" Will asked.

Somewhat reluctantly, Hollingsworth handed him one of the thirty round magazines. Will didn't blame him for his hesitation. Will was inexperienced with automatic weapons, and he'd wasted a lot of ammo so far. He was determined to be more careful.

"Isabella, you go first, and then Stephens, Betley, and… I forgot your name?" Hollingsworth said.

"Will."

"Stephens, you got Betley? I need Will's help watching our six."

Will released Betley's arm and stood beside Hollingsworth as Stephens and Betley followed Isabella and Bordonski out the door. A refreshing breeze hit Will in the face as he stepped outside. The building had been stifling hot, but he'd barely noticed until now. The sun beat down on them as the others ran south across the parking lot toward another row of military vehicles. Hollingsworth and Will remained near the building, with Hollingsworth watching for hostiles to their left and Will scanning to their right. When the others disappeared between vehicles, Hollingsworth tapped Will on the shoulder, and the two took off after them.

They were within ten feet of the row of vehicles when the shots rang out. Hollingsworth shoved Will to the ground seconds before several rounds hit the Humvee to Will's right. The pinging noise it made caused Will's butt to pucker. He and Hollingsworth crawled between the vehicles and waited for the firing to stop. When it did, Hollingsworth stood to a crouch, placed his rifle on the bumper, and fired several rounds.

"Go!" he shouted.

Will ran, trying to locate the others but saw no one in the maze of vehicles.

Seconds later, Hollingsworth appeared at Will's side. "Keep moving. That way," he said, pointing to the end of the row twenty-five feet ahead.

Will ran in that direction but kept peering between vehicles for Isabella and the others. He didn't like getting separated from the rest of the group. "Where are the others?" he asked as he ran alongside Hollingsworth.

"They know where they're going." That was all he would say.

"We need to catch up to them."

"We need to not get flanked by those assholes shooting at us first."

Hollingsworth turned south before reaching the end of the row and ran between vehicles to the parking lot's edge. Ahead was an open field, and beyond that were rows of airplane hangars. Isabella and the others were nowhere in sight. They had to still be within the maze of trucks and Humvees.

"Shit!" Hollingsworth cursed. He pressed the button of the radio attached to his vest as he turned back toward the parking lot. Before he could speak, a barrage of gunfire erupted.

"Alpha two-six. What is your position?" Hollingsworth yelled into his mic.

They ran toward the gunfire, but it was hard for Will to pinpoint where it all was coming from.

"Alpha two-six!"

No response came.

"Alpha two-seven," Hollingsworth radioed. "Santos!"

"Bravo two-three. Bravo two-three. We're on the northeast corner of the parking lot, taking heavy fire. We've got at least a dozen advancing from the northwest corner of Building F. There are more making their way across from the front. Two-six is down surgical."

"Shit! Shit! Shit!" Hollingsworth said, pacing back and forth.

"Alpha one-niner. This is Bravo two-three. How copy? Over."

Will didn't hear a reply from Alpha one-niner.

"Will, we're going to head down the row. I'm going to take the rear of the vehicles. You stay in the aisle and move from vehicle to vehicle. Call out if you see anything. We have to get to them before those reinforcements do."

"Alpha one-niner. This is Bravo two-three. Alpha two-six is down surgical in the southeast parking lot of Building F. We need a litter and transport to the aid station. Over."

Will still didn't hear a reply. He hoped Hollingsworth did. If he didn't, that meant they were in a lot of trouble. His mind imagined the worst, conjuring images from all the war movies he'd ever watched. Scenes from films like *Lone Survivor* and *12 Strong* made his knees nearly buckle. It had looked like hell on earth, and they'd had the ability to call in air support. What hope did he and this group have?

"Eleven o'clock. Eleven o'clock. Fall back! Fall back!" Hollingsworth yelled, chopping the air with his hand. Will stood there, unsure who he was talking to.

"Fall back, Will. Four hostiles advancing on my eleven o'clock."

Will pivoted and ducked between two Humvees. "Where are the others?" Will yelled as Hollingsworth came into view.

A moment later, Will heard one of the Humvees start. His first thought was why in the hell hadn't they taken one in the first place. Going on foot had been like a suicide mission.

"There," Hollingsworth said, pointing.

Will took a step toward the vehicle seconds before hearing the thud, thud, thud sound of the Humvee's .50 caliber turret-mounted weapon. Someone was unleashing a barrage of firepower on the advancing enemy. He shifted to his left to see if he could tell who was doing the shooting. Betley spun the turret clockwise to engage a group coming at them from the front of the museum. Will prayed that Isabella and Stephens were in the Humvee and not pinned down somewhere out in the open. He strained to see inside but could see nothing more from his position.

The Humvee rolled forward a few feet before coming to a stop, and Betley opened fire again. He must have fired over a hundred rounds. Yet the insurgents still returned fire from their positions behind a row of small steel box containers.

"Alpha one-niner. This is Bravo two-three. We are taking heavy fire from multiple locations along the northern parking lot of building F. Bluebird one's location is unknown. Bluebird two is returning fire with the fifty cal. Over."

Crack! Crack! Crack!

Rounds struck the truck in front of Will, causing him to have to hunker down between vehicles. He felt powerless to help Isabella and Stephens wherever they were.

"Can you see them?" Will asked.

"We have a group at our two o'clock and eleven o'clock."

"No. Isabella and Stephens."

"Negative."

"We have to find them," Will said.

"We're pinned down. We've got hostiles less than fifty meters. If we move left, we'll be in their line of fire. Betley is engaging with a group advancing from the front parking lot."

"Is help on the way?"

Hollingsworth shook his head. "I couldn't raise anyone on the radio."

Panic crawled up Will's spine and threatened to seize him by the throat. He swallowed hard and drew in a deep breath. If they were on their own, he needed to be clear-headed. All he could think of was he may never get to tell Cayden how sorry he was and how much he loved him. He should have said that to him that every day. How would he make it without his parents? Regret filled Will. He wasn't ready to die. He'd made a promise to Melanie to take care of their son. It had been her dying wish. Never had he thought that helping two women in distress would lead to all this? How could he have known?

If he hadn't rushed in and pulled Isabella from her burning car, he and Cayden would be safe at the lake house—but Isabella would be dead. Would she die anyway? Would they all be killed in the enemy's fight to take Houston? Will clenched his jaw. Not if he could help it. He'd fight and keep on fighting for as long as it took. He had no other choice.

"Peel back. Peel back—they're flanking. We can't let them get behind us," Hollingsworth yelled. He continued firing as he moved back toward Will. Hollingsworth fired around the front bumper, dropping a man dressed in dark-colored street clothes.

Will wasn't sure how he would tell who were friendlies and who were hostiles. Then the man pulled himself upright onto one knee and attempted to lift his weapon into firing position. Will fired multiple rounds before remembering he needed to conserve ammo.

"How much ammo do you have?" Hollingsworth asked.

Will patted his chest, looking for spare magazines. He pulled an empty from a pouch and held it out. "Just what I got in my rifle."

"Shit! Shit! Shit!"

Hollingsworth pulled a magazine from a side pocket of his tactical pants and tossed it to Will as they continued to move south down through the parking lot, weaving in and out between vehicles. Hollingsworth opened the doors of each of the Humvees they passed, each time cursing loudly as he slammed them shut.

"What the hell? Why is there no ammo in these? Geesh!"

At the end of the row were more twenty-foot-long steel shipping containers. Will wondered how the military had moved all that equipment there so quickly after the EMP and then remembered the long convoy he'd seen on the bridge that day. It appeared they had all this equipment but not enough people to fight back a few insurgents. Was it just a few? He'd seen at least fifty. How many more were fighting to get past the checkpoints and over the walls?

Hollingsworth ran to the nearest shipping container and yanked on the handle. "Shit!" he screamed. He fired at the lock, causing sparks to fly, but the lock held.

"Alpha one-niner. Alpha one-niner. We are pinned down, taking heavy fire from multiple locations. We need immediate extraction. Bluebird one is in the wind. I repeat Bluebird one is in the wind. Over."

Almost immediately, the radio crackled to life. "Bravo two-three. Secure Bluebird one and hold your position. Echo Team is heading your way."

Will could barely make out what the man was saying over the sound of constant gunfire and explosions on his end. They must have been in one hell of a battle themselves.

"We need to locate Stephens and get her inside the building," Hollingsworth said.

Will felt comfortable with that plan. They could barricade the doors and move to the middle of the building.

"You ready?"

Will nodded.

"Let's move up."

TWENTY-SIX

Will

DAY SIX

Will was surprised when Hollingsworth took the time to drop beside the enemy combatant and pat him down. Will stole quick glances as he concentrated on firing over the top of the hood of one of the Humvee's nearest the man.

"Got it. Let's go," Hollingsworth yelled, holding up two magazines of ammunition.

Will scooped up the man's rifle as he ran by him. Hollingsworth made a quick right and disappeared between vehicles. Will's stomach flip-flopped for a second before he made the turn himself and spotted Hollingsworth scanning the opposite aisle between rows. He chopped the air and ran across the open space. Will held his breath and took off after him, surprised when he made it to the relative safety of the next row of vehicles without being shot.

"How are we going to locate them?" Will asked. If they were smart, they would be well concealed—even from them.

"Stephens," Hollingsworth shouted.

A second later, Will spotted the top of Stephens' head poking above the hood of one of the Humvees five or six vehicles away.

Relief washed over him. He started to rush towards her, but Hollingsworth held out his arm to stop him.

"Pull security," he said, pointing back to their south.

"What?"

"Watch my back," he said as he slowly moved closer to Stephens.

All Will wanted to do was rush to Isabella and get the hell back inside the museum, but he held his position and watched for movement in the fields between the parking lot and the hangars.

Seconds seemed like hours as he waited for some signal from Hollingsworth to join him. Will spotted Stephens and Isabella emerging from between the vehicles flanked by two other soldiers. He pivoted his head slightly to make sure Isabella wasn't injured. She looked terrified as Stephens wrapped an arm around her shoulder and they took off toward the building. A round whizzed past Will and then another. He kept his eyes on Isabella and Stephens as he dove for cover, praying that they somehow made it to safety. He popped up and begun returning fire on several insurgents. They were firing at them over top of a low wall at the south end of the building. Hollingsworth dropped down beside him, and he too opened up on their location.

"What a shit show," he yelled over the reports of the rifles.

"Did they make it?" Will asked.

"Yeah. They're safe. We just need to hold these assholes off until Echo Team arrives."

"I sure the hell hope they send more than a couple of soldiers this time and a ton of ammo," Will said.

"Don't worry. Lieutenant Sharp will come loaded down. He does shit right."

For some reason, hearing a familiar name brought Will some measure of comfort. He didn't know the man that well and certainly didn't know how he was as a soldier, but his first impression of Sharp had been that he was a tough, no-nonsense type of guy. And he was aware of the importance of the information

Stephens carried. He might be more motivated to rescue them, to retrieve it—at least he hoped that was the case.

Will and Hollingsworth dropped to a crouch as the firing stopped. He could no longer hear Betley and the .50 cal. The hostiles could be advancing on them from that position, and they wouldn't know it, hunkered down as they were. Will considered crawling under one of the Humvees but feared getting trapped under there if they were overrun. No, he'd make his stand alongside Hollingsworth come what may.

His mind went in multiple directions as they waited. He kept telling himself that Cayden was safe and help was on its way. Soon this would be behind him, and he and his son would leave this wretched city. He had to believe they would. His son was all that had kept him going—that and his desire to protect Isabella. She'd had his back and helped him get Cayden to safety. He owed her. Neither of them had signed up for this. But somehow, here they were. So far, they'd survived—by pure luck and determination, they had survived. How long would that luck hold? Long enough for Sharp and his men to arrive? Will prayed so.

The insurgents to their south suddenly stopped returning fire. Will wasn't sure why. He was reasonably sure that he and Hollingsworth hadn't killed them all.

"Let's try to make it inside," Hollingsworth said.

"What about Betley?"

"There's too many. We can't get to him. Our best chance is to make it inside and secure the doors."

Will hesitated, not willing to abandon the agent.

"Go. I'll cover you," Hollingsworth said.

Hollingsworth was right. There was nothing he could do for Betley. Will hoped the Humvee would provide him enough protection until Sharp could arrive and rescue him.

Will rose and stepped away from the safety of the vehicles, spotting two men running toward him from the end of the row near the front of the building. He raised his rifle to fire, but before he could get off a shot, the two men dropped to the ground. Will looked behind him and saw four soldiers quickly moving toward him in a crouch.

"Go, Will!" Hollingsworth yelled, tapping him on the shoulder.

Will took off toward the building right behind him but immediately came under heavy fire. The rounds struck the wall of the museum and kicked up pieces of dirt from the grass. Will and Hollingsworth once again fell back to the safety of the Humvees as the arriving soldiers ran past them, heading toward Betley's position. A second later, Will heard Lieutenant Sharp barking orders.

"Owens. Barkley. Ten o'clock. Ten o'clock. Concentrate your fire toward the plane."

Will rose just enough to see where he was talking about. He hadn't even noticed the NASA plane on display fifty yards from them. There was a clump of trees maybe ten yards beyond that where insurgents had concealed themselves.

"Hollingsworth. Where's Betley?" Sharp asked as he ran up.

"Second row. About the fourth Humvee in. He's out of ammo. None of the others have any either. The nearest ammo resupply point is near those hangars," Hollingsworth said, thrusting a thumb over his shoulder.

They'd need to cross several hundred yards of open field to reach it. There was no way to make it.

"We've got some fifties and a few mortars. Move on me. Let's get to Betley and then take out those assholes firing at us from that cluster of shipping containers there," Sharp said.

"You. Civilian. When I start firing, you're going to run like hell toward the building. Don't stop until you're inside. Got it?" Sharp asked.

Will nodded.

"Got it?"

"Yes!" Will said. "I got it."

Sharp chopped the air, and he and two other soldiers took off

No Other Choice

running north. They stopped about ten yards ahead and began firing before moving again.

"Go, Will," Hollingsworth yelled as he took off to follow them.

Will stepped out then looked back south to make sure no one would shoot him in the back before taking off across the parking lot toward the museum. A loud boom sent him scrambling back for cover. When he poked his head up, Sharp and the others were running toward Betley's direction. Gunfire was coming from everywhere, so much of it that Will had no choice but to keep his head down.

He spotted movement in the next row and pivoted. The man carried a rifle but wasn't in uniform. Will raised his rifle in the man's direction, and he stopped. It was then that Will could see his face. Rage. Pure hatred. Will squeezed the trigger but missed. The man jumped back out of view. Will waited, but he never reappeared. Should he go after him? He wasn't trained for this. All he could do was stay there, hoping not to get shot or blown up.

Will once again heard the thudding sound of the .50 caliber machine gun. They'd made it to Betley. Next, he heard a thump and then witnessed a massive explosion of a building on the other side of the airplane. A thick cloud of smoke rose into the air, but the automatic gunfire persisted seemingly everywhere around Will. There was no doubt that more than a few insurgents were still alive. It felt more like a whole army had descended upon them. Was this an invasion? Were they too late leaving the city? He feared they'd be trapped and never get out if that was the case.

The next time Will saw movement, it was two soldiers moving south carrying Santos. His head was bandaged, as were his leg and arm. His head was lolling to the side, and he was barely conscious though he cried out as one of the soldiers shifted him to bring his rifle up. Out stepped the insurgent who'd fired upon Will. He raised his rifle and began firing.

The two soldiers scrambled backward, dragging Santos toward the row of vehicles while attempting to return fire on the shooter.

Will ran toward them, firing at the man as well. Someone's rounds hit their target, and the man crumpled to the ground. Will turned his attention to Santos. He was lifeless at the soldiers' feet. One of them felt for a pulse, then shook his head. It was unlikely that he would have survived his wounds from what Will had seen, but he understood that they had to try. They dragged him between the vehicles and, without a word, took off running toward the front and the concentration of gunfire.

Will stood there, staring down at the dead soldier. He was sick of death. Sick of all the bloodshed. He feared that this was only the beginning. The enemy had initiated this fight. It was apparent to him that they wouldn't stop until they reached their objective. Exactly what that was, Will was afraid to even guess. What would it mean for them if the Chinese won? It was unthinkable. They couldn't let that happen even if every man, woman, and child had to take up arms and fight. They had to defend their country, or they would never be free again.

"Will!" Hollingsworth called. "Sharp told you to get to the museum."

Will turned. "I tried. I nearly got my head shot off."

"Shit. Go. I've got your back."

TWENTY-SEVEN

Will

DAY SIX

Will and Hollingsworth had barely made it five steps before having to drop to the ground. A massive explosion hit one of the shipping containers, and flames shot into the air. Will felt his bones rattle.

"They hit the genny," Hollingsworth yelled.

Will could barely hear him. He worried that his hearing might be permanently damaged from all the noise.

Another explosion hit somewhere in the direction of Betley and Sharp. A few seconds later, soldiers began running past Will. "We're falling back. They're hitting us with mortars."

Sharp and Betley came into view. Betley was doing his best to keep up but was lagging behind. He tripped and fell. Will took off toward him. One of the soldiers ran past and scooped Betley up by the collar of his shirt. He was dragging him back towards cover when an explosion rocked the vehicle nearby them. Will dropped to the ground and crawled to cover, expecting the next one to hit his location. The air was thick with smoke.

"Two-three. Get Bluebird two and haul ass to Building F," Sharp barked.

"Owens. Get those damn mortars on that container and stop those bastards."

Hollingsworth ran into the smoke and disappeared. Will stood there for a moment just staring at the soldier, loading a mortar into the bipod supported firing tube. Seconds later, he heard a loud thunk, and the weapon launched a mortar into the air. Through all the smoke, Will couldn't see if it hit its target.

Hollingsworth and Betley appeared, and Sharp gestured toward the museum. "Get him inside."

Will followed Sharp and the three soldiers as they took off after them. Hollingsworth and Betley were within ten feet of the door when a mortar dropped on the building. Will was hit by something, and he fell to the ground. He was stunned. He could make out faint voices, but not what was being said. He searched through the smoke for Hollingsworth and Betley but saw nothing but twisted metal and debris. That was when he realized that the museum had been hit. Another explosion hit the building, and Will watched in horror as the southeast side of the museum collapsed in on itself.

Will opened his mouth and screamed Isabella's name. He tried to get to his feet, but he was dizzy and disoriented. The voices and gunfire around him sounded muffled. Sharp was waving his arms and chopping the air with his hands, directing soldiers' movements. His mouth was moving, but Will couldn't hear anything he was saying.

The soldiers manning the mortars continued loading and firing while others took off after the enemy. Sharp pivoted and lifted his rifle. Will saw his arm fly up and his feet come out from under him. Will's head spun to his right, and he spotted two men rushing toward them. He fired and continued firing until they were both down. He turned back to Sharp, who had pulled himself up to a seated position. Will ran over and grabbed his left arm, pulling him to his feet.

Sharp immediately ran to where they'd last seen Hollingsworth and Betley. Will followed, and the two begun pulling debris off the two men. They discovered Hollingsworth first. He was on his stomach. Underneath him, Betley lay lifeless. Sharp rolled

Hollingsworth over. From his appearance, there was little doubt he was gone. The sight nauseated Will but he pulled Betley out from under him and turned him facing up. His eyes were open. From his chest protruded a four-inch piece of steel. Will felt his neck for a pulse only to confirm what he already knew, Betley too, was gone. For better or worse, the fight for him was over. He hadn't lived to see their victory or defeat. At least if they failed, Betley wouldn't suffer under a communist regime.

Sharp turned and ran toward the gaping hole in the side of the building. Fire smoldered within it. Somewhere inside were Isabella and Stephens. Maybe they'd moved away from the blast. They could still be alive. Alive and trapped.

"We need to get in there," Will said. "We need to help them."

The front of the building was gone. In its place was a pyramid of rubble. A ten-foot-wide hole in the ceiling, through which dangled broken pipes, electrical wires, and twisted metal, allowed light to flood in. Ignoring the sick feeling of dread in his gut, Will pulled on the enormous sheet of metal blocking his way and tossed it aside. Piece by piece, he continued.

"Isabella," he called, tossing a slab of drywall aside. "I'm coming, Isabella. Hold on."

Will climbed over the top of the pile when a space large enough for him to crawl through opened up. Isabella could be anywhere beneath him. How much time did she have? Could she find a pocket of air under all that debris? He held on to that hope as he continued clawing at chunks of ceiling tiles. His hands were bloody but Will didn't stop. He kept digging, trying to reach her.

He fought back flashes of the worst day of his life as his wife slipped away from him, his grief as fresh as it had been that night. He hadn't known Isabella long, but they'd gone through a lifetime of hell together already. Cayden adored her. How would he explain this? He couldn't give up on her. He couldn't walk away without knowing he'd done all he could to save her.

Will wasn't aware of precisely when all the gunfire had stopped. His singular goal was to dig his way into the building and find Isabella. Minutes passed as metal and glass cut his hands and ripped at his clothes. Sharp and the soldiers joined him and began handing debris back one piece at a time to make entry into the heart of the building.

"Isabella!" Will yelled every few minutes. All work would stop for a moment as they listened for a reply. They were long agonizing seconds, and then work would begin again. He lost all sense of time. Had it been five minutes? An hour? Half the day? With every second that passed, his desperation rose. It was as if he'd entered a primal survivor mode. He felt almost detached from reality. It was too much to comprehend. At times, he found himself confused and thought he was searching for his wife. At one point, he'd stood and repeatedly called Melanie's name, and Sharp grabbed his arm and pulled him aside.

"Take a break, man—just a minute. Get a drink of water. The heat is getting to you. We'll keep digging. Don't worry."

Will stumbled back and took in the scene. Sweat was pouring off him. His breathing was rapid, and his tongue clung to the roof of his mouth. Someone shoved a bottle of water into his hand and his fingers relished the chill. He placed it against his forehead and rubbed it down his cheek. Tears stung his eyes. He turned and caught sight of Betley's body, overwhelmed with the loss of life he'd witnessed.

It appeared that the soldiers had somehow taken out the insurgents in their area. Four soldiers were standing guard at each end row of vehicles. Soon more soldiers arrived and joined the others pulling debris from the building. Will wanted desperately to cling to some hope that Isabella would be removed from there alive. If not, how was he going to tell his son? Just as Cayden was opening up, now this devastating blow? How much more could the kid take? How much could he take?

"I think we have something," someone called out.

Will pushed forward and stepped around people to move closer. His heart raced as he waited.

"It's O'Reilly. He's KIA."

O'Reilly. Not Isabella. There was still hope. She could have been farther back in the building in the parts still standing. But why hadn't she answered when he'd called her name? Why hadn't Stephens, Santos, and the other soldier answered them?

"Maybe they ran through the building and got out on the other side," Will said, turning to Sharp. "Stephens was solely focused on getting to the hangar and getting that computer away from here. Maybe they're at the hangar right now."

Sharp's expression said he disagreed.

"Baxter. Elmworth, take your team and go check out the hangar. See if Stephens made it out and ran there."

"Thank you," Will said softly. He was torn. He wanted to join the soldiers and look for them at the hangars but felt compelled to stay and be there if they found them in the rubble instead.

As the soldiers headed across the field toward the hangars, Will moved closer, climbing over a small debris pile trying to get near where the others were digging. He made his way past them and began clawing and grabbing at anything and everything that might be covering Isabella and Stephens. If she was there, he was going to find her.

"She has to be alive," he repeated to himself. "Please, God. Let her be alive."

As the minutes and hours ticked past, Will found it harder and harder to remain hopeful. In his mind, he knew the odds of finding anyone alive were slim. Everyone was tired and dehydrated from the relentless heat. Still, the soldiers remained determined to pull Stephens and Isabella from the rubble.

His body was giving out. It was becoming increasingly difficult to keep going. He was in a crazy amount of pain, and every cell in his body said, 'quit.'

"Here, drink," Sharp said, handing Will a bottled water.

"They could still be alive under there," Will said.

"Yeah. We'll find them."

A few times, Will considered asking if someone could bring his son to him, but Cayden didn't need to see this. That would be selfish on his part.

Will returned to removing debris. This time even more desperate and hurried. The clock was ticking for Isabella and Stephens. He didn't have time to waste going easy.

TWENTY-EIGHT

Will

DAY SIX

Will smeared blood across his forehead as he wiped the sweat from his brow. He held out his hands and inspected them. He was bleeding from dozens of cuts but didn't feel them. He blocked out all pain and kept digging, sure he was getting close. Any second, he'd pull back a piece of metal or sheetrock, and her gorgeous face would be staring back at him. He couldn't bear the thought of anything else. He pushed away images from the night of the accident. The ones that had haunted him for the last two years. That wouldn't be the case here. He could save Isabella. He could find her in time.

"Here! I've got something here," someone shouted.

Will stood tall, trying to see over the rubble. "Is it them?" he called back. "Is it Isabella?"

"I've got a leg," someone called.

"Who is it?" Will asked, desperation growing in his gut. He had to know if it was her. He started moving in that direction. The pile shifted under him, and he stopped. "Are they alive?" he asked as he stretched his neck to see.

"I think it's Santos, Lieutenant."

Will abandoned his pile and scrambled toward where the others were gathering. A large steel beam lay across twisted metal sheeting. Protruding from the edge of it was a boot and partial pant leg. Not Isabella's. A soldier. Will watched as several men struggled to lift the heavy beam. They managed to get it high enough for someone to pull on the boot. He was lodged in tight.

"Shush! I heard something," one of them said.

Everything quieted. Will heard nothing but his hearing had only improved a little since the earlier blasts. He leaned forward, straining to listen.

"It's faint, but I definitely hear tapping."

"Let's get some more men in here and get this damn beam off them," Sharp yelled.

Minutes later, two dozen military personnel were working to move the beam. Will crawled closer, looking for any opening. The beam moved a few inches and then a few more, then the piece of sheet metal was pried back. Will gasped. Santos' body was a grisly sight. No way anyone survived those injuries. Beneath him, Will spotted something pink. As the soldier's body was lifted, Will thought he saw the object beneath him move. He narrowed his gaze and focused on it then drew in a breath and held it. A wave of joy washed over him, and then fear as he waited to see if it was just the debris shifting beneath Santos. As Santos was removed, first a bloody arm came into view and then a torso, followed by a face. A beautiful face.

"Isabella," he said sharply. "Can you hear me? Open your eyes."

Will looked for any sign that she heard him. He started to panic, heart racing, stomach churning.

"Oh, God. No!" He couldn't lose her now.

Blood trickled from a cut on her forehead. Black dust covered her face. Will burst into tears and scrambled toward her, calling her name over and over. He pushed a female soldier aside and reached for Isabella. Will grabbed her arm, and she cried out. Her eyes popped open.

No Other Choice

"I'm sorry. I'm so sorry. Where does it hurt?" Will said through his tears.

She smiled through gritted teeth. "Everywhere. My arm," she whispered.

The one with the burn, he thought. All the dust and dirt in it would make the infection worse.

"Can I get some water? I need water over here," Will yelled.

The soldiers continued digging around her, pulling sheetrock and metal away to free her legs.

Will felt such a rush of emotions. She was alive. They'd found her. She was going to make it out of there. The miracle of it all wasn't lost on him. Death hadn't won this time. They were alive despite all that had been thrown at them.

Someone nudged him in the back with the water bottle, and he reached back and retrieved it. He opened it, poured some in the cap, and slowly trickled it into Isabella's mouth.

"Try not to move just yet. We need to make sure you don't have a spinal injury," Will said.

"What happened?" she asked.

"Mortars."

"Stephens?"

"We haven't found her yet."

Will poured another capful and gave her a drink.

"That soldier saved me. He dove on top of me and pushed me to the ground." Isabella choked up. Tears glistened in her eyes.

Will didn't know what to say. "You're going to be fine. We're going to get you out of here, and we can get you home."

"Home? I just want the hell out of this town," she said.

"I know. Me too."

She scrunched up her face and cried out as pieces of debris were tugged out from around her. Will leaned forward and put his face near hers.

"I'm sorry. It won't be very long. Everything is going to be all right. We're going to make it through this. I promise. I won't let anything happen to you," he whispered in her ear.

She turned her head slightly and kissed him on the cheek. "Does your sister happen to have hot water at her place?" she asked. "Please tell me I get to take a shower when we get there. I'm sick of smelling BO."

"Sorry," Will said, moving back away from her.

"Not you—not just you. I can't stand the smell of myself. I don't think I've ever sweated this much."

"Yes. Savanah has hot water. She has a cistern that collects heat from the sun and pumps it through black pipes that run into the house. My grandfather designed it years ago. It works great in the summer."

"I cannot freaking wait."

With Isabella's legs free, four soldiers gently pulled her from her tomb and placed her on a litter. Will held her hand as she was loaded into the back of an old white pickup where medics began assessing her wounds.

Her hand looked broken for sure, but apart from that and a few scrapes on her face, they said she looked good. Will couldn't believe it. How could someone have a building collapse on them and come away with relatively minor injuries?

"We found Stephens. She's alive. I need a medic," someone yelled.

Sharp disappeared back into the building, and a few minutes later, Stephens was carried out on a stretcher.

"Is she all right?" Isabella asked, struggling to sit up to see for herself.

"She might have some broken ribs and a pretty nasty cut on her leg, but I think she'll recover fine," the medic said.

Isabella let out a sigh of relief and then turned to Will. "Isn't that great news?"

Will smiled and nodded.

Isabella's head swiveled right and then left. "Where's Betley?"

It hurt Will's heart to see Isabella's pained expression as she slowly lowered herself to the ground beside Betley's lifeless body. Tenderly, she placed her hand on his chest. Her head lowered, and her shoulders shook. It was as if she was letting out the agonizing grief and pain from all the losses she'd experienced over the last week. She lifted his hand to her cheek and rocked.

It was unbearable. Will struggled with his own jumble of emotions. Grief was an all too familiar emotion for him. This time, though, he had someone else to direct his anger at. He wasn't the one responsible for the loss; the murderous enemy that had invaded his country was. But as much as he wanted to see them pay, he couldn't get lost down that hole just yet. He had to get to Cayden and get him away from the city. There'd be more of them, Will was sure of it. They wouldn't stop until the military could get reinforcements and run those bastards straight into the Gulf of Mexico.

Will knelt and slid his arm around Isabella's shoulders. "We have to go now. I need to find Cayden. We have to get away from Houston—leave now while we still can."

Isabella's gaze flicked up and then returned to Betley. "There's so much death. There's no going back, is there? Life as we know it is over."

"We'll get through this. You'll get through this." They'd seemed like such hollow words when he'd heard them two years ago. Will hadn't believed them then. There had been days recently that he'd doubted them as well, but now he knew that you had to keep going and live day by day.

"What if I don't want to? If this is all there's ever going to be, what the hell's the point?"

"I have to believe that things will get better. Remember how awful things look after a hurricane blows through. But with time and hard work, people can rebuild. That is what we are going to have to do here. We'll have to rebuild."

"You have to believe that, you've got a kid."

"I do, but I also know how resilient we are as a people. We've been knocked down before. Look what happened with the Civil War and then World War One and World War Two. People held on, and when it was over, they rebuilt."

"It's just too hard."

Will nodded. It was too hard, and if he wasn't a father, he might be feeling the same way. He didn't have that luxury. He'd already spent too much time wallowing in his grief and self-loathing and letting his son suffer in the meantime. He wouldn't fall prey to that again. He wouldn't let Isabella either if he could help it.

"I'm too tired. I'm tired of the violence and suffering. I don't have it in me to keep going like this."

"You have to. There's no other choice."

"You don't have a choice, but I do."

"You won't be doing it alone," Will said, reaching out and stroking her hair. "You have Cayden." He turned her head to face him. He ran a finger down her cheek and lifted her chin. "And me," he said softly. He kissed her gently on the lips and then pulled her into his arms. He felt her shoulders slump, and then the sobs began again. "We can do this, Izzy."

She straightened and swatted him on his arm. "Don't call me that. I hate that nickname. Kevin only told everyone that was my name to annoy me." The corners of her mouth turned up. "No nicknames, okay?"

"Got it." Will laughed.

As he stood, Isabella reached over and placed Betley's hands across his chest. Will had never been sure why people did that to the dead. He'd been told that it was to make them appear to only be sleeping, but who slept like that. They hadn't had an open casket at Melanie's funeral and Will had searched for hours and hours to find the right photo to display next to her during the service. He'd finally settled on the one of her and Cayden at the beach that summer. Her hair had been pulled back into a ponytail, and she'd worn her big floppy beach hat, but she looked radiant as she stared at Cayden and the Hogwarts sand sculpture they'd built together.

"Are you ready?" Will asked, holding his hand out to her.

Isabella took his hand, and he pulled her to her feet. "Thank you," she said as she wrapped her arms around his neck. "Thank you for getting me out of that rubble and talking me off the ledge."

"My pleasure."

"Let's go get Cayden," she said as she released him.

Will wasn't sure what they'd face after leaving Houston. Without cell phones or the internet, it was difficult to know what the rest of the country was facing. For them, it could be more like the normal aftermath of a storm, at least until their food ran out. Will knew that most people didn't stock much in their pantries. Many shopped for groceries every few days, expecting the stores to be fully stocked every time they went. The grocery stores themselves had turned to the "just in time" deliveries of goods to supply every day rather than holding too much stock themselves and would all have been cleaned out by now. Somewhere, there had to be massive warehouses filled with undelivered goods. If a person was smart, they'd go there first.

"McNally can drive you over to pick up your son," Stephens said.

Will nodded.

Stephens held out a hand to him. "Thank you for your help."

Will looked back over his shoulder at Betley. "It wasn't enough."

"What's going to happen to that colonel and staff sergeant who were working with the Chinese?" Isabella asked.

"They'll be court-martialed," Stephens replied.

"What's that mean?" Isabella asked.

"They will have a military trial and be executed."

"Hung or shot?" Will asked.

"Shot," Stephens said, flatly.

"Good," Isabella replied.

Will opened the door and stepped through then poked his head back inside and asked, "What about that general?"

"General Dempsey will be dealt with, eventually."

Isabella grabbed Will's hand. "They're waiting for us."

"Good luck, Stephens. I hope you succeed. We're all counting on you to root out all those assholes so we can start to rebuild this country."

She smiled. "I'll do my best."

TWENTY-NINE

Will

DAY SIX

Will took in the grounds around the demolished flight museum as the female soldier led him and Isabella to the vehicle. The soldiers had already started collecting the bodies—first their comrades and then the enemy that had mercilessly attacked the base. There were so many of them. When Betley had discussed the possibility of insurgents attacking strategic positions within the city, Will had imagined bands of six or eight, not dozens and dozens. Maybe as many as a hundred or more insurgents lay dead just in that location. That wasn't accounting for those that the military was battling along the perimeter and out at the checkpoint. For the time being, it looked as if the army had been successful at taking them out.

It didn't take a military expert to tell that this was considerably more intense than a ragtag insurgency. This was an invasion though they hadn't seemed all that well-armed to Will. From what he could tell, they had a few RPGs and some mortars, as well as rifles. But an invading force would bring much more sophisticated weaponry, wouldn't they?

The Humvee was already running when they reached it. Behind the wheel was a kid who looked not much older than Cayden. He stepped out and opened the door for Will and Isabella. "Do you have any water?" Isabella asked.

As the soldier reached in to retrieve his canteen, Lieutenant Sharp approached them. "I didn't get a chance to thank you," he said.

"Thank me?" Will asked.

"You fought hard. Betley said if you two hadn't stepped up and helped, we'd have never retrieved the flash drive."

"I hope it was worth it," Isabella said.

"I believe it will be."

"Are you going to be able to stop them?"

Sharp smiled. He looked as if he'd aged ten years. His uniform shirt was stained with blood and his hands were cut up like Will's. "We were successful today. It may take time, but we'll track them all down and secure this city, the state, and then the nation."

"What about the traitors?" Will asked.

A surprised look crossed Sharp's face, and then a smile returned. "We have them in custody. Someone will deal with General Dempsey in due course." He patted Will on the shoulder and extended his hand. "You two take care out there." Will shook his hand and stepped aside to allow Isabella to say goodbye. Instead, she walked around the back of the Humvee and climbed inside. Will was about to get in himself but stopped and turned.

"Hey. I never got my weapons and gear back. The soldiers that brought us here took it from me."

Sharp glanced from Will to the female soldier. "Have someone get his gear."

"Thanks," Will said as he closed the vehicle's door.

Sharp pounded on the side of the Humvee. "Take this man to get his boy."

As the Humvee weaved and swerved around debris and vehicles, heading south across the base toward the Johnson Space Center, Will grew more and more nervous about what they might find there. Stephens had assured him that Cayden was safe there,

No Other Choice

but until he laid eyes on his son, his stomach would remain in knots.

Pulling into the NASA complex, Will was reminded that he had never ceased to be amazed at the hub of human spaceflight. He'd been there numerous times and was still in awe every time he visited. Seeing the famous Mercury, Gemini, and Apollo 17 space capsules, along with the Skylab, where astronauts used to train to go into space, always brought him a sense of astonishment at what mankind had accomplished. Could they somehow come back, even from this? What if the technology was dead forever?

The Humvee weaved through the complex and pulled up to the Space Vehicle Mockup Facility, home of the International Space Station modules, where astronauts prepared themselves for their missions on the space station. Usually, he would be excited to tour the facility again, but this time all he wanted was to see his son's face and hold him in his arms. He'd never felt so helpless in all his life as when Stephens had separated them when they arrived at the base and now, finally, the long hours waiting to make sure he was okay were about to come to an end.

Practically as soon as the wheels of the Humvee stopped rolling, Will jumped from the vehicle and ran toward the door. He was greeted by a soldier with his hand out to halt him, but Will wouldn't be denied. He heard Isabella call his name, but he didn't turn. He had one singular mission, and he was getting to his son.

"Step aside and let him in. He's the boy's father," the female soldier said.

Will didn't wait. He shoved the man and pushed past him calling Cayden's name.

Will ran through the building, frantic to find him. Finally, Cayden stepped out of the Skylab Trainer, and a huge grin spread across his face. "Dad. You've got to see this."

Will ran to him, wrapped his arms around him, and lifted him off his feet. Nothing mattered but that moment. Hope returned.

Hope that somehow—someway they could overcome, adapt, and begin a new life.

Will placed him back on the floor and put his hand on Cayden's shoulder. "I'm so glad to see you," he said, wiping tears from his face. "I love you, son. I'm so sorry. I haven't been there for you. I'm sorry for—"

"It's okay. I love you too."

Will somehow managed to choke back the years' worth of tears that threatened to burst to the surface, feeling a weight lift at hearing those words. From that moment on, he was determined to be a better father, to not avoid the hard discussions, and be there for his son both physically and emotionally.

Cayden stepped back and examined him. "You have blood on you—again."

"I'm fine," Will said.

"Isabella?" Will could hear the fear in his voice.

"I'm fine too," she said as she approached.

Cayden sidestepped Will and ran to her. He threw his arms around her and immediately began telling her all about his tour of the Space Center.

As he watched them, Will was overtaken with gratitude. He was so relieved that Stephens had separated them and sent Cayden there safely away from the base. He hadn't had to witness all the carnage and see what had befallen Betley. He was alive and well. They were together now, and that was what mattered.

Cayden pulled a chunk of drywall from Isabella's hair and held it out.

"Boy, do I have a story to tell you. Later, though. I'm starving. How about we go back to my place and warm some soup over the grill."

"Ew—soup again?!" complained Will.

"The soldiers gave me an MRE, Dad. It wasn't all that bad. It had a chocolate bar."

"That does sound much better than room temperature soup," Isabella said.

"I'm sorry. I should have saved you some."

"No. Don't be."

"Are you ready, sir?" the female asked. Will hadn't even been aware of her standing there.

"We're ready."

Just as they were loading back into the Humvee, Cayden turned and ran back to the door. He and the soldier fist-bumped, and then Cayden handed him something.

Two soldiers rode in the front and one in the turret. Will glanced past the gunner's legs to Isabella. Cayden would have to ride in his lap but it wasn't that far and he wasn't too heavy.

The gunner standing in the turret spun to his left and then right as the Humvee pulled from the parking lot. Cayden leaned and looked up at the soldier. "I bet that thing is loud."

"It is from out there. I don't want to hear it from in here," Isabella said.

"Let's all hope we never do," Will replied.

THIRTY

Savanah

DAY SIX

Of the twenty or so houses along her road, they'd only made it to four of them by nightfall. What Savanah had seen so far had angered her and ripped her heart out at the same time. Two of the houses had already been thoroughly looted. There'd been no sign of their residents and Savanah hoped they had fled before Spring Hill's posse had descended on their homes. She'd been encouraged when Pete Ashby and his three sons had agreed to join them. They'd heard about the trouble at the other farms and had taken steps to secure their place.

The Ashbys' was more like a family compound with several generations occupying the one-hundred-and-twenty-acre farm. It had been in their family for over a hundred years and the Louisiana Century Farm sign hung proudly above the gate as she entered. Thick woods stood between the road and houses, obscuring them from view. The Ashbys were obviously very private people.

Ashby's son, Beau, recognized Savanah as soon as they approached the pipe gate spanning the entrance of the gravel drive. He was Kendra's age, and fortunately, they'd been on co-ed soccer teams together since they were three. If they hadn't, they likely wouldn't have made it close enough to reach the gate.

"How can I help you, Mrs. Fontenot?" Savanah thought she saw a hint of facial hair growing above his lip. Gone was the babyface that she remembered watching kick the ball around the field every weekend.

"Is your daddy around, Beau? We've got a problem that I'd like to discuss with him."

Beau crawled off his all-terrain vehicle, stuck two fingers into his mouth, and whistled loud enough to wake the dead. "Hey, Pops. Will you let Dad know Kendra's mom and some dudes are at the gate and want to talk to him?"

Jason hung back behind Rod and Luca, making Savanah wonder if there might be an issue between him and the Ashbys. She hoped not. They really needed their help. Beau approached and leaned against the large pipe gate, throwing his hands over it and resting his chin on his arms. "Is this about those old boys looting farms?" he asked.

"Yeah. Have they been by here?" Savanah asked.

"Hell no!" He covered his mouth. "I'm sorry."

Savanah gave a dismissive wave.

"I mean, no, they haven't come around here. They wouldn't. My uncle gave Robbie Thompson a beatdown two nights before the lights went out. He and that brother of his stole stereo equipment out of my cousin's car. He caught them red-handed. Of course, they threatened to call the police with them being underage and all, but he told them to go right ahead because my cousin is a deputy."

"Beau, go on up to the house and help your momma carry out that wash water," Pete said as he walked up. He was a big guy, standing at least six-five and nearly three hundred pounds. But it was the way he pointed the shotgun at them that had Savanah concerned.

"What do you folks want?"

Savanah stared at his massive forearms as she tried to speak, feeling her tongue cleave to the roof of her mouth. She swallowed hard and was about to explain when Jason spoke up.

"The Blanchards set themselves up over at Spring Hill. They're running a crew of kids around out here causing trouble."

"I heard about that already. What the hell does that have to do with me and mine?"

"Nothing if you don't want it to," Jason replied.

Savanah shot him a dirty look. That wasn't how Savanah wanted this to go. Jason was making out like it was no big deal. It was a damn huge deal. They needed Pete's help. She wanted to plead with him to help them. "They killed Mr. Johnson and others. They came after Mr. and Mrs. Bertrand. Jason and I intervened and brought them to my place. They're not going to stop until they kill us all and take everything we have," Savanah said.

Pete looked back over his shoulder.

"We're ready for them. Let the bastards try to take what's mine and I'll blow their asses back to Blanchardville." He glared at Jason. Savanah was right, there was some history there, but at that moment, they didn't have time for old grudges.

Savanah thought she'd try a different approach. "I understand. I'm glad. We were hoping that you might have some idea as to how we might block the roads and stop them from coming around."

Pete pulled a pack of cigarettes from his pocket, tapped it on the back of his hand, pulled one out, and lit it. Luca huffed and took two steps back as if afraid of being poisoned by second-hand smoke.

"Well," Pete said, rubbing a stubble chin. "First off, you need some firepower. Hunting rifles and pistols ain't gonna do a whole lot against the ARs those guys have. Then you need a few well-placed claymores and some—"

"We need a roadblock and someone to man checkpoints," Luca interrupted. "Do you think you could help with that?"

Pete scoffed. "Roadblocks ain't gonna do shit. They'll just

walk around them. They ain't driving down the middle of the road. They're coming in on the back roads and trails on quads and UTVs. Hell, I took a shot at one on a horse just yesterday. The boy had an armload of live chickens. That horse reared back and dumped his ass on the ground. Ole boy's eyes got big as saucers. Well, he dropped those chickens and took off, kicking up dirt as he ran."

Savanah felt all the life drain from her as overwhelming hopelessness hit her. She couldn't sit back and wait for them to come for her and her children. But where on earth could they go? How were they to survive this mess without the farm?

"You need to take the fight to them," a male voice said.

Savanah scanned the area behind Pete to see who'd spoken. His father suddenly appeared through the bushes and stood beside him. "Only way to deal with a bully is to fight back. Can't wait for them to catch you alone and pick you off. You need to roll right up in there and confront them. Either kick their asses and send them packing or wipe them off the face of the earth." His eyes moved to Jason.

"We can't do that. We don't have the people or weapons."

"Well then, I guess you'll have to tuck tail and run," Pete said.

"Pete," his wife, Kathy said, stepping out, and Savanah strained to see who else might be hiding behind the bushes. "Pete, you two have been talking for days about going over there and taking care of those old boys. High time you two stop talking and partner up with these folks to do something about it."

Pete's forehead furrowed, and his father hung his head.

"We got plenty of weapons and enough ammo to fight an army. You go round up some of those drinking buddies of yours, Pete, and go wipe ass. Lord knows you can talk a good game, now prove you ain't just a blowhard."

Savanah covered her mouth to conceal an ear-to-ear grin. Kathy had spunk, and Savanah was getting the picture of who ran their household. Kathy held her hand out to Luca. "You that new couple that moved in the Cliftons' old place. "

"We bought it from their son," Luca said.

"Did you rip down all that hideous wallpaper yet?"

"Working on it." Luca grinned.

She turned to Savanah. "Don't you worry. We'll gather up some folks to help get rid of those vermin." She turned and stepped back through the bushes. "Tell Mrs. B that I said hi, will you?"

Pete stood with his arms crossed while his father made circles in the dirt with the toe of his boot. An uncomfortable silence settled over them.

"Okay, well, we're going to stop and visit with the Masters and Herberts before it gets too dark to find our way home," Savanah said.

"We'll be over your way at first light. We can figure out a plan to take those boys on," Pete said. He turned to Jason. "You gotta problem with that?"

Jason shook his head.

"They're your kin."

"They stopped being family when I walked away," Jason said flatly.

Savanah couldn't imagine how much it hurt him to say that. Blood was thick in southwest Louisiana. You didn't just walk away from family like that. She wondered if he ever had second thoughts. How did he handle Mother's Day and Christmas? She'd lost most of her family. Will and Cayden were all she had left. She couldn't imagine willingly walking away like Jason had done. Her thoughts drifted to her brother and nephew so far away in Houston. She prayed they'd somehow made it to the lake house and that they weren't running into the violence she'd witnessed since the lights went out.

∼

No Other Choice

With Pete's commitment to help, Savanah assumed that getting the rest of the neighbors on board would be easier. It wasn't. No one wanted to go to war with the Blanchards. By the time they'd made it back to Savanah's, even Luca was having second thoughts.

Savanah kicked her boots off and lowered herself down onto her grandmother's porch swing. She missed those simpler times, snapping green beans, and listening to the frogs croaking. Her grandparents had been the first 'homesteader' type people Savanah had ever met. Their goal to live off the land and be self-sufficient here on their little acreage had inspired her to do the same. The lifestyle was filled with hard work, but she loved it here. She wasn't ready to give it up and hated the thought of being run off by thugs.

Luca and June leaned against the porch railing. They too had been pursuing a self-sufficient lifestyle. They knew what she'd invested with blood, sweat, and tears.

"I'm not willing to go in there guns blazing and kill people. That's not what I'm about. June and I have discussed it. We're going to load up what we can carry and head to my mother-in-law's. Maybe we'll be back when all this dies down."

"You mean with the rest of us taking care of the problem that you don't want to get your hands dirty with?" Rod asked.

Frankly, Savanah was surprised that Rod was contemplating the plan himself. He'd never struck Savanah as being all that brave but Luca and June leaving did concern her. If Pete didn't show, she and her children might just be packing up and following them, except she didn't have a mother-in-law to run to. Well, she had one, but she'd never go there. That woman was as evil as her husband and son.

Savanah was struck by how absolutely rotten people could be and the depth of depravity they were capable of without law enforcement to keep them in check. She pictured the kid they'd buried out in her pasture. She didn't feel guiltless, but they'd come after her family. She was grateful Jason had been the one to do the deed. She wasn't sure if she could have. That would need to change if they were going to survive this. She would have to change.

"If you leave, can we come to get your animals?" Kendra asked.

Savanah smiled. Her daughter was so intelligent and pragmatic.

"Yeah, can I have your rabbits?" Kylie squealed, jumping up and down.

June picked her up and swung her around. "If we go, you can have them all."

Savanah noticed that she'd said, "if." Maybe the issue wasn't as settled as Luca made out. Maybe there was still hope for them to build a strong community—one family at a time.

Savanah wasn't going to give up on her homestead so easily. She had too much invested in the place. It could very well be the only hope her children had to outlast this mess. She had to give them a fighting chance.

"Dinner's ready," Mrs. B called, and all the children took off toward the back of the house.

"You coming?" Savanah said, turning to Jason.

"I'll be along in a minute."

Savanah lingered a moment before joining her children. Jason had things to work out in his own mind. She dreaded what they faced if they did indeed have to go up against the Blanchards. But no matter what, she was grateful to him for sticking by her and helping protect her children.

THIRTY-ONE

Will

DAY SIX

The Humvee pulled into the parking lot and stopped in front of Isabella's building. They were back where they'd started that morning. So much had happened in such a short time. The reality of it all was so much worse than he'd imagined. He was still determined to leave the city as fast as possible, but at the moment, he was just too exhausted. He feared he wouldn't be able to make it two miles before collapsing. Fighting for his life had taken everything out of him. He had nothing left, and the likelihood of encountering trouble out on the road was high.

"Jaz!" Isabella squealed, throwing open the door.

Jaz met her at the bottom of the stairs. "I thought you guys would be gone by now." The women embraced.

"Gus went with Lloyd and Stuart to find a working car."

"And he left you here all by yourself?"

"No. Raul came to babysit me." Jaz pointed toward her apartment.

A man and woman stepped forward, both armed with AR-15 rifles. The man waved. Isabella waved back then turned to the Humvee.

"We have to go, miss," the soldier driving said.

"Thank you for bringing us home," she replied.

Will and Cayden exited the Humvee and stood beside Isabella and Jaz.

"You both did great out there today," the soldier said before rolling up his window and driving away.

"We did do good, didn't we? We made it out battered and bruised, but alive," Isabella said.

"Yes, we did," Will replied.

"You guys look like you've been through a war. What the hell happened?" Jaz asked.

"Not much. I just had a building collapse on top of me, shot a few bad guys, and came home." Isabella chuckled.

Will was glad that she could make light of it now. He knew that what they'd been through might break some people and was pleased to see that Isabella wasn't one of them. When shit got real, she stepped up to the plate and wouldn't back down. She'd done that for Cayden, and Will was enormously grateful as well as greatly relieved that she'd finally agreed to go with them to Louisiana. He knew she and Savanah would get along great.

"What's the plan now?" Jaz asked.

Isabella grimaced as she raised her arm slightly. She sniffed her pits and screwed up her face. "First, I'm going to strip off these clothes and use every wet wipe I have to get clean. Second, I'm going to find a way to make a good pot of coffee."

"You might want to lay off the caffeine so you can sleep. We'll need to be fully rested if we're going to head out tomorrow," Will said.

"Are we still leaving in the morning?" Cayden asked. "Shouldn't we wait a day or two and let everyone heal some?"

In the best of worlds, that would be a prudent plan. But they'd need much longer than a few days. Will still had bruised or cracked ribs and the bruises on his stomach had merged, turning nearly his entire abdomen purple. Isabella was still fighting off infection from her burn and now had a broken hand, along with who knows what injuries from being buried in the rubble back at the base. Will's gaze turned to Cayden. Other than his hair sticking up every which way, he looked great. The fact that his son wasn't injured or killed brought tears to Will's eyes. A wave of panic shot through his gut at the thought of what could have happened and what they still faced in the days ahead. He prayed that his luck would hold, and he'd be able to get Cayden safely to Savanah's. He knew he could not do that alone and Cayden was right. They needed to be in better shape to take on the challenges ahead of them.

"Maybe we should take the day tomorrow to rest and resupply," Will said.

"Are you sure? Don't do that on my account. I can handle it," Isabella said.

"I know you can, but these old bones of mine could use a little more time," he said, patting his ribs.

"I'll come up and let you know when we head out then, Izzy," Jaz said, turning to go.

"Okay, Jaz."

Isabella waved to Jaz as they began their climb toward the third-floor landing. At the top, Isabella stopped and looked out over the parking lot. "We should go out tomorrow and try to find a car," she said.

"That might be risky. People with running vehicles might be willing to fight to keep them," Will said, joining her at the railing.

"You're right, but we aren't going to make it far on bicycles, Will."

She reached down and pulled up her pants leg. Cayden gasped. Will bent and examined the four-inch gash to the side of her calf. She had tied some type of cloth around it. Dried blood trailed down to her ankle. He hadn't noticed that she was limping more than usual. They were all moving rather slow. She was right. There was no way she could ride a bike one hundred and fifty miles.

"Isabella, why didn't you say something? We could have had the military docs treat that," Will said.

"You need stitches," Cayden added.

She shrugged one shoulder.

"I just wanted away from there before any more trouble popped up."

Will had been in a hurry for the same reason. After being cut off from Cayden during the firefight, he'd been anxious to get him far away from the insurgents' target—the military. "Let's get you inside and get that wound cleaned up," Will said.

"We have those butterfly bandages you brought back from the pharmacy," Cayden said as he grabbed Isabella around the waist.

"We'll have to take a look after we get it irrigated. We may have to use them until we can find a doctor to close the wound properly." Will held the door to Isabella's apartment open as Cayden helped her inside. "You still have the antibiotics I gave you, right?"

"Yeah, and I should still have some in my bloodstream from that shot the medic gave me, right?"

"I don't know, maybe. It might help, but you'll need to take some for the next week or so, I'd imagine. Now is not the time to get a second infection. Your body is still fighting the one from your burn."

"We are a mess, aren't we? We're going to roll up to your sister's looking like hell."

"I can't wait to get to Aunt Savanah's. I'm diving in the pond first thing. I'm tired of all this sweat on my body," Cayden said.

While Isabella headed straight for the bathroom, Will grabbed the trash bag filled with the pharmacy's medicine and supplies. By the time she returned, he'd laid out the gauze and bandages they'd need. She'd changed clothes, combed her hair, and pulled it into a messy bun on the top of her head. Will stared at her. He couldn't take his eyes off her. She'd been nearly burned to death in her car, shot at, survived a hurricane, had a building blown up around her, and she could still stand there looking radiantly beautiful. Isabella's face flushed. He'd embarrassed her by staring.

"Dad!" Cayden had said something, but he hadn't heard him. Will turned to him. "What?"

"These are all amoxicillin."

"How do you know?" Will said, taking a bottle from him.

"It says so on the capsule."

He handed one to his dad. Will turned it over. "Amox five hundred," Will said.

"There's gotta be at least five hundred in this bottle, and I've found five bottles so far."

Relief washed over Will. It would buy them some time. His first order of business after getting to Savanah's would be tracking down Doctor Guidry. Savanah would likely want to treat Isabella's wounds with some of her homemade concoctions, and he didn't have a problem with that, but Isabella needed a doctor to close that wound, pure and simple. He hoped to convince the old guy to stay with them on Savanah's farm. The way things were looking, he'd have plenty of work.

"I'll head out in the morning and see about rounding up a vehicle," Will said. "If I find one, we could be at Savanah's by lunchtime."

"Oh my gosh. I can't wait to have a fresh salad from her greenhouse. I'm dying for a tomato," Cayden said, licking his lips.

"That would be nice. I'm looking forward to ham and eggs with a glass of goat's milk," Will said.

"Will you two stop. I'm freaking starving, but I'm sick of canned soup already."

"Just wait until you try my aunt Savanah's gumbo. It's the best."

Isabella's gaze dropped to the floor. Cayden frowned. "I'm sorry."

A single tear slipped over her eyelid and spilled onto her cheek. "Kevin didn't really care for Cajun food. He just ate it so as not to offend the band. I adore it. I'm looking forward to meeting your aunt and cousins. And I would kill for a salad right now."

Will wanted so much to believe that they could find a somewhat normal life at Savanah's. She had everything necessary to feed them long term. What they couldn't grow, he could hunt or catch. It would be good for Cayden to be with family. They should have moved back there a long time ago. He stopped himself before he could start recounting all his regrets. He would choose to be positive and focus on the future. They were strong and determined. He would do whatever was necessary to make sure Cayden had the best life possible even in this apocalypse, and he was more and more convinced that Isabella would too.

"Let's get that wound taken care of and then get some rest. Tomorrow, we start our big adventure to Cajun country."

Thank you for purchasing *No Other Choice*, book two in the *Fall of Houston* series. **The story continues in book three, <u>No Turning Back</u>**

If you enjoyed *No Other Choice*, I'd like to hear from you and hope that you could take a moment and post an honest review on Amazon. Your support and feedback will help this author improve for future projects. Without the support of readers like yourself, self-publishing would not be possible.

Don't forget to sign up at tlpayne.com for my spam-free newsletter to receive a FREE ebook copy of Sudden Chaos: A Post Apocalyptic EMP Survival Story and to be the first to know of new releases, giveaways, and special offers.

Have you read my Days of Want series yet? If not, keep scrolling to read a sample or CLICK HERE to order your copy today.

Sample Chapters

TURBULENT: DAYS OF WANT SERIES, BOOK ONE

Chapter 1

Chicago O'Hare International Airport
Chicago, Illinois
Day of Event

Terminal Three of Chicago's O'Hare International Airport was filled with pissed-off passengers. After a four-hour delay, Maddison Langston was feeling cranky herself. Her flight from San Diego had arrived at eleven that morning. By three that afternoon, her connecting flight was still not boarding, even though the plane was at the gate.

When the lights in the terminal cut out and the flight departure screen went blank, Maddie sighed.

Looks like my flight will be delayed. Again.

Sitting in the dim light, Maddie pulled her cell phone from the Silent Pocket Faraday backpack Uncle Ryan had given her. Although she had promised him that she would keep her phone in the bag while she was in the airport, she was having social media withdrawal. She was not as concerned about a thief scanning her RFID chips as he was.

She pulled the charging cord from the pack and started to plug it into an outlet before realizing that it wouldn't charge with the power off. Maddie tapped a social media app on her phone, but it wouldn't load. Her phone did not have a signal. After shutting it down and restarting it half a dozen times, it still wouldn't connect to her wireless service provider.

To pass the time, she listened to songs from her music library. She usually listened to her favorite music using streaming services. Luckily, she had a few games on her phone.

Maddie looked up to see an angry man in a sport coat and trousers with one knee on the American Airlines service counter. The terrified woman behind the desk had her back pressed against the wall as far from the out-of-control passenger as possible.

Maddie pulled the earbuds from her ears.

Two men had gripped the arms of the angry man, who was yelling obscenities at the woman, as the woman yelled for security.

"Why can't you tell us what the hell is going on? My flight was supposed to leave three hours ago. Now the lights are out, and it is freaking hot as hell in here," another passenger yelled at the petite woman.

"I do not have anything to tell you. I am in the dark too," she said.

"Oh, is that your attempt to lighten the mood? De-stress the situation? Did they teach you that in customer service school?" the man mocked.

"My cell phone isn't working. I need to use a phone. I have to call my husband. He'll be expecting us to arrive in Nashville any minute," a woman called out.

A tall man in a sports jersey and jeans stepped forward. He towered over the other passengers. Holding an arm up, the man said, "Listen up, folks. All this yelling and getting aggressive with customer service isn't going to get us answers that the woman clearly doesn't have."

"Well, someone sure as hell better start explaining pretty damn fast," the man in the sport coat barked, shaking his arms loose from his captors.

"Look around you. It is a chaotic mess in here. It's not just American Airlines' flights that are delayed. No planes have taken off or landed here in over an hour. The power is out to the airport, and something has disrupted the phones, including cell phones."

Just then, an explosion rattled the windows. The ear-piercing sound of metal on concrete was followed by the cockpit of a jet skidding down the runway. It hadn't occurred to Maddie that planes might collide mid-air without access to tower control for guidance. People rushed from the shopping area of the terminal, dragging their wheeled bags behind them, and huddled near the window to stare at the burning wreckage of the plane on the tarmac.

Maddie slowly rose to her feet. Grabbing her backpack from its position beside her, she flipped it over her shoulder and reached for the extended handle on her suitcase. The terminal was in darkness, lit only by the windows where a surreal show of flames and black smoke was casting long shadows toward the center of the concourse.

As Maddie stared out the window with her mouth open wide at the flaming, smoking, twisted mass, a second Boeing 737 dropped from the sky in pieces, scattering onto the runway and bursting into flames. The lights were out, there was no cell service, and planes were colliding in the sky above them.

Maddie came to a startling realization. It had happened. The EMP—the electromagnetic pulse—her dad and Uncle Ryan talked about had really happened. Her hand shot up to cover her mouth. Maddie's feet would not move, even though her brain said run.

She couldn't catch her breath. While her fellow travelers stood with eyes peeled to the horrid sight and their mouths wide in shock and terror, Maddie ran.

Her bag's wheels skipped off the floor of the concourse as Maddie bolted toward a family restroom. Her backpack smacked the wall as she spun around to turn the lock. Maddie dropped her pack and suitcase by the door and slid to the cold tile floor. Hugging her knees to her chest, she sobbed, rocking side to side. Mixed with the crushing fear was a pang of guilt. She had mocked her dad for his paranoia. A wave of grief threatened to crash over her without mercy. As she cried, the years of repressed grief burst to the surface as she recalled the training and warnings her father had tried to communicate to her over the years.

Maddie hadn't cried this much since the accident. The day her dad died. The day her world changed forever.

As the tears flowed in torrents, Maddie rested her head on her arms. She was startled by loud banging behind her. She jumped to her feet and spun to face the door, her heart pounding against her chest. In the blackness, she couldn't see her hand in front of her face. Maddie pulled her phone from her back pocket and activated its flashlight feature. Holding it over her head, she turned and looked around the small room.

I can't stay in here forever.

How long before a plane came crashing through the terminal? How many were up there circling the airport? How many had diverted from their flight paths to land after they lost their navigation system and contact with the control tower? Pilots would only have line-of-sight to avoid a mid-air collision. How soon would it be before they ran out of fuel? Maddie's thoughts raced.

She had to get some place safe right now. That was what her dad always told her. The longer she hesitated, the more dangerous it would be.

Maddie stood and blew her nose. She bent over to reach for her pack.

She froze.

Maddie's heart dropped. She was stranded in one of the country's busiest airports in the middle of one of the most populated cities. And she had never felt more alone.

Maddie turned and put her back to the door. She slid once more to the floor, curling her arms over her head.

Dad was right.

Her friends had called her father, Greg Langston, a doomsday prepper—a title that brought Maddie embarrassment. Before he died, her father had taught her and her brother, Zach, survival skills and how to prepare for disasters. She never took it as seriously as she should have.

"What do I do, Daddy? What do I do?" she cried.

Her mind raced, searching for answers. Images of her rolling her eyes as her dad lectured her and Zach on what to do in a world-ending scenario brought a new round of guilt and shame.

"You were right, Daddy. I am so sorry I mocked you. I didn't listen to you, and now the shit has hit the fan, and I don't know what to do."

She curled into a fetal position. Time seemed to stand still in the tiny, cold room. She stared at the shadow cast by her cell phone. Her mind went blank. She slid into a familiar numbness. Sleep had been her comfort, her only solace in the days and weeks after her dad died. She wanted to go there. She let her breathing slow.

She was shaken back to reality by the sound of the growing chaos outside the bathroom.

Maddie heard her dad's voice in her head.

"Maddison Grace Langston, pay attention. Someday, you might find yourself alone when the shit hits the fan and you will need to know how to survive and get home."

She sat up, brushing loose strands of hair from her face.

The get-home bag her dad had given her containing all the essentials to survive on the road was in her dorm room in Ohio. It would do her no good now. But she had the everyday-carry items with her. Uncle Ryan had picked up where her dad left off in making sure carrying her EDC was a habit. Maddie looked down at the plain, waterproof backpack on the floor next to her. There were times in the last few years when she had resented Ryan for trying to take her dad's place. At that moment, she was grateful he had.

Maddie got to her feet and walked over to the sink. She looked in the mirror. Mascara streaked her face, and her hazel eyes were bloodshot. She ran her hand through her long, blonde hair, pulling it into a messy bun on top of her head and securing it with the hair tie from her wrist. She stared at herself in the mirror.

"You've got this, Maddie. You can do it."

She pointed to the mirror with her index finger.

You have to.

Unzipping her carry-on bag, Maddie was relieved that she had brought her hydration pack on the trip. Knowing she would need to run every day to maintain her current level of endurance, she had thrown it in her bag. Pulling the vest pack from her suitcase and emptying all the pockets and pouches, she quickly inventoried its contents. With the Jelly Belly Sport Beans, sports gels, and energy bars, she had about ten thousand calories with her. Her hydration bladder and water flasks held at least two liters of water. She added the weight up in her head. She would be carrying around ten pounds.

When running a marathon or endurance race, she didn't take the hydration bladder or as many energy gels. There was an aid station along the route, and her crew would take position between stations in case she needed a quick pick-me-up. But Maddie had carried that much weight when she did backcountry and trail runs, so she knew she could.

In a Ziploc bag were two headlamps, extra batteries, a compass, and a multifunction mini tool—all requirements from her last race. From her every-day carry pack, she removed the emergency bivvy bag, her Sawyer MINI water filter, and a LifeStraw personal water filter. Maddie shoved them into the kangaroo pouch of her vest pack, along with a Ziploc bag of socks and thermals. The last thing in was a weatherproof jacket.

Maddie undressed and pulled on her running tights. After putting on a tank top, she put on a fresh pair of socks and slid on her running shoes. She wished she hadn't chosen to bring the red ones. They would stand out too much, but there was nothing she could do about that now.

Gathering up the water flasks and bladder, Maddie filled them in the sink. She pushed the bladder into the pouch and placed it in the hydration vest pack.

Placing her arms through the arm holes of the vest, she adjusted the straps across her chest. Her runner's pack was a vest-style. It wrapped around her, fitting snugly against her body. She tugged on the cords. It felt secure. After placing the soft flasks in the front pockets, she strapped one squeeze flask to her wrist. Lastly, she pulled on her dad's Marine Corps Marathon headband and adjusted it to cover her ears.

She looked down at the half-empty suitcase and her clothes strewn about the floor. She picked them up and threw them into the bag. Maddie did not consider herself overly materialistic, but her suitcase contained some of her favorite clothes. It pained her to just leave them there.

This is crazy. How am I going to run all the way to St. Louis?

From her Silent Pocket Faraday backpack, Maddie retrieved her earbuds, car keys, and a pack of gum. As she placed them in the right-side pocket, her hands shook so badly that she dropped her car keys on the floor. She was alone in Chicago and the end of civilization as she knew it had occurred—just as her dad had predicted. She was scared shitless and was not afraid to admit it. Maddie shook her head, attempting to fight back the tears that threatened to spill down her face.

Harden up, Maddie.

No one was coming to save her. If she was going to make it,

she would have to protect herself. She couldn't afford to let self-doubt and indecision keep her prisoner in the airport.

St. Louis was about three hundred miles away. The previous week, she had run the New Hampshire 100-mile endurance race in twenty-six hours. So, with needing recovery time between runs, it would take at least a week or more to get home.

How long will it take if I have to avoid dangerous people?

She wanted nothing more than to sit back down on the cold tile floor, curl into a ball, and stay there until her mom came to her rescue.

Mom is not coming, Maddie. Mom is stranded in California.

She had gone with her mother to San Diego. They had brought her grandmother home from the hospital. Her mother wanted Grand to enjoy her last days at home in her own bed surrounded by the things she loved, including her one-eyed dog, Jack. The sudden realization that her mom might not be able to make it back home to Missouri shook her to her core. She had been so focused on herself that she had not even thought about where her mom and brother were. When she had last received a text message from Zach, he had been coming back from his school field trip to Washington, D.C.

Maddie placed her hands over her face and rubbed her forehead.

Where did he say they had stopped?

Maddie retrieved her cell phone from the floor beside her suitcase, opened her messages app, and clicked on the last message from Zach. He had been in Marshall, Illinois, right before the lights went out.

Maybe the lights aren't out there?

Although she was unsure where Marshall, Illinois, was, she doubted it was anywhere near Chicago. His bus had been heading southwest back to St. Louis.

He will be all right. There were six teachers on the trip. They'll get him home.

She checked for cell service one last time before putting her phone in the front pouch of her vest. The light from the phone shined through the mesh fabric. She patted her pockets, adjusted her straps, and pulled the cords tight.

Time to get going.

Maddie slowly unlocked and cracked opened the door. The scene out in the corridor was even more chaotic than before. She could hear raised voices and crying.

How long was I in there?

She checked her watch. It was four o'clock. She had at least two hours before it would be dark. Walking down the terminal toward the main hall, she could see that most of the activity centered on the restaurant area of the concourse. People were fighting over what was left of the food.

She needed a map. She had seen a place that sold books and newspapers when she'd gotten coffee earlier.

They should have maps. There are tourists here, right?

Maddie raced around a corner and saw a floor to ceiling mural of the city of Chicago. It wouldn't replace a paper map that she could take with her, but it would give her a direction to head out in at least. Not knowing the scale of the map, she made a fist and stuck up her thumb, using it as a ruler to calculate distance.

"Which way are you heading?" a man asked.

The voice startled her, causing her to jump. She twirled around to find a man in his mid-thirties. Beside the man stood a woman, maybe a little younger than him, and a girl of about ten years old.

"Um— I— South," Maddie stammered.

She chastised herself. She had just given out critical information to a stranger. She could hear her father scold her.

OPSEC, Maddie, her dad would say.

Operational security meant keeping your big trap shut about what you have and where you plan to go. She was sucking at this already. She looked at her feet.

"Your dad serve?" the man asked, pointing to Maddie's Marine Corps buff.

"He did. Did you?" she asked, pointing to the U.S. Army National Guard Minute Man logo on his hat.

"I did."

"Two tours in Iraq and four in Afghanistan," the woman added.

"Yeah, my dad spent a lot of time in those places too."

"Is he with you?" the man asked.

Maddie looked away and swallowed hard, resolved to fight back the tears. She would give anything to have her dad with her right now.

"I'm Rob Andrews, by the way, and this is my wife April and our daughter Emma."

Emma gave a timid wave as April stepped forward and extended her hand. Maddie shook it and said, "I'm Maddie Langston."

"Look, it is getting bad in here. It's going to get worse in the city very soon. We're not going to wait around for the lights to come back on. We're getting out of here, and it looks like you have the same idea," Rob said.

"Um… Yeah. I mean, I was thinking about it. With the airplanes crashing, I was trying to decide how to leave to avoid the runways. I need to head toward Interstate 55, but that is southwest, and it looks like most of the runways are in that direction."

"You could go due south and then cut over, say, around here." Rob pointed to 143rd Street on the map mural.

"I wish I had a map to take with me, in case I have to adjust course quickly."

"I have a map. We're heading south too. We live about fifty miles from here. You're welcome to join us until you need to head west."

"I don't know if I should."

"You shouldn't be out on the streets alone. It's not safe on a regular day, but now with the power being out…"

Maddie was leery of leaving the airport with strangers, but he was right. It wasn't safe to go alone. Safety in numbers, as her dad would say.

She looked the man over. He had been in the military like her dad. He had his wife and daughter with him.

It should be all right, right?

"Okay. When do you want to leave?"

∼

Chapter 2

San Diego, California
Day of Event

Beth's drive back to her mother's house after dropping off her eighteen-year-old daughter at the San Diego airport was difficult. The doctor had put her mother on hospice care just days before. She hadn't had time to adjust to the news that her mother would not recover from cancer this time.

Beth's mother, Florence, had beaten breast cancer twice. The third time, it was in her bones. Her mother was sixty-eight and had led a full, vibrant, active life before this most recent diagnosis.

The traffic was heavy—heavier than Beth remembered from when she had lived there before marrying her first husband, Greg Langston. But that was ages ago. She had lived all over since then, settling in Missouri. When Greg left the Marines and took the job in St. Louis, Beth had been thrilled.

For the first time in their marriage, they had been able to settle in the place of their choosing. To be honest, though, St. Louis hadn't been her first choice. She could think of much nicer places to live, but Greg had received a great job offer from a military defense contractor. The job allowed him to be home with Beth and their children, Maddie and Zach.

Beth pulled the car into the third bay of her parents' three-car garage. She unloaded the groceries and placed them on the marble countertop.

"Beth, is that you?"

"Yes, Mom, it's me. Can I bring you some juice? I stopped at Panera Bread and bought you some of the chicken and wild rice soup you like."

"Maybe later, dear. I…"

She was getting weaker and sleeping longer. Beth wasn't sure if it was because of the cancer or the pain meds. She was incoherent a lot when she was awake. Beth had moved the dining table and china cabinet out of the dining room to set her mother's hospital bed up there. Her stepfather, Frank, was set up in the den, where he spent most of his time. He had suffered a stroke the year before, leaving his left arm paralyzed.

Beth finished putting the groceries away and went into the den to check on Frank.

"Frank, can I get you some soup or a sandwich?"

He didn't answer, so she said it louder. The television was blaring, so she had to yell to be heard over the commentator's gloomy newscast.

"Frank," she yelled.

"What? Why are you yelling at me?" Frank asked, glowering over his shoulder.

He turned back to stare at the television before she could finish her sentence. She rolled her eyes and went back to the kitchen.

"I'll just make him a tray, and if he's hungry, he'll eat it," she said out loud, exasperated.

"What did you say?" Frank called from the den.

Beth shook her head and pulled a bowl from the cabinet next to the sink. She made Frank a tray and set it on the coffee table in front of him.

"You're blocking the television," Frank barked, craning his neck around her.

Sample Chapters

China's president, Xi Jinping, is said to have facilitated the talks between North Korean leader Kim Jong Un and the United States. U.S. State Department spokesman, Robin Payton, said Monday that the president had rejected calls from China, Russia, and North Korea to lift sanctions imposed on the isolated state. The U.S. remains committed to only doing so when Pyongyang makes further progress toward denuclearization on the Korean Peninsula. Further talks between Chairman Kim and President Rhynard have yet to be scheduled.

"You can't trust those damn commie North Koreans. Are they nuts or something? What the hell are we talking to them for anyway," Frank yelled at the television.

Beth had never been so tired of listening to the news in her life.

Why in the world did they invent twenty-four-hour news stations, anyway? All they do is repeat the same bad news over and over.

Sandy, the hospice nurse, arrived shortly after one o'clock that afternoon. She took Florence's vitals and adjusted her morphine pump.

"She is sleeping most of the time now. Is it from the meds?" Beth asked as she walked Sandy to her car.

"Her urine output has decreased again. I increased her fluids, but I think her kidneys are shutting down."

The nurse put a hand on Beth's shoulder. Her eyes were full of sympathy.

"It is just a matter of days now—maybe three or four. If you have family to call in, I'd say now would be the time. She will likely slip into a coma in a day or two."

Beth inhaled and held it. She had known those words were

coming. She had felt it in her heart, and she'd thought she was prepared for it. Beth thanked Sandy and walked back into the house. All she wanted to do was go upstairs to her room, crawl into bed, and pull up the covers. That was what she had done after her husband, Greg had died. She had shut down. Sleep was her only comfort. She didn't have the luxury of retreat today, however. She had ill parents and a lazy, one-eyed dog to care for.

Jack slept in the bed with Beth's mother. He rarely left her side. She stroked the dog's head as she stared down at her mom. He lifted his head, shifted position, then put his head on Florence's leg. Feeling sorry for her mother's furry child, she decided she would reheat the chicken and rice she had made him the day before.

"Jack, you want some lunch?"

Jack's paws hit the wood floor, and a flash of white fur streaked by her feet. Jack loved food.

"What are we going to do with you, little guy?"

She hated the thought of taking him to an animal rescue, but her husband, Jason, would never allow her to bring him home with her. They already had a dog he didn't like.

As Beth followed Jack into the kitchen, an ear-piercing emergency alert tone came from Frank's television. Beth's first thought was the alert was for a wildfire. They hadn't had rain in a while. Beth placed the kitchen towel she held in her hand onto the counter and walked into the den just as the emergency alert message began to scroll across the screen.

We interrupt our programming. This is a national emergency. The Department of Homeland Security has issued a national emergency alert. Residents are asked to shelter in place until further notice. Stay tuned to this channel for updates. This is not a test.

Beth heard the alert tone on her cell phone and ran to the kitchen to retrieve it.

Presidential Alert
THIS IS NOT A TEST. This is a national emergency. Shelter in place until further notice.

"What the hell?" Frank said.

Beth clicked the news app on her phone to check for news about the emergency alert but found none. She opened the Facebook app and scrolled through the messages. She stared down at her phone as her news feed refreshed. A story from a San Diego station informed the city that the nation had been attacked. Beth dropped to her knees, her cell phone skidding across the floor. Crawling over to pick it back up, she leaned against the kitchen cabinets and read the article.

San Diego Daily News has been informed that at approximately twenty-three minutes past three this afternoon, a nuclear device exploded in the atmosphere above the United States. Information is still coming in regarding the extent of the damage this detonation has caused and the areas affected. But right now, we know that communications with most of the nation have been interrupted. An official with the governor's office has told Daily News that they have no information regarding further attacks. A state of emergency has been declared, and residents have been ordered to shelter in place until further notice. We expect a formal statement from the governor later today. Stay tuned for further details.

Beth kept scrolling through her news feed, hoping for more news. She tapped on contacts, selected Maddie's cell number, and pressed the call button. The call failed, so she couldn't even leave a voicemail. She opened her message app and typed a message to Maddie and Zach, then tapped the send button. She waited. A moment later, a message appeared telling her that delivery had failed.

Beth buried her head in her hands. Being cut off from her children during a national emergency was beyond any heartache she had ever experienced. Rocking back and forth, she tried to control her panic. She repeatedly tapped the message's send button, hoping desperately that it would go through.

Placing her hands on the counter, Beth pulled herself to her feet. She ran her hands through her hair. Her mind wanted to go numb, but she couldn't give in to that. Walking over to the sink, she washed her face and dried off with a kitchen towel. She heard a news anchor discussing the shelter in place order and headed back to the den.

Frank was unusually quiet as he and Beth sat staring at the television screen. All anyone could say was that no one knew what the damage was throughout the rest of the country. All planes had been grounded, and a state-wide curfew had been ordered. No one was allowed out of their homes except essential personnel.

It was hours before news reports came in about the blackout caused by the EMP. A so-called expert explained the effects of an EMP detonated at a three-hundred-mile altitude. As far as they had determined, the unaffected areas include parts of California, Oregon, Washington, and Alaska. Beth didn't need to listen to the rest. She understood the effects of an EMP. Her deceased husband, Greg had studied it as one of the possible scenarios he foresaw happening.

She was cut off from her children and her current husband, Jason. She was two thousand miles away, and there was nothing she could do to protect them. Worse yet, they were both away from

Sample Chapters

home and separated from each other. Zach would have his teachers for help and support, but Maddie was stranded in an airport in a large, densely-populated city.

Beth paced the room. No matter how hard she tried, she couldn't think of a single thing she could do to help her children or even try to get to them. The roads were shut down. The authorities were not allowing anyone to travel. Walking two thousand miles without any gear was impossible.

"Beth? Where are you, Beth?"

"I'm right here, Mom. I'm coming."

No matter how desperately she wanted to get home to her children, she knew she could not leave her dying mother, and it would be foolish to go alone anyway. She wouldn't make it out of California, let alone across four states of chaos and devastation.

Even though every cell in her body wanted to get to her children, she would have to stay there and care for her parents.

Turbulent is book one in the Days of Want series. If you've enjoyed this sample of Turbulent, CLICK HERE to order your copy today!

Also, don't forget to check out my Gateway to Chaos series.

Also by T. L. Payne

Days of Want Series

Turbulent

Hunted

Turmoil

Uprising

Upheaval

Mayhem

Defiance

Sudden Chaos: A Post Apocalyptic EMP Survival Story

(Newsletter signup required)

Fall of Houston Series

A Days of Want Companion Series

No Way Out

No Other Choice

No Turning Back

No Surrender

No Man's Land

Gateway to Chaos Series

Seeking Safety

Seeking Refuge

Seeking Justice

Seeking Hope

Survive the Collapse Series
Brink of Darkness
Brink of Chaos
Brink of Panic
Brink of Collapse
Brink of Destruction: A FREE Novelette

Desperate Age Series
Panic in the Rockies
Getting Out of Dodge
Surviving Freedom
Trouble in Tulsa
Defending Camp
This We'll Defend: A Desperate Age Novella
(Newsletter signup required)

Reign of Darkness Series
A Conquer the Dark Companion Series
Endure the Dark
Escape the Destruction
Evade the Ruthless
Engage the Enemy (Pre-order Now!)

Last Light: A Reign of Darkness Novella

(Newsletter signup required)

Conquer the Dark Series

A Reign of Darkness Companion Series

Collapse

Ruin (Pre-order Now!)

Carnage (Coming Soon)

Desolation (Coming Soon!)

About the Author

T. L. Payne is the author of several bestselling post-apocalyptic series. T. L. lives and writes in the Osage Hills region of Oklahoma and enjoys many outdoor activities, including kayaking, rockhounding, metal detecting, and fishing in the many lakes and rivers of the area.

Don't forget to sign up for T. L.'s VIP Readers Club at www.tlpayne.com to be the first to know of new releases, giveaways, and special offers.

T. L. loves to hear from readers. You may email T. L. at contact@tlpayne.com or join the Facebook reader group at https://www.facebook.com/groups/tlpaynereadergroup

Join TL on Social Media

Facebook Author Page
Facebook Reader Group
Instagram
Follow me on Amazon.com
Website: https://tlpayne.com
Email: contact@tlpayne.com

Printed in Dunstable, United Kingdom